I CAN

DO

IT!

The sky's the limit!

Roberta Cava

Published by Cava Consulting

info@dealingwithdifficultpeople.info

www.dealingwithdifficultpeople.info

Cava, Roberta

I can do it!

The sky's the limit!

National Library of Australia
Cataloguing-in-publication data:

ISBN: 978-0-6485408-3-0

BOOKS BY ROBERTA CAVA

Non-Fiction

Dealing with Difficult People (24 publishers – in 17 languages)
Dealing with Difficult Situations – at Work and at Home
Dealing with Difficult Spouses and Children
Dealing with Difficult Relatives and In-Laws
Dealing with Domestic Violence and Child Abuse
Dealing with School Bullying
Dealing with Workplace Bullying
Retirement Village Bullies
Keeping Our Children Safe
Just say no
What am I going to do with the rest of my life?
Interpersonal Communication at Work
Change? Not me!
Creative Problem-Solving & Decision-Making
Customer Service that Works
Teambuilding
Before tying the knot
How Women can advance in business
Survival Skills for Supervisors and Managers
Human Resources at its Best!
Human Resources Policies and Procedures - Australia
Employee Handbook
Easy Come – Hard to go – The Art of Hiring, Disciplining and
Firing Employees
Time and Stress – Today's silent killers
Take Command of your Future – Make things Happen
Belly Laughs for All! – Volumes 1 to 6
Wisdom of the World! The happy, sad and wise things in life!

Fiction

That Something Special
Something Missing
I can do it! The sky's the limit!
Trilogy: Life Gets Complicated
Life Goes On
Life Gets Better

Prologue

This is a true story. To protect her children and relatives, Jenny Harper requested that all the characters in the book remain anonymous.

It is a story about the ongoing battles she had to fight throughout her life. She'd climb one hill, only to fall off a cliff and find herself needing to start over again. Jenny is a fighter and I hope you enjoy reading about her lifelong struggles to be free of tyranny and become the woman she dreamt she could be.

I can do it! The sky's the limit!

One

Jane Robertson glanced at her granddaughter and smiled as she thought how much she reminded her of her younger self. Despite the cold -20 F. weather, Jenny had not hesitated to drive the icy streets to bring her grandmother over for dinner. It was a ritual, and one that Jane looked forward to very much. It was good to be around Jenny, as she could brighten the dullest of days and break the monotony of the long lonely days spent in her room at the senior centre. January was always a sad month as the festivities were over and there were now several months of frigid weather ahead.

Jenny was dressed for the weather in a full-length navy coat and she wore the lilac scarf and gloves that Jenny had bought her for Christmas. Jenny had tied back her long blonde hair, leaving a few tendrils to escape from beneath a white beret. Her long slim swimmer's legs were clad in tight black leggings and knee-high burgundy boots, which matched the little leather bomber jacket she had zipped up to her neck. Jane could see that Jenny was concentrating on navigating the icy roads, so she did not engage in any of their usual chatter, but rather scanned the road ahead.

They were heading down the street where Jenny lived, but Jenny had made sure that they both had their lap belts tight. There were no shoulder harnesses or air bags in those days, but the lap belts at least kept them from bouncing around on the rutted side roads and would provide a modicum of safety in the event of an accident.

Cars were parked on the left lane of the street and normally in the summer there was sufficient room for two cars to pass each other. However, this was the middle of winter and there was only room for one car to be on the road. With only one navigable lane open, Jenny was travelling at low speed and prepared to stop and pull over if another car approached. Even her safe driving could not prevent what happened next. An out-of-control driver was driving far too fast and could not pull into a space between the parked cars. As soon as he hit the brakes, his car careened across the road heading right at them.

'Oh my God Gran, he's coming right for us!' Jenny screamed as the threw out her arm to try to protect Jane from the impending impact.

Jenny closed her eyes and prepared for the crash. The other vehicle hit so hard that even though Jenny was prepared for the crash, she was propelled forward with great force. There was an ear-splitting noise as the two massive metal objects collided and Jenny and her grandmother were pelted with shards of glass as the windshield shattered. Then just as suddenly, there was absolute silence.

Jenny knew she must have been knocked unconscious for a few seconds because the first thing she noticed when she regained consciousness was that she was draped over the steering wheel facing the driver's door. Her face and ribs hurt terribly as did her right knee. She tried to open her eyes but could only open her left one. Her right eye was held shut by the pressure of her face against the steering wheel. As she looked down, she could see blood dripping onto her left knee below.

'This is going to ruin my slacks,' she thought just before she chastised herself by thinking, 'What a stupid thing to worry about. I've obviously been injured - and it really hurts!'

When she peered upward, she could see the dash of the car, but that was all. She attempted to sit up but found she couldn't do so. She seemed glued to the wheel and ached all over. Her effort to move made the world spin. She felt terribly dizzy and nauseous and hoped she wasn't going to be sick.

The impact had thrown Jenny forward over the steering wheel and she could not see her grandmother. *'Oh, please let her be all right,'* she silently prayed.

Fighting consciousness and trying to forget about her own injuries she focused her attention on how her grandmother might be after the accident. Jane was a feisty seventy-year-old and had seen Jenny through many scrapes in her life. *'She has to be okay,'* Jenny thought. *'What would I ever do without her?'*

As Jenny lay helplessly draped over the steering wheel, she was just about to ask her grandmother how she was, when she heard a lap belt retracting and a car door opening. Jane looked at her beautiful granddaughter and tried desperately to stop the tears as she saw the gash on her face and her swollen lips. Her white beret had fallen off and lay on her lap covered in blood. 'You'll be all right Jenny, you're made of tough stuff, just like your old gran.'

Jane squeezed Jenny's shoulder with far more confidence than she was feeling. Then she heard a young woman's voice asking if anyone was hurt.

'Please call an ambulance. My granddaughter has been badly hurt.' she heard her grandmother cry as she climbed out of the car. Jenny assumed that her grandmother was not seriously hurt. She saw her own door open and a young woman peered at Jenny in horror.

'I'm going to call an ambulance.' she said to Jane. 'Stay beside her and try to keep her awake. Don't move her because I think she may be seriously injured.' The young woman turned around and Jenny's grandmother took her place.

'The other driver seems to be okay – he wasn't hurt.' They learned later that the driver was only eighteen and was driving a friend's car. It too was a write-off.

Then all Jenny felt was blackness closing in on her.

When Jenny woke up after the car accident, she peered around the room and identified from her surroundings that she was in a hospital room. She was lying on her back and panicked when she realized she couldn't move her head. The reason became clear as she lifted her right hand and felt the cervical collar around her neck. As she investigated further, she found that bandages covered most of her lower face. The nurse in the Intensive Care Unit (ICU) seeing her move, quickly came over to her side. Jenny tried to speak but her mouth was so sore and swollen that all that came out of her mouth was garbled words. The nurse urged her to not try to speak, then stated, 'Your husband and parents are here. Do you want to see them?'

She mumbled a 'Yes' and soon her husband Russ and her parents Ian and Martha Harper entered the room. 'How's grandma?' she tried to say and thankfully Martha understood.

'Your grandma is okay – just a little shook up. They brought her to the hospital with you and checked her over. Your brother came and drove her home.'

They turned as a doctor entered the room carrying several X-rays. 'Hello Jenny. I'm Dr. Warren. I'm the orthopaedic specialist on duty today. We've examined your X-rays and are concerned by the swelling in your spinal column, both in the neck area and between the fourth and fifth vertebrae in the lumbar region of your lower back. You'll have to wear the cervical collar until the neck swelling goes down.' he stated. He checked to see that Jenny was absorbing what he was saying, and then continued, 'I'm sure it hurts when you breathe. Two of your ribs were broken, so I've taped them up. You were lucky and didn't fracture your jaw or cheekbone when your face hit the steering wheel, however when you were still unconscious, we stitched up several cuts on your face. Do you understand so far?'

Jenny mumbled, 'Yes.

Jenny could feel him' remove the sheets around her feet, but wasn't sure what he was doing until he asked, 'Can you feel this?'

Confused, Jenny replied, 'No I can't feel anything. What are you touching?'

'I'm using a sharp instrument on the bottom of your feet. Are you sure you don't feel anything?'

Jenny began to cry when she realized what this meant. She quietly replied, 'No. I don't feel a thing.'

'We'll put you in traction to relieve the pressure on your spine and hopefully that will allow you to feel your legs again.'

'Will she be able to walk again?' her mother asked.

Dr. Warren frowned and admitted, 'At this stage we can't tell whether the injury is permanent or not. We'll know better in about a week. In the meantime, we'll get Jenny settled into the orthopaedic ward.'

'Will I be having any physiotherapy?' Jenny asked.

'No, we don't think physiotherapy will make any difference to your ability to walk again.' he replied.

Jenny cried and cried while her family comforted her. She fell asleep after a nurse gave her some pain relief in her drip.

After her parents left, Jenny couldn't help but wonder what was going to happen to her and how she would cope if she was permanently paralysed. Swimming would be impossible if she couldn't move her legs. More importantly, would Russ want to stay married to her now that she might not be able to walk? They'd only been married for six months and had no children, so he might not want to stay with her. She wished she could go back to that morning when she was fine and cursed the driver of the other car for the pain and suffering, she was going through.

The nurse arrived with her 'dinner' that was given intravenously. It was impossible for Jenny to open her mouth wide enough for even a straw. She wasn't very hungry anyway, so was not disappointed that she couldn't eat. She did crave a good cup of tea but realised that it would be some days before she could enjoy food or her favourite beverage.

The next day, she was able to leave the ICU and was taken to an orthopaedic ward on the fourth floor. As the attendant wheeled her bed into the room, he introduced Jenny to her roommate. 'Your roommate's name is Elaine Harrington. Elaine – this is Jenny Carponi.'

'Hi Jenny.'

After Jenny had been settled, Elaine said, 'I broke my ankle skiing and it's really a mess. They pinned it and put it in a cast but say it will be months before I'll be able to walk properly.'

The attendant told Elaine about Jenny's difficulty in speaking until her mouth healed and explained the one blink for 'yes' and two for 'no' communication system. He also suggested that, because it would be difficult for them to communicate unless Elaine was standing beside her bed and Jenny being prone on the bed, that they change the communication system.

'Jenny, why don't you raise your right arm for 'yes,' and your left for 'no?'' he suggested.

'Sounds good to me.' Elaine replied as Jenny raised her right hand.

They soon settled in for the night. Shortly after midnight, Jenny woke up to find herself wrapped up in her traction device. Somehow, in her sleep, she'd turned over and now lay helplessly on her stomach. She knew she shouldn't be lying that way, especially with her head turned slightly towards her right side. She tried to find the bell to call a nurse for help but couldn't find it. Thankfully, she remembered she had a roommate who could help her.

'Elaine,' she mumbled. There was no reply. 'Elaine,' she shouted again. It hurt tremendously to speak, but she needed to get help. Finally, Elaine sleepily replied, 'What's the matter Jenny?'

Jenny said, 'Nurse – bell.' Elaine looked over at Jenny and realised what had happened and immediately pushed her bell to call for help.

A nurse arrived and advised Jenny that she was going to get help to turn her over. Two nurses and an orderly unhooked her traction device, carefully turned her over onto her back and re-attached the traction weights.

'How do you feel,' asked the nurse when Jenny was hooked up again in the right position. 'How is your neck? Does it hurt?'

'No.' Jenny signalled by raising her left hand. Then she raised her eyebrows, shrugged her shoulders and put both hands out palm up.

'We've called Dr. Warren to see if there's anything else we should do to stabilise you.' the nurse responded.

The nurse returned a few minutes later and explained, 'Dr. Warren has ordered another X-ray series to see if there's been any damage done when you turned over.'

X-Rays were taken and processed. Jenny lay in her bed wide-eyed and fearful that she had caused more damage to her already fragile spinal column. An hour later, her nurse came back to Jenny's room, 'The X-ray technician has assured Dr. Warren that you have not caused further damage to your neck and back.' Then she added, 'I've got something that will stop it from happening again.'

She placed two rather large rubber wedges beside Jenny's head, so she could not inadvertently turn over in her sleep again. Jenny received another injection for the pain so she could sleep during what remained of that night.

The next morning, Jenny was terribly embarrassed when she smelled that she'd had a bowel movement during the night. She buzzed for the nurse who came and cleaned her up. It was then that Jenny realised she was wearing adult diapers. Her urine wasn't a problem because she was catheterised, but she needed the diapers in case she had a bowel movement. They had placed her on medication to keep her bowels from becoming constipated, but she could not feel when her body was releasing its contents. How embarrassed she felt – so helpless and dirty.

Shortly after, the nurse brought Jenny a large glass with a straw. 'This is your breakfast. It's high calorie and should keep you going till lunch. Now let's make sure your mouth isn't too sore to suck on the straw.'

Jenny tried drawing the food through the straw and was pleased that it didn't hurt too much. Because she needed to stay flat on her back, it was necessary for the nurse to stay with her while she drank the fluid in case she choked.

After breakfast when the nurse had gone, Elaine said, 'You sure did a good job of tying yourself up last night. You looked like a trussed-up turkey ready for basting.'

Jenny and Elaine got the giggles and Jenny ended up with tears running down her cheeks but not wholly from the funny idea, but because it hurt her ribs so much when she laughed.

The days passed slowly, and Jenny still didn't have feeling from the waist down. So, two weeks later, when Dr. Warren entered her room, she steeled herself knowing that he might bring her bad news. The look on his face confirmed this and he sadly said, 'Jenny, I'm afraid I have bad news. I've consulted with two other orthopaedic specialists and we all believe that you will not be able to walk again.'

Jenny burst into tears and he awkwardly patted her on the arm. Shortly afterwards, he left, and Jenny sat for a bit almost paralysed with sadness, anger and hurt. 'What did I ever do to have this horrible thing happen to me? What kind of a life am I going to have, living the rest of my life in a wheelchair depending on others for the rest of my life?'

She cried and cried and finally phoned Russ and her parents to give them the news.

I can do it! The sky's the limit!

Two

All Jenny wanted to do when she grew up, was to get married and have children. Even though her parents had offered to pay for a university education, having a career wasn't in her plans. She wanted a marriage – one just like her parents had where the gender boundaries were blurred, and everyone pitched in when there was a job to do. Her man would call his wife 'Hon' and would never fail to give his wife a kiss when he left home and when he returned. That's what her father did. His wasn't a long-drawn out kiss, but a loving peck on the cheek and a pat on his wife's shoulder to show her he loved her.

Both her parents set a good example for their three children. The year after their marriage, their first child, a son they named Jeff, was born with a club foot. Jenny arrived fifteen months later in 1939, one week before World War II started and their unexpected baby Susan arrived in 1949 when Jenny was ten.

Jenny's mother, Martha and her grandparents had been born in Canada, but her great-grandparents had been born in Ireland. Jenny often wondered whether her mother's life would have been different if the tradition of her day hadn't discouraged women from working after marriage. Before her marriage Martha had worked at Eaton's Department Store in their catalogue sales department. She excelled at mathematics, so Jenny believed she would have made an excellent accountant. Her large vocabulary was gleaned from pouring over crossword puzzles most of her life. However, her mother seemed to enjoy staying at home with her children – keeping herself busy doing volunteer work for the Red Cross or preparing bandages for the Cancer Institute when the children were in school. She was the first to volunteer to look after sick relatives or visit them in the hospital.

Jenny's father, Ian, had been seventeen when he emigrated from Scotland, but had worked hard since he was thirteen. Ian came from a rather large family that had been raised mainly by his mother. The oldest in his family was Jack, then Joan, Jane, Ian, Mark and George. Ian's father and one brother had died of diphtheria when he was only six. The family worked hard to be able to pay for their passages and immigrate to Canada. The children contributed to buying their mother's ticket and after several years they all settled in or around Winnipeg, in the centre of Canada. His close-knit family continued their strong work ethic and remained close throughout their lives. Their families continued the tradition that if a chore required doing in a home, everyone pitched in – no gender boundaries.

Ian worked hard all his life and passed on his work ethic to his children who learned that 'You don't get what you don't work for.' When World War II started, Ian Harper was employed as a police constable with the City of Winnipeg Police Force. Even though he was thirty-five and would not likely have been called up to serve in the armed forces right away, he volunteered to go to war in early 1942. He was stationed in Britain and because of his police background, was posted to the Provost Corps and rode a motorcycle.

Jenny had only been three when Ian left for England and had no idea who he was when he returned to Canada in 1945. But it didn't take long for Jenny to adore her father because he always made her feel important and encouraged her with praise and support. After the war, Ian made the decision that he didn't want to be a police officer all his life. At the age of forty, while still working full-time as a railway police officer, he enrolled in courses that would qualify him as a stationary engineer. His older brother, Jack had already qualified and encouraged Ian to do the same. After two years of agonisingly hard study, he passed his exams and took a position as the stationery engineer at a veteran's hospital near their home in St. James, a suburb of Winnipeg. Jenny always hoped that she would marry a man like her father

Jenny's brother Jeff had a difficult time as a baby and young child. She remembered when he was about six years old hearing him grunting as he tried to turn over in the bunk bed below her. It was very difficult for him to do so because the shoes on his feet had been attached to a board that forced them to point outwards. Jeff had already suffered through three operations to try to correct his club foot. The boots were to encourage his left foot to slant slightly outwards as his right one did normally. To accomplish this, he had to wear the cumbersome device while he slept.

He'd ripped many sheets before his parents realised that if he wore long heavy socks under the shoes attached to the board, his feet could be left out of the sheet and blankets that covered the remainder of his body. This enabled him to turn over in his sleep. Because Martha had a knitting machine that she used to make socks for the soldiers during the war, she was able to make as many socks as Jeff required. However, it was still impossible for him to sleep on his side.

Jenny was only five but slept on the top bunk bed in their bedroom. It was simply impossible for Jeff to manage the ladder to the upper level and the room was too small to have the beds side-by-side. Because he couldn't get up during the night if he needed to go to the bathroom, it was Jenny's responsibility to wake one of their parents, so they could help him. To accomplish this, Jeff pulled on a cord that rang a little bell next to Jenny's pillow.

Jeff couldn't take part in any sports until his leg was fully healed, but he hoped that this would be the last of his suffering. He was stoic about his situation and found other things besides sports to occupy his time. He became so good at cards that he often beat his parents and friends. He had a mathematical mind and excelled in math at school, so much that he was advanced a year because of his proficiency.

Life hadn't been kind to Jeff. Ian had explained why the calf of what he called his 'bad leg,' was so scarred. When he was just two, he'd been put in a leg and foot cast after an operation. That night he screamed and screamed. When he was still screaming at midnight, the parents knew something was terribly wrong. It was Saturday night, and their doctor's office was closed, so they bundled him off to the emergency ward. The doctors could see the agony Jeff was in and immediately removed the cast. As he removed it, some of the skin from Jeff's calf came with it. Someone in the operating room had put iodine on his surgical area instead of mercurochrome and it had eaten away at the skin under the cast.

In today's medicine, the doctors would have been charged with a malpractice suit, but in those days, most people didn't know that such a thing was possible.

I can do it! The sky's the limit!

Three

In July 1956, Jenny was working as a typist in the typing pool at the Veteran's Hospital where Ian worked. Part of Jenny's job was to go into various wards of the hospital to collect the medical records that were typed by the women in the typing pool. Although it was a veteran's hospital, it also had younger military men as patients, and she often received wolf whistles as she walked down the halls of the wards. Jenny smiled and knew that they had little to smile about, so took the whistles in good humour.

She was given the responsibility of typing reports for the Recreation Department, and for several months had collected records from Bill Beckam. One morning her typing supervisor said, 'Jenny because you know basically how the Recreation Department works, I want to know if you would like to oversee looking after the Recreation Department while Bill is away on holidays for two weeks? He's asked if you can do it for him.'

Jenny was surprised that her supervisor thought she was mature enough at seventeen to take on such a monumental task. She knew how many responsibilities Bill had. But it was a wonderful opportunity for her, so she replied, 'Sure, I'll do it.'

The next day, Bill showed her how to record the recreational activities that were offered and who would take part in those activities. He had already ordered the bus for the upcoming football game, but she would have to check that it was the right size of bus to accommodate the final number of patients that had signed up.

He showed her another list he used to keep track of the needs of the patients. If a patient smoked, he was supplied with adequate cigarettes for his use while he was in the hospital. If he needed shaving lotion, a deck of cards, a comb or a housecoat, those too were supplied. 'You would have to keep track of all new patients while I'm gone. You'll get their names every morning from the admissions department and visit their wards to interview them so you can get them anything they require. Here's a list of the things we can supply to them at no cost.'

On her first morning on the job, Jenny settled herself into Bill's office and got to work. She had her typewriter brought to the Recreational Department, so she could remain there in case someone needed to talk to her. The job required her to do a lot of paperwork and involved considerable interaction with the patients, but at the end of the two weeks, Jenny felt she had done an excellent job of staying on top of the paperwork and activities.

On the afternoon of the day Bill was supposed to return, a representative from the hospital Human Resources Department arrived at the door. Jenny had been puzzled that morning when she went to the Recreational Department and saw that Bill was not there.

The man said, 'I've just spoken with Bill, and he's advised us that he won't be back. He's been offered and has accepted a position in Vancouver and won't be back.'

Jenny didn't know what to say.

'We're wondering if you would look after the Recreational Department until we find a replacement?' he asked.

'I guess so. There haven't been any plans made for more sporting outings. I'll have to look over Bill's old records to see what kind of activities he normally schedules for this time of the year. But yes, I can do it.' she finally said.

That night she excitedly told Ian and Martha about her new assignment. Ian was particularly proud and went around the next morning to see Jenny in her new office.

On October 23rd, the week she met her future husband, the Hungarian revolt began in Budapest. A student demonstration mobbed the parliament buildings in Budapest and Soviet Security Police fired on the students. This initiated the Soviet retreat from Budapest. Many of those injured in that revolt were taken to other countries for treatment. A lovely Hungarian seventeen-year old student, Magda Zhukov was admitted with gunshot wounds to her leg and arm to a ward at Jenny's Veteran's Hospital. Her parents had been killed the day after she was shot so she had no one to care for her.

Jenny visited her to see if there was anything she needed. She knew that Magda did not speak English. Magda was approximately the same size as Jenny, was blonde and had the same pale skin colouring as she, so she'd prepared accordingly and came bearing gifts.

'Hello Magda. I'm Jenny.' she said pointing to herself.

'Jenny,' replied Magda.

First Jenny handed Magda a package of makeup she'd purchased for her.

Magda looked at it then glanced up at Jenny with tears in her eyes. It had been a terrorising time for her, and she was overwhelmed by the kindness of the many Canadian people that had helped her. She held Jenny's hand and nodded her thanks.

Then Jenny handed her another package that was a lovely silk housecoat with matching slippers. The tears flowed again.

The next day, Jenny arranged to have a Hungarian interpreter come to help them communicate. The interpreter learned that Magda's fourteen-year-old brother Mikhail was still in Hungary and she was very fearful for his welfare. Through the interpreter, Jenny assured her that she would be contacting the Red Cross, so they could find out how he was.

Ten days later, Jenny entered Magda's room with a big surprise. Mikhail was all smiles as he greeted his sister. The Red Cross had flown him over and found a family willing to care for him and later for Magda after she recovered from her injuries.

It was after that incident that Ian spoke with Jenny, 'It looks as if the hospital is taking advantage of you. You've been working at a managerial level but are still paid as a typist. That's not right. I think you should apply for the position and if given it, should receive the same salary as Bill received.'

Jenny agreed and made an appointment to speak with the Human Resources Manager who had put her into the temporary position. Within two weeks, he hired another person to do the job. Jenny was devastated when she was overlooked for the position after she had worked so hard to do such a great job. 'Well – if I can do this job, I can do another more suited to my ability. If they don't appreciate my hard work, I'll find another employer who will.'

Young as she was, she was not prepared to work below her capabilities of anyone.

Jenny was so terribly disappointed that within a week, she'd applied for and was offered a new position as a secretary to a Wing Commander at the nearby Air Force Base. Her boss, Wing Commander Warren was a lovely man who treated Jenny with respect and as if she was one of his daughters. He was kind and thoughtful to her and the other staff. Once he apologised to Jenny when he realised that she would have to file a document that had comments on it that annoyed him. He had written the word 'balls' over the document and Jenny was touched that he was so sensitive.

On occasion Jenny took dictation from two squadron leaders in the section. Squadron Leader Henderson was a staid middle-aged gentleman who always appeared to be standing at attention. He was very proper in his behaviour with his staff, but always insisted that every 'T' was crossed and every 'I' was dotted. Jenny learned to double-check everything she did for him.

Then there was Squadron Leader Patton. For some reason Jenny did not like this man. He seemed to have a smarmy, paternalistic attitude towards women in the department. One day he stopped by Jenny's desk and asked her to come to his office to take a letter for him. Jenny nodded, picked up her shorthand notebook and followed him down the hallway to his office. When he entered his office behind her, he closed the door and Jenny was astonished to see that he also locked the door. She sat apprehensively as she waited for him to start dictating the letter to her. Instead he stood behind her and placed his hands on her shoulders. Jenny stiffened in protest and when he slid his hands down to her breasts she panicked. She could hear his breath in her ear as he placed his face beside hers. Her heart began thudding so hard she could feel it in her head.

'*What should I do?*' she wondered.

Then her shock turned to rage. She took a breath and in a steely voice said, 'Take your hands off me or I will scream blue murder.'

He released his hands and Jenny bolted to the door, unlocked it and almost ran down the hallway to her desk. Her heart was pounding so hard her vision blurred and she was afraid she was going to pass out. Her first intention was to go to her desk until she recovered from the shock, but instead found herself swerving left until she stood at the doorway of Wing Commander Warren's office. He was in a meeting with two other officers, but when he looked up and saw Jenny's white, shocked face and heard her quavering voice as she said, 'I need to speak with you sir.' he stood up and said to the other men, 'We'll have to continue this later today. I'll phone you when we can get together.'

Jenny stood to the side of the door, even more upset because she had barged into her boss's office when he was in the middle of a meeting. The men passing by her gave her curious glances. They could see that there was something drastically wrong and hoped the Wing Commander would enlighten them later when they met again.

Wing Commander Warren came over and stood beside Jenny, and gently took her arm to guide her into his office. She peered up at him, wide-eyed and teary and said, 'I'm sorry sir. I didn't realise that you were in a meeting.'

'It's okay Jenny. What's wrong? Come and sit down.' he said as he led her to a chair that had just been vacated by his visitors. He looked again at Jenny, then went to the door of his office and closed it. It was obvious that Jenny was terribly upset by something and he was determined to give her privacy while she explained it.

'Sir, I can't... do work any more for Squadron Leader Patton. If I must, I will have to give you my notice.' she hiccupped the words out.

'What happened?' he asked full of concern.

Jenny explained what had happened and watched as his face change from the kindness he had shown her, into a rigid mask. She wondered if he was mad at her, but his next comment reassured her. 'You will never have to do work for him in the future and neither will any of the other secretaries. I want you to stay right here until you feel better. I'm going to talk to him right away.'

Jenny sat in the chair taking big breaths wondering what he was going to say to the man who had molested her. It wasn't long until she heard his angry voice from down the hallway as he chastised the man. Even though the door was closed in Squadron Leader Patton's office, his voice carried along the hallway to where Jenny was sitting. His anger prevented him from keeping his voice down. 'How dare you act that way with any female employee? From now on you will type and file your own letters and I will be reporting this to the proper authorities.'

Jenny realised that most of the people in the department must have heard the shouting. When the Wing Commander returned to his office, Jenny looked shyly at him. She had never seen him angry before. He sat at his desk and took several deep breaths then said, 'I guess we've both had a rotten time of this. I don't remember losing my temper like that for several years. I hope I didn't frighten you.'

'No sir,' she replied. 'I was just pleased that you believed me when I told you what had happened.'

'Well, it's over now. Please let me know if he tries anything again like that in the future.' he said as he rose and kindly patted Jenny on the shoulder.

'I'll get back to work now.' said Jenny. 'I was in the middle of typing the report you gave me this morning. I'll finish it now that I've calmed down. Thank you for being so understanding.' she added as she stood up and left the room.

The office was buzzing with gossip about what had happened, and Jenny just wished it hadn't happened. Several asked her what had happened, but she refused to talk about it. Soon their interest went to other things and the office returned to normal. Squadron Leader Patton was disciplined, transferred to another post and warned not to use such behaviour in the future.

Four

When Jenny was seventeen, she was popular and attended many community club dances. While she was at one of these dances, when she noticed 'him' across the room that October evening. She and her friend Adele giggled as Jenny ogled him. His tall, dark, handsome looks and football star build attracted her as soon as she spotted him. Jenny was tall herself and felt most comfortable when she dated tall men.

Russ was rather introverted and was not comfortable in such a noisy, bustling environment and knew he would probably leave early as usual when the chaos became too uncomfortable for him. He worked in an all-male environment, and had little chance to meet eligible women, so had gone outside his comfort zone by coming to the dance. When he first spotted Jenny across the room, his heart began beating like a trip hammer. Her tall good looks, slender but shapely legs and confident manner as she stood talking with several other girls made him want to meet her. When she sat down at her table, he decided to ask her to dance.

Jenny watched as the gorgeous looking man kept eye contact with her as he walked over to her table. 'Hi, my name is Russ – would you like to dance?' he asked.

'I'd like that,' she replied as she smiled and rose from her chair – giving a sly look at Adele and rolling her eyes. They danced quite well together, and Jenny was glad she had worn high heels that night. Their dance turned out to be a spot dance. At the end of the dance when the head of the band walked across the dance floor seeking the spot he had chosen earlier. Jenny and Russ were surprised when he stopped in front of them and gave them the prize.

'What a beginning!' she thought. They walked back to Jenny's table to see what they had won. It was a box of chocolates that they shared with others at their table.

'Do you mind if I join you?' Russ asked.

Jenny nodded, 'Sure, have a seat.'

They sat together chatting and dancing for the rest of the evening. Although Jenny was still in high school, Russ was already working for the railway and she learned that he was two years older than she.

He seemed so much more mature than the school kids she'd dated so far and appeared to have his life in order. After they danced the last dance, he asked 'Can I drive you home.'

Jenny nodded her head. This was another plus. Most of the boys she dated didn't have a car – but Russ did, and she was impressed especially when she saw his Ford Mustang sports car. When they got to her front door, Russ gave Jenny a quick peck on the cheek and asked, 'Would you go out with me tomorrow night? There's another dance at the Silver Heights Community Centre.'

Jenny nodded her head and said, 'Yes, that sounds great. What time does it start?'

'It starts at eight, so I'll pick you up about then. See you tomorrow.' he said as he waved goodnight and walked back to his car.

The next day, Jenny bubbled over as she told her girlfriends about the new man in her life. Several of them had been at the dance and agreed that he was very good looking and that they made a lovely couple. She tried on three different outfits until she found just the right one that was feminine but not overly sexy.

Russ picked her up the next night and they had a lovely evening at the dance. As they entered the community centre, they were given an admission ticket and were told to keep it because there was going to be a door prize. Later that evening – to their surprise, they won the door prize. *'This relationship is destined to be a success!'* she thought.

Jenny and Russ were soon dating each other exclusively. Very early in their relationship Jenny made it plain to Russ that she had no desire to have sex before marriage. Like most virile males he made several attempts when he became too aroused during their occasional petting sessions, but never failed to stop going further when she said 'No.'

Time passed quickly, and Jenny realised that a year had gone by since she'd met Russ. One Wednesday night in October when they cuddled up watching television in her family's rumpus room, Jenny said, 'Do you realise that this is our anniversary? It's been a year since we met. The time has flown by so fast I can hardly believe it.'

Russ reached over and took her hand. 'I know it's a year, and I waited until tonight to ask you something.'

Jenny held her breath in anticipation – she thought she knew what he was going to say and wondered if they were ready to take a step forward. Was she mature enough to become a wife and eventually a mother? When he asked, 'Will you marry me?' she hesitated. 'We're very young to get married, and we may get some flack from our parents,' but finally she hugged him and said, 'Yes, I'll marry you!'

'When do you want to get married?' he asked as he gave her a big kiss and hug.

'Well because I'm just eighteen, people might think we 'had' to get married if we get married too soon. Why don't we plan on a June wedding? That way, we'll have time to prepare and won't have to rush things.'

Her parents were upstairs playing a card game called canasta. 'Shall we tell my parents?' she asked.

'Yes, why don't we.' he replied.

Jenny expected some resistance from her parents because she would still be eighteen in June, but she thought she was mature enough to get married. 'Mom, Dad we have something to tell you.' she said then noticed the look that passed between her parents. 'Russ has asked me to marry him and I've said yes. We wanted you to be the first to know.'

She watched her parents faces and could see their concern, so she continued, 'I know you think I'm too young and probably wonder if I'm pregnant – well I'm not. And we want to wait until June for the wedding. Please say you approve of us getting married.'

Ian and Martha looked at each other, nodded their heads and gave their approval.

'Oh, I'm so glad you approve,' she beamed as she hugged them both.

Her father stood looking up at Russ and shook his hand, 'Welcome to our family, son.'

Russ beamed, and his smile told it all.

'When are we going to tell your parents?' asked Jenny.

'Well, you're invited to my home tomorrow night for dinner – why don't we tell them then?'

Russ picked her up that Thursday night and before they went into his family home, he gave her a big hug. 'I know you're worried about telling my parents – especially my Dad. But they both like you even though you aren't Italian. My dad always hoped that I would marry an Italian woman.'

Russ's father, Frank Carponi had been married before he met Russ's mother. Jenny learned later that this marriage had ended when his wife committed suicide. That marriage produced a son – Dario who at sixteen ran away from home shortly after his mother died. A few years later, Frank met and married Nellie Brown, a forty-year-old spinster who had just emigrated from England. Frank was five feet eight inches tall and Nellie was barely five feet tall, but two years later they produced a son, Russ, who grew and grew and grew until he was six feet four inches tall.

Nellie's brothers were all over six feet tall, so he obtained his genes from his mother's side of the family. Their second son, Antonio arrived eighteen months later. He had his father's genes and looked very much like his father and ended up the same height as his father.

It hadn't taken Jenny long to understand that Frank was supreme ruler of his family. His wife and two sons were expected to obey his every command. This didn't overly concern Jenny, because Russ acted very differently with her.

At dinner, the evening when they were going to announce their engagement, Jenny was apprehensive during the first part of the meal. She kept sneaking looks at Russ wondering when he was going to tell his family. His younger brother Antonio kept watching them, until he said, 'What's up with you two. You're acting very strange tonight?'

'Well, we do have an announcement to make.' said Russ, 'I've asked Jenny to marry me and she's said yes.'

For a while, nobody said anything until finally Antonio said, 'I had a feeling that's what was going on – welcome to the family Sis.' he stood up and came around the table to give her a big hug.

His parents were obviously not expecting this announcement and sat quietly at the table.

'Mom, Dad, what do you think about our decision?' prompted Russ. He could tell from their reaction that they were not happy about his announcement.

Frank looked at Russ and said, 'You're awfully young to think about getting married.' Then he turned with a scowl on his face and looked directly at Jenny, 'Are you pregnant?'

Nellie gasped and grabbed Frank's arm in reprimand. 'Frank, you don't ask a question like that!'

'It's okay Mom. 'No, she's not pregnant.' replied Russ. 'So, people won't wonder about that, we aren't getting married until June. Now do we have your approval to get married?'

Jenny could tell that Russ was annoyed at his father's reaction and his facial expression announced it clearly. His father realised that Russ would go ahead with the marriage with or without his approval, so reluctantly decided to give his approval. It's not that he didn't like Jenny, but he'd expected Russ to marry an Italian woman. Instead, Jenny's lineage was from Scotland and Ireland.

Frank looked at Nellie – who nodded, and he replied, 'Yes, we give our permission. Now, let's get on with our meal.' he said dismissing any further conversation about the upcoming marriage.

Jenny felt slighted at his abrupt way of giving his approval. He had used the word 'permission' as if he was the one that decided whether they did or did not get married. He didn't seem to understand that they were both legally able to marry with or without parental approval. She knew that in his home he was 'lord and master' and his quiet unassuming wife obeyed him without question.

As Russ drove her home that night they discussed where they would live and what they would need to buy for their home. Russ explained, 'Most of my paycheque I give to my parents. The rest has been spent on buying and running my car and of course taking you out.'

'Do you have any money in a savings account?' Jenny asked.

'I have a couple of thousand dollars. Some of that will have to go towards your engagement ring and our wedding rings. How about you?'

'When I was younger, I babysat a lot, and since I started my job last June, I've been able to buy my bedroom suite. It's a queen-sized bed with two dressers. I should have enough in my savings account to buy a kitchen and living room suite by the time we get married. And I think my parents will let me take the television set from my bedroom.'

Jenny and Russ sat down and made a budget of what money would be coming in and what they anticipated their expenses would be. They were sure they could manage somehow to buy whatever else they needed and of course there would be wedding presents from both sides of the family.

Later, Jenny's parents asked them whether they would like to rent the one-bedroom downstairs unit in a two-story rental property they owned in a nearby suburb. It was an investment property that they and their family had lived in a few years ago. When they moved out, they divided the home into two suites, one upstairs and one downstairs. It sounded ideal and the monthly rental was within their means. Jenny knew that her parents could get much more rent than they were asked to pay and gave them a big hug when she confirmed that they would love to live there. Besides, she'd lived there before, so knew the neighbourhood and how to get around in that area of the city.

Soon, Jenny and her mother started making plans for the wedding.

'Do you want to buy your dress, or do you want me to make it?' Martha asked. Her mother was an accomplished seamstress and Jenny knew that she would do a good job of making it for her. After several weeks of examining bridal patterns they chose one that took advantage of Jenny's trim figure.

Her dress was made mainly of snowy white satin. Its strapless hand-embroidered bodice was beautifully fitted to the dipped waist. The skirt was full, and the overskirt of white satin was gathered up in the front to the dipped waist and flowed downwards towards the sides and ended up in a short train. In the area below this overskirt was a full underskirt of meters of fine silk that had matching embroidery to the top. Being five feet seven inches tall, Jenny was able to wear high heels and still be much shorter than Russ. A shoulder-length veil attached to a smart cloche hat that showed off her beautiful features completed her outfit.

After completing Jenny's wedding dress, they both worked on sewing a going-away ensemble, several other new outfits for Jenny, and Martha's and Susan's wedding outfits.

Russ and his ushers wore white tuxedoes. His brother Antonio was best man and Jenny's brother Jeff and Hugh McKenzie were his ushers. Jenny's matron of honour was her best friend Adele Morrow and her bridesmaids were her cousin Ruby Connelly and Sylvia Collins. Her eight-year-old sister Susan was their flower girl and Ian gave the bride away.

The wedding went off without a hitch and everyone had a wonderful time. For the first time in many years all her father's brothers and sisters were together, along with some of their children and even grandchildren. His brothers Mark, Jack, George and two sisters Jane McCaulley and Joan Henderson had come from distant cities. They did not know it, but this was the last time all six of them would be together.

Jenny had met many of Russ's Italian relatives when she and Russ attended his cousin's wedding in Thunder Bay two months before their own wedding. She'd enjoyed meeting them and had fun dancing with all his cousins at the wedding. The male cousins seemed to vie for the opportunity of dancing with this blonde beauty that was soon to marry their cousin. Many of them were invited and came to Jenny and Russ's wedding and insisted on dancing with the bride.

Shortly after midnight Jenny threw her bridal bouquet (that Doreen caught) and Russ laughingly retrieved the garter from under her skirt and threw it for the men waiting to catch it. Hugh scrambled and was successful in catching it. Two weeks later Hugh and Doreen eloped and were already a married couple by the time Jenny and Russ returned from their honeymoon.

Then it was suddenly time to say goodbye to their family and friends. They all waved goodbye as they gathered around the limousine that drove off with the bride and groom. The couple would spend the night at The Fort Gary Hotel, next door to the train station. Because Russ worked for the railway and had a railway pass, they would leave the next day for their honeymoon train trip to Vancouver. Jenny's father would deliver their travelling bags to the train station, but they each had an overnight bag with them in the limousine.

I can do it! The sky's the limit!

Five

When they entered their honeymoon suite at The Fort Gary Hotel, Jenny was suddenly very shy. She and Russ had not had much to drink at their wedding. Jenny had been kept so busy dancing with relatives and friends that she had only wanted water or soft drinks because of her thirst. However, she was glad to see that the hotel had supplied a bottle of champagne for the honeymoon couple. Russ gestured towards the bottle and Jenny nodded her approval. He popped the cork and poured drinks for them. After they finished their first glass, Russ reached for her glass and placed it on the table. 'I've been waiting so long for this night. I want you so badly I ache.' he murmured, as he snuggled into her neck.

'I have too.' she admitted, 'but I'm a bit scared too. I've never made love before.'

'That makes two of us!' he exclaimed. 'We make a good team, don't we?' he said as he laughed.

They both chuckled and shared another glass of champagne. 'Shall I get undressed?' she asked. He nodded and watched as she gathered her nightgown and toiletries and went into the bathroom. She brushed her hair and cleaned her teeth.

Jenny had shopped carefully for her satin nightgown and decided that it had to be symbolically white rather than a sexy black or red. When she slipped it over her head, she glanced at the mirror. The image staring back at her from looked frightened and her face had a pinched, nervous look to it. She forced herself to smile and taking a deep breath, she opened the door.

Russ's eyes lit up when he saw her in her beautiful nightgown and walked over to her. As he gazed at her, longing shot through him, in the same urgent way it always did whenever he was near her. He had never wanted a woman as much as he wanted her.

'You're so beautiful.' he said as he tilted her chin for a deep kiss. When he pressed his lips against hers, she opened her mouth slightly so that his warm tongue could enter. As he kissed her more deeply and passionately, she felt his hard manhood press almost painfully against her.

Unexpectedly, his kisses stopped. He quickly undressed, throwing his wedding outfit on the chair. Jenny stared apprehensively when she saw him standing naked before her. She had never seen a naked man with an erection before and Russ's manhood seemed very large to her. *'How can that fit into my body?'* she wondered sceptically.

He gazed at her beautiful slim but curvaceous body. Her breasts were young, taut under the satin of her gown and her nipples stood out clearly under the silky fabric. He stood back and slipped the nightgown straps over her shoulders. The gown slithered to the floor and lay like a shimmering pool of satin at her feet. The sudden cool air made her nipples stand fully erect and she shivered.

'You're getting cold,' he said as he lifted her and carried her to their marital bed.

He kissed her deeply. The blood rushed through him and his desire for her was overwhelming. He moved over her body and slipping his hands under her body, lifted her closer to him. He groaned as he spread her legs, clasping her buttocks tightly as he searched to find the entrance to her. He took her urgently, needing to be joined to her, needing to make them as one.

Jenny gritted her teeth and almost screamed with the sudden unexpected searing pain. Russ had not given her time to become ready for penetration. Her body had not produced the lubrication necessary to have painless intercourse. But Jenny didn't know this because she was a virgin and had no knowledge of how Russ should have prepared her for a pleasant introduction to intercourse. She felt him pumping in and out of her, each time causing her more and more pain until he moaned, became rigid and lay still. After he released her and lay back panting on the pillow, she lay beside him with tears streaming down her face and her body bruised, torn and bleeding. He seemed oblivious to the pain he had caused her and was still in the throes of sexual ecstasy.

Jenny reached for the box of tissue beside the bed, grasped several tissues and placed them on her throbbing body. She could feel something oozing from her body. As she rose from the bed, she saw the large red circle of blood on the sheets. She threw the covers back over the ugly stain then staggered into the bathroom, still quietly sobbing.

As she sat on the toilet letting the blood and semen flow into the toilet she sobbed and shivered with emotion. When she felt rid of it, she then wondered what she should do. Her clothing was still in the bathroom, so she reached for her panties and stuffed them with more tissue. A hotel chenille bathrobe hung on the back of the door, so she put that on and wrapped it snugly around her. Then she flushed the toilet, lowered the toilet seat and painfully sat down. She sat there for about five minutes when she heard a quiet tap on the door. It was Russ.

'Can I come in?' he asked.

'Okay.' she replied quietly as she prepared to leave the room. Her mind was in a quandary, and she was shaking all over.

Russ stood aside as she stepped through the door. He closed the door and used the toilet. As he left the bathroom, he saw Jenny sitting on the end of the bed and heard her sobbing, 'What's the matter?' he asked as he examined her tearstained face.

She went to her side of the bed, pulled back the covers and pointed to the red circle in the bed. Russ gave her a puzzled look. 'Why did that happen?'

'You hurt me badly. Why did you have to be so rough? You know I've never made love before? Couldn't you wait a bit, so I was ready for you?'

'I didn't know I would hurt you. I thought you enjoyed it as much as I did.'

'Well, I didn't.' she sobbed. 'I feel very upset that you only considered your needs and rushed things. If this is lovemaking, I don't like it. We must be doing something wrong. I expected we would have love making, not violent sex.'

Russ said, 'I'm so sorry. I'm not good at this.'

With tears still running down her face, Jenny looked at him before she added, 'I think it's because you rushed into it without any romance or time for me to get ready. In the future, I hope you'll take more time to make sure I'm ready.' she sobbed. She went to the bathroom and returned with a bath towel that she placed over the red stain on her side of the bed. She was embarrassed to think what the hotel maid would think about the stain.

Climbing back into the bed, still in the housecoat, she turned her back on him. Russ placed his hand on her shoulder, but she shrugged it off. He gave up trying to placate her and was soon asleep and snoring loudly.

She hardly slept that night and was glad when morning came. After having a shower and getting dressed, she realised she was still bleeding. As she passed by Russ she said, 'I'm going downstairs to the little shop. I have to get something.'

She purchased sanitary pads to absorb the flow that was still coming from her body. The flow wasn't heavy, but she was terribly sore and had to force herself to walk normally.

When she returned to their room, Russ had already ordered breakfast from room service. She really didn't have much of an appetite but forced herself to eat. Because both sets of parents had promised to come to the train station to see them off that morning. She tried to make herself more cheerful, so they wouldn't know how upset she was. Her biggest concern was that Russ didn't seem to think he'd done anything wrong – that it was just because she was a virgin that she hurt so badly. She wondered if he could be right.

They checked out of the hotel and Russ carried their overnight bags next door to the train station. They'd just picked up their travelling luggage and put them on a trolley when Ian and Martha arrived. Russ and Jenny had just been contemplating whether they should find their compartment on the train, so were relieved to see them.

Martha noticed how pinched and white Jenny's face was, and when she hugged her, she asked quietly, 'Is everything all right?'

Jenny nodded, but the mother in Martha knew that something was terribly wrong. Unfortunately, she was not able to talk privately with her daughter before she left because it was soon time for Jenny and Russ to board the train and find their compartment. She gave Jenny another extra-long hug trying to convey that she hoped she would be all right.

'We'll pick you up when you get back from your honeymoon,' Ian said as they boarded the train.

Just before boarding the train she and Russ searched the platform for his parents, but they did not arrive before their train left the station. Jenny could tell that Russ was very disappointed that they had not bothered to come as promised.

Russ's railway passes came in handy for our trip to Vancouver. They were able to obtain a compartment that made into a bed at night.

That night as they prepared for bed, Russ became amorous and obviously expected to have sex again. Jenny backed away from him shaking her head and said, 'Not tonight – I'm still bleeding and I'm far too sore to do it again.' After a perfunctory kiss, they lay spooning throughout the night.

They arrived in Vancouver and spent time exploring the city. It took several days for Jenny to mend and stop bleeding and another day before her internal bruising went down. Russ kept asking whether she was well enough to try again and promised to be gentler with her. On the fourth day of their stay, Russ went to a pharmacy and bought some lubricating cream to see if that would help them. That night they tried again. Jenny was so apprehensive that she found herself tightening up so found that again she didn't enjoy it at all. The lubrication did help somewhat, but Russ still entered her far too soon, just minutes after they'd gone to bed. No foreplay except a few kisses – no romantic words, no caresses, no fondling, no stroking. Jenny kept thinking, '*If this is love-making I don't like it at all!*'

All too soon, their honeymoon holiday was over, and it was time to head back to Winnipeg.

It was Saturday when they returned to Winnipeg. Ian and Martha greeted them at the train station and Ian helped Russ with the luggage. Martha had worried about Jenny the entire time she'd been gone and was glad to see that she looked better – not entirely happy – but better than she'd seemed at the beginning of their honeymoon.

'How was Vancouver?' she asked as she walked beside Jenny.

'Vancouver was wonderful Mom. We explored and really enjoyed the sites there. The weather was perfect.'

'How are you?' her mother asked concern showing on her face.

Jenny shrugged her shoulders and said, 'I'll talk to you about it later, Mom.'

Her parents delivered them to their new home, the downstairs portion of a two-story rental property they owned. They introduced them to the couple, Patrick and Rayna Dorsett who rented the upper floor of the large home. While they were on their honeymoon, Ian had moved her bedroom suite into the home and Martha had been there when their new kitchen and dining room suites were delivered. They had left their wedding gifts on the new dining room table and elsewhere in that room Martha had also gone to the store and stocked the fridge with necessities – even two T-bone steaks they could have that evening for dinner. They didn't stay long but invited Jenny and Russ for dinner at their home the next evening.

The next day, when they arrived at her parent's home, Jenny and her mother went into the kitchen to prepare dinner. As Russ and her father walked through the kitchen her father asked Russ to help him with a problem he was having with his car. 'Call us when dinner's ready.' Ian said. He knew that Martha was very concerned about Jenny and wanted the opportunity of speaking with her privately.

As soon as the men left for their garage, her mother took that opportunity to speak with Jenny. It was obvious that something had gone wrong and her mother was anxious to know if there was anything she could do to help.

'All right; we're alone. Now I want you to tell me what's going on. You looked like death the morning you left for Vancouver and I can't say you looked much better when you got back.'

Jenny hesitated, wondering how much she should tell her mother. Then she decided she had to speak to someone and probably her mother was the best one to talk to.

'Mom, you may or may not have known that I was a virgin when I got married.' she said shyly.

Her mother nodded her head. 'I was quite sure you were – but these days you never know.'

'Well I was and every sexual experience I've had since my wedding night has been horrible.' she said as tears started pouring down her face.

'What happened to make you feel this way?' she enquired.

Jenny told her the complete story and as she explained what had happened, Martha became more and more anxious. 'Is that the way sex is with you and dad?' Jenny asked.

'Oh goodness no! Your father is the best lover a person could ever have – so gentle, never expecting me to have sex unless we both want it. He always waits until I'm ready.' She said, her face a rosy red with embarrassment as she remembered that this was her daughter she was talking to.

'Then what happened with Russ that I hate it so much?' she asked tremulously.

'Honey, a man has to wait till a woman is ready to have intercourse otherwise all he's doing is relieving his own sexual tensions at the expense of his partner. You're going to have to insist that Russ take the time to make sure you're ready for sex. What he's doing to you is not lovemaking. It's pure sex!'

'Okay Mom. I'll talk to him about it. Maybe I can buy some books that explain how important it is for me to be ready. Thanks, Mom. I was embarrassed to speak to anyone about it, but I'm glad we had time to talk about this.' she said as she hugged her mother.

Meanwhile, Ian asked Russ, 'How was your honeymoon?'

'Oh, it was great. We had a great time in Vancouver.' Russ replied.

'Jenny didn't look too good the day you left. I hope she didn't drink too much bubbly and was hung over.' Ian asked as he pointed to a tool he required.

'Oh no. She hardly drank anything at the wedding and we only had two glasses of champagne at the hotel.' he replied as he passed a spanner to Ian.

'Was she ill during the trip?' Ian asked.

'No, she was fine.' Russ wondered where Ian's questions were heading, then frowned as he considered, 'Could Jenny had told her parents about their sexual problems?'

Ian saw that Russ was becoming upset, so decided not to delve more into the situation. Russ was glad when Ian changed the subject and began discussing the problems he was having with his car.

When they joined their spouses for dinner, Ian was glad to see that Jenny looked better. He knew that she and Martha must have taken the opportunity to discuss whatever problem had been bothering Russ and Jenny. He also knew that Martha would share the problem with him. Later when Jenny and Russ had left, she did discuss it with him, and he was furious about the rough way Russ had abused Jenny.

A week later, Jenny made an appointment with Russ's doctor to be fitted for a diaphragm, so she wouldn't become pregnant. As he examined her, he noticed the tear in her vagina and asked her about it. She shyly explained what had happened on her wedding night and asked him if there were any books about intercourse and foreplay.

He shook his head in sympathy, 'This should never have happened. I'm sorry you had such a sad introduction to intercourse. Here are two books I think you should buy or borrow from the library. You need to emphasise to Russ that his total disregard for you during intercourse in interfering with your love life.'

Jenny bought and read the recommended books. Suddenly she understood how intercourse should really be between a couple and realised how selfish Russ was being by not waiting until she was ready.

The next Wednesday night when they went to bed and Russ reached for her, she held him off. 'We have to discuss things. I saw your doctor earlier this week to be fitted for a diaphragm. He asked me about the tear I had in my vagina and said that it would not have happened if you had taken the time to prepare me for intercourse. He's recommended that we read these books.'

She showed him a chapter she'd read that would help him understand what he needed to do to help her become aroused. He read it and promised to change. When Jenny mentioned that she was turned on by some men's cologne, Russ replied, 'You don't expect me to wear that sissy stuff do you?'

Russ did try and improved somewhat but he still hurt her because he was so rough when he tried to stimulate her with his hands. He never took enough time, nor did he do anything romantic to put her in the mood. He never complimented her about how she looked or for all the things she did to make his life comfortable. His efforts didn't seem to do much to improve the situation for Jenny and he soon reverted to his 'wham bam, thank you ma'am' habit of having sex.

During her marriage, Jenney never reached a climax during intercourse with Russ. However, during her visit with the doctor, he had encouraged her to masturbate to bring herself to a climax and she had to accept that this was the only way she could alleviate the sexual tensions that often built up in her body.

Six

Jenny found her marriage to Russ far from ideal and her life was full of turmoil. When she met him, she thought he was her knight in shining armour, and he was during their courtship, but throughout her disastrous honeymoon and marriage Russ used a different set of behaviours than he'd used during their courtship. Russ cloned his father's unacceptable behaviour – refused to help around the house even though they both worked full-time.

The Monday after Jenny and Russ returned from their honeymoon, they both had to return to work. Jenny worked from eight to four o'clock and Russ worked the four-to-twelve shift, so they didn't see each other at night except Wednesday and Thursday evenings, and Saturday and Sunday during the day.

That morning, Jenny prepared their breakfast and was just heading out of the kitchen to leave for work when Russ tapped his spoon on the side of his coffee mug. At their wedding, people had tapped their spoons on the side of their wine glasses, which meant that the bride and groom had to kiss. 'Okay, one kiss - then I have to go.' Jenny said.

'No, I don't want a kiss – that was to tell you I want another cup of coffee.'

Jenny aimed an astounded look at him. She couldn't believe what he'd said.

'Russ, we're in a partnership now. We both work; so, we both pitch in at home. If you want another cup of coffee – there's the coffee pot – help yourself.' she added disgustedly as she snatched up her purse and left for work.

She soon learned that Russ was hopeless around the home. His mother had made his bed, picked up after him and had done everything around the home to make him comfortable. It was soon clear that he expected the same behaviour from Jenny. He'd come home from work and step out of his work clothes and leave them lying on the floor. If they went out socially, he left those clothes over the back of a chair.

The Thursday evening after they returned from their honeymoon, two of their friends came over for dinner. Before they arrived, Jenny was kept busy preparing the meal, setting the table and getting dressed. She'd waited an entire week for Russ to pick up his clothes but saw that they were still lying all over their bedroom. Disgustedly, she went to the back porch, got a large black garbage bag and stuffed Russ's clothes into it including his suit. Then she disgustedly threw the bag into their bedroom closet. Two days later, Russ asked where all his work clothes had gone – that he didn't have any clean ones left.

'Where did you leave them?' asked Jenny innocently.

'In our bedroom.' he replied

'Where in the bedroom?' she said as she stood with her hands on her hips.

'In that corner.' he said as he pointed to the corner where he normally threw his work clothes.

'Don't you know where dirty clothes belong? The laundry basket is in the basement next to the washing machine. And did you expect me to hang up your suit?'

'Well, where are my clothes?' he asked as he peered around the room.

'I only had a few minutes to clean up your mess when our friends arrived for dinner on Thursday. I couldn't leave our bedroom with your clothes all over the room, so I put all the things you'd left lying around in a plastic bag. It's in the closet.' she said as she pointed to the closet then added, 'Clothes do not magically get clean; magic hands don't take them away to wash them and return them all ironed and hanging up. The least you can do is put them in the laundry basket, I'll do the rest.'

After that, he improved a bit, but always acted as if it was an imposition – not his job to clean up after himself. There were all sorts of household duties to sort out between them. With lots of resistance and complaint, they found a system for clearing up, doing laundry and shopping.

When they purchased a dishwasher, Jenny automatically took her dishes and placed them in the dishwasher. Russ left his where they were on the table and they were still there when he came to breakfast the next morning. 'Why did you leave these dishes on the table?' he asked.

'I didn't – you did. I put mine in the dishwasher. I guess you forgot to put yours in there before I washed the rest of them.'

Shortly after her marriage, Jenny realised that their life had changed in many other ways. Their social life was not what it had been before their marriage. She kept encouraging Russ to do the things they had done before they were married, but he kept explaining that they didn't have to do those things any more – that they were married. Why buy her flowers when they had some in their garden? Why take her out for dinner, when they could have it at home? Why should they go dancing when he hated dancing?

Four months after their marriage Russ reluctantly promised Jenny that they would go out to dinner the following Saturday night. He arranged to change shifts with a co-worker, so he could have Saturday and Sunday nights off for a change.

About three o'clock that Saturday afternoon, Jenny started preparing for their night out. After having a leisurely bath using scented bath salts, she fixed her hair in a special way, and slipped into her sexiest dress. By five o'clock, she was ready. Their restaurant reservation was for six so they would have to leave soon.

She went down into Russ's basement workroom and asked, 'When are you going to have a shower and change?'

'What for?' he asked suddenly noticing she was all dressed up.

'We've got a dinner reservation in one hour.'

'Well, we can't go. I'm in the middle of something and don't want to leave it.'

'Are you telling me we aren't going out for dinner after you promised me that we would?'

'That's right.' he said as he turned away from her and continued sanding the piece of wood he was working on.

'When you give me your word, I expect you to keep it!' she threw at him as she climbed the basement stairs.

She now knew that she had not paid enough attention to the warnings she should have recognised when she met Russ – how different his upbringing was from the family life she'd enjoyed before her marriage. He expected to be 'Lord and master' of his home and Jenny was having none of it.

Jenny checked her purse to make sure she had some money, phoned the restaurant, cancelled their reservation and walked to the nearby bus stop. *'Where can I go?'* she wondered, then decided she would visit Adele and her husband Jim. She wished she'd had an opportunity to phone to warn her that she was coming but decided to take the chance that it would be all right. If they weren't home, she would just go to a movie.

It took three busses, but she finally arrived at Adele's home. Adele answered the door and immediately could see that Jenny was upset. 'Come in.' she said as she opened the door.

'What's the trouble?' she asked as she noticed that Jenny was all dolled up.

Jenny explained what had happened and Adele said. 'Jim and I will be having a couple over for dinner. They'll arrive soon. You're very welcome to join us.'

'Oh no. I couldn't do that.' Jenny replied as she stood up to leave.

Adele pushed her back onto the sofa. 'Oh yes you are. You're staying for dinner. No arguments.'

Their friends Jessie and Aaron Millar arrived and the five of them had a lovely evening. Several times Jenny attempted to go home but was encouraged to stay longer. When it was time to go, Aaron offered to drive her home. 'It's not much out of our way – and it will save you the long trip home.'

So, they drove her home. Jenny peeked at her watch along the way and realised that it was after midnight. As they drew up to her front door, she saw a light on in their front window and with a sigh entered the front door. She was not looking forward to what she knew would either be glaring silence or an argument.

There was nobody home, even though the lights were on and she thought she'd seen a shadow through the front window. She prepared for bed and had just turned out the light when Russ came in. He was furious, and she could tell from his breath that he had been drinking.

'Where the hell have you been?' he bellowed.

'Out.' she replied, just as angrily.

'Who were you out with? I saw you arrive in some guy's car. Don't deny it.'

'You were home then when I arrived?' she countered.

'Never mind that – who is he?' he shouted.

'It was they – Jessie and Aaron Miller.' she said as she turned over in bed away from him.

'Well you're not going to get away with it.' he said as he roughly turned her over. He was astride her before she could move. He ripped away her silk pyjama bottoms, but she was so mad that she was determined that he would not rape her.

'Do you get enjoyment out of raping your wife?' she screamed. 'Does it make you feel manlier, if you take me by force?'

He gave her a shove and crawled off her. That night he slept on the sofa in their living room.

I can do it! The sky's the limit!

Seven

The next morning the air was frigid. They were to have dinner at his parent's place that night and because he had promised his father that he would help him dig his garden, they'd left their home shortly after having their lunch. As soon as they arrived at his parents' place, Russ went into the back yard to help his father. Jenny was left with his mother, Nellie. Nellie was rather a chatterbox and with Jenny's raging headache she didn't want to be rude to her mother-in-law. She loved the woman but couldn't tolerate her constant chatter – not today anyway.

'I promised a friend that I would stop in and see her this afternoon. Seeing Russ is busy this afternoon, it will be a good time for me to go see her.'

Jenny got in their car and drove to Adele's home that wasn't far from her in-laws' place. She wasn't home, so Jenny went to a fast food place and had a cup of tea. She returned to her in-laws home less than an hour after she'd left. As she drove into the yard, she saw that everyone was gathered around the back door of the home. Russ's dad, Frank strode over as Jenny was exiting the car.

'What are you doing driving Russ's car without his permission?' he shouted.

'*Just what I need*.' she thought. She'd just calmed herself down but was instantly angry again. How dare this old man tell her what to do!

'This is now my car as well as Russ's, and I have every right to drive it whenever I want to.' she tried to say calmly.

'Russ bought it, so he owns It.' was Frank's curt retort.

'So, I suppose he should ask my permission every time he sleeps in the bed I bought or eats at the kitchen table or sits on the sofa I bought?' she roared back.

Russ suddenly stepped between them. He was still furious at Jenny for what she'd done the night before, 'Don't you dare talk to my father that way!' he shouted at Jenny as he lifted her bodily from the ground.

His fingers gripped her upper arms so tightly she couldn't move. He carried her this way for fifty feet until he reached the public sidewalk at the front of his parent's home. He placed Jenny's feet roughly on the ground, turned her around, and kicked her in the buttocks with his work boots. 'Get out and stay out!' he bellowed.

No one in his family had attempted to intervene. Jenny thought that at least Antonio would have stepped in to help her. She staggered a few steps then regained her balance and kept walking away from Russ – tears streaming down her face. Her purse was still in the car, so she had no money. What was she going to do? Where was she going to go? She just knew she couldn't go back to his parent's home. When she got to the corner of the street, she peered back to see whether anyone had followed her. No one had.

Her own parents lived about ten blocks away, so she started walking towards their home. She noticed that Russ's fingernails had pierced the backs of both her upper arms and they now had rivulets of blood running down them. As she passed a filling station, she decided to ask whether she could use their washroom facilities to clean up her arms and use their phone to call her parents.

The elderly male attendant at the filling station took one look at the distraught young woman and immediately thought '*Rape. This girl has been raped,*' and rushed over to assist her. She was as pale as a ghost and he led her to a chair behind the counter and brought her a glass of water. Everyone in the place was staring at her. The man asked a female customer to get some wet paper towels from the washroom, so he could clean up her arms. Then he went to the first aid kit in the staff room, applied a disinfectant and carefully dressed her wounds.

'Thank you so much,' murmured Jenny. 'Would you please let me use your phone? I want to phone my parents.'

'Of course, you can. Do you want me to call the police?' he asked.

Jenny gave the man a startled look then suddenly understood why he'd said what he did. 'No, that's not necessary. My parents will look after this.'

Jenny didn't want anyone at the filling station to know what had happened to her, so when Martha answered the phone she said, 'Mom I'm at Jackson's filling station on Davidson Road. Can you please pick me up right away?'

Martha could hear from Jenny's voice that something was dreadfully wrong but didn't question her. 'I'll be right there.'

Martha arrived in record time and was upset to see Jenny in such a condition. 'What happened?' she asked the attendant.

'We don't really know. She just walked in here asking to use the washroom and phone. But she had blood running down both arms and looked as if she was going to pass out. I've cleaned the wounds and dressed them. I hope she'll be all right.' replied the concerned attendant.

'Well thank you for taking such good care of her,' added Martha.

As soon as they were driving, Jenny told her mother everything that had happened since the evening before and as soon as they arrived home Martha phoned Ian at work. He worked only minutes away and came right home. Jenny explained again what had happened. 'Do you want me to drive you home to get some of your clothes?' he asked.

'I don't have my purse, so don't have the keys to get in.' she replied.

'That's all right. Seeing we're your landlord, we have an extra set.'

They quickly drove over to Jenny's home, retrieved a suitcase from the garage that Jenny filled with work, casual clothes and toiletries. She saw her father glancing at the torn pyjama bottoms that were still lying in their bedroom floor and shook his head. 'I'll kill him if he ever hits or harms you again!' he raged.

'Dad, since you gave us the portable TV, I think we'd better take that with us.'

'Okay. Now let's get out of here. I don't want to run into Russ the way I feel right now. It could get very nasty.' he added indignantly.

They left, and Jenny returned to her parent's home. They put her things into her old bedroom, and she slept well that night. Martha phoned the filling station and thanked them again for looking after her daughter. She didn't elaborate on what had happened – just thanked the attendant for his kindness.

The next morning, Jenny returned to work, but made sure she wore a long-sleeved outfit so her bandages would not be visible. The Air Force base was not far from her parent's home, so in good weather she was able to walk to work. As Wing Commander Warren passed her desk on Monday morning, he noticed that she seemed to be upset about something. He beckoned to her to come into his office, and then closed the door. 'You look so sad today. Is there anything I can do to help? Do you need some time off?'

'Oh no, just some trouble at home – it will settle down soon, but thanks for your concern.' she replied. He was such a kind man.

He nodded and repeated, 'Just remember if I can help in any way, just let me know.' She nodded as she rose from the chair and returned to her desk.

For six days she didn't hear from Russ. Finally, that Saturday morning he phoned. Ian answered the phone when he called.

'Can I speak to Jenny please?' Russ wanted to know.

'I doubt if she wants to talk to you after what you did to her.' was Ian's reply.

'I want to apologize to her for my behaviour and ask her to come home.' he said earnestly.

Ian turned away from the phone, 'Jenny, do you want to talk to Russ?'

First, she shook her head, but when her father told her what Russ had said, she agreed to speak with him.

Russ repeated his apologies and told her that such a thing would never happen again. 'Can I come over to see you?'

Jenny looked at Ian, 'He wants to come over to see me.'

'Just remind him that your mother and I will be here, and he'd better not start any trouble.' he added worriedly.

Russ promised he wouldn't and arrived a short time later. Even though Ian was six inches shorter and many pounds lighter than he, Russ was intimidated by the man and almost turned back instead of ringing the bell. However, he built up his courage and rang the bell. Ian met him at the door and ushered him into the living room. Jenny and her mother stayed in the kitchen. Ian stood before Russ and said plainly and clearly, 'If you ever harm my daughter again, so help me I'll make you wish you weren't alive!'

Russ nodded his head, 'I promise I will never harm her again. Now can I talk privately with her?'

'Yes, but remember we'll be in the next room.' was Ian's reply as he glared at Russ.

'Okay.' Russ said as he looked at the carpet.

Ian went to fetch Jenny and she squared her shoulders before she left the kitchen. She was apprehensive about being in the same room with Russ, knowing the kind of a temper he'd revealed to her that past Sunday afternoon. But when she entered the room, she saw that Russ was sitting on the sofa with his head in his hands sobbing. He looked up when she entered the room with such anguish on his face, that she couldn't remain furious with him.

He stood up and cautiously approached her, 'I'm so sorry I hurt you. I shouldn't have done what I did either Saturday night or Sunday. Did I hurt you very much?' he asked as he started examining her.

She'd waited till that morning to take the bandages off her arms, but the marks and bruises still looked very sore and tender. 'Oh my God.' he said as he looked at them. 'I can't believe I did that to you!'

'Well you did, and I need you to promise that you'll never do anything like that again.' she admonished him.

'I do. I do. Can you ever forgive me?' he said contritely.

'I'll forgive you this time, but I will walk out for good if you ever hurt me again.' was Jenny's emphatic reply.

Jenny gathered her things, gave her parents a big hug and went home with Russ. Before she left, she told her parents that Russ was truly sorry and had promised that he would never harm her again. Ian just shook his head as he said, 'Time will tell. Time will tell.'

For a while they went out socially the same as they had before their marriage. Russ bought her flowers, told her he loved her and spent much more time with her. The only thing that didn't improve was their sex life.

At first Jenny refused to go to Russ's parent's home for their usual Sunday noon meals, but after several weeks Russ begged her to go, so she relented. Jenny and Frank were never destined to be close. Frank had refused to apologise for his outburst and Jenny certainly wasn't going to give in to the tyrant. She had to steel herself before each visit, telling herself that she wouldn't argue with him. Frank and Jenny seldom if ever spoke directly to each other and you could cut the air with the hostility between them. Nellie sat looking from one to the other shaking her head and was upset that their feud was not resolved.

Within two months, everything in their life went back to the way it had been before their separation and Jenny realised their honeymoon was over and the man she married, was not the man she thought she'd married. Because they seldom went out socially and their friends had drifted away, Jenny was very lonely and seriously thought about leaving Russ.

Eight

However, fate had other plans, as she now lay in a hospital bed having just been given the devastating news that she may never walk again. Her Orthopaedic specialist, Dr. Warren had said, 'Jenny, I'm afraid I have bad news. I've consulted with two other Orthopaedic specialists and we all believe that you will not be able to walk again.'

What a horrible announcement that had been. When she was younger, Jenny had trained for six years with an Olympic swimming team so was very physically fit. The thought of spending the rest of her life in a wheelchair sent her into a deep depression and the least little thing seemed to end up with her sobbing. After she was released from the hospital, Martha came over every day to help her with physiotherapy, but her calf muscles deteriorated quite quickly.

Jenny realised that she was furious; furious at the other driver; furious about not being able to walk and furious about life in general. She placed a pillow over her abdomen and pounded it repeatedly. She felt so defeated and depressed that she didn't want to go on living.

'What did I ever do to deserve this?' she wailed. She cried for a long time. Then her fighting spirit kicked in and she mentally prepared for her next battle.

The afternoon, before she was released from hospital, Dr. Warren explained that he'd arranged for a carer to be with her to help her manage at home.

Russ drove her to their home. He'd made several changes to their home so that Jenny to manage easier. They were home only a short time when the doorbell rang. It was her carer, who introduced herself, 'Hi, I'm Janet Blakely.'

They shook hands then Janet explained what would happen. 'I'll come in the afternoon just before Russ leaves for work and will stay until he returns shortly after midnight. I know he's off Wednesday and Thursday, so I won't come those days. I'll do this for two weeks and the third week will come only Friday, Sunday and Tuesday. After that you'll be on your own.'

She noticed Jenny's look of panic and quickly added, 'But you can call me any time after that if you need further help.'

Janet taught Russ and Jenny how to get her into and out of bed from her wheelchair. Soon Jenny was able to accomplish these tasks without assistance using the bar that had been installed over her bed. Janet also showed Jenny how to move herself out of her wheelchair into and out of a chair that was set up in her shower. 'It's very important that you remember to put the brake on your wheelchair, so it doesn't roll away from you when you are transferring to and from it.'

Then she explained to Russ the importance of moving things down to lower cupboards, so Jenny could reach the items she required to perform her everyday tasks and activities.

At first, Jenny had problems propelling herself around in her wheelchair, and her arms and shoulders ached from the effort. She had not developed the muscular shoulders and arms that modern swimmers have because her training had not included weightlifting. But soon Jenny was able to do most of the things she had to do for herself without Janet or Russ's assistance.

After Russ left for work on her first day alone, Jenny felt a bit of panic wondering whether she could cope by herself. She sat in her wheelchair looking around her empty home feeling very frightened and alone. To help her cope, she decided to phone Elaine and see how she was doing. Elaine heard the panic in Jenny's voice.

'Would you like me to come over?' she asked. She was able to drive even though her left foot was still in an ankle cast.

'That would be great!' exclaimed Jenny, so pleased that she wouldn't have to spend the evening alone.

Elaine was very glad to hear from Jenny. They had a wonderful evening laughing over silly things. At the end of the evening when Elaine had gone home, Jenny realised that it was the first time she'd felt happy since before her accident. Elaine was also pleased that she had come and vowed to do so regularly in the future. She and Jenny kept in touch, called each other at least once a week and Elaine drove over to visit Jenny many evenings when Russ was at work.

After helping Jenny for three weeks, Janet said, 'This is my last day with you. However, if you find you need more help here's the number you can call for assistance.' She gave Jenny a hug and they said goodbye.

Jenny found it quite intimidating being on her own at first. However, her parents had spoken with Jenny's next-door neighbour Agnes

Evans who agreed to be on call should Jenny need anything or if she felt unwell. Agnes also helped by stopping by to see if there were any groceries or supplies Jenny might need.

Jenny, always an avid reader, found she now had time to read as much as she wanted to. She read novels, magazines and the daily newspapers. The second evening when she was on her own, she was reading the newspaper when she spotted an interesting article about a new revolutionary medical breakthrough called biofeedback. The article explained that physical therapists used biofeedback to help stroke victims regain movement in paralysed muscles.

'I wonder if they could help me?' she wondered as she continued to read the article. The article said that biofeedback was based on the idea, confirmed by scientific studies, that people have the innate potential to influence with their minds many of the automatic, involuntary functions of their bodies.

Jenny was so excited she could hardly restrain herself. 'I must look into this,' she thought. The next morning while Russ was out buying groceries, she phoned the hospital she'd been in just three weeks before.

'Hello, I'm Jenny Carponi. I was a patient in your hospital until three weeks ago. Can you tell me whether you have a biofeedback specialist on your staff?'

'Sorry we don't, but we have a list of them we can give you and you can choose one you think might be helpful. Now let me see… where did I put that list? Ah – here it is.'

The receptionist gave Jenny a list of three specialists she might want to call. Jenny jotted down the three specialists' phone numbers and addresses and decided that the one nearest her home would probably be the best one. When she called to make an appointment, they were able to fit her in the next morning. The day of the appointment, she told Russ she had an appointment at another specialist's office but didn't let him know that her orthopaedic specialist hadn't referred her to him. He left her at the office while he did an errand saying he would be back in an hour to get her.

How enlightening was her visit, and how uplifted she felt after that first appointment! Dr. Bowles hooked her up to a machine and showed her how it worked, and how she could eventually be able to use the techniques herself without the need to be hooked up to the machine. After their session and Jenny was back in the waiting room waiting for Russ, she knew she had to stem her excitement, so Russ wouldn't know what she was up to.

She had several sessions that week and was hopeful that biofeedback would work for her. However, she didn't want Russ or her parents and get their hopes up that she could walk again, so she didn't tell them about this special treatment.

When she was alone, she practiced biofeedback at least four or five times a day concentrating mainly on moving her feet. She realised she'd have to push herself hard if she wanted to walk again. And she was going to walk again, if she died trying!

In addition to the biofeedback sessions, Jenny devised a way to drape a towel under her feet so that she could lift them up one at a time to exercise them. She asked Russ to help her, but he always seemed to find some excuse not to help so she began to have doubts whether he still loved her or wanted her to improve.

Her parents had offered to help but she felt so guilty taking advantage of them when Russ was the one who should be helping her. After all he was her husband and it shouldn't be left to them to drop everything, so they could help her. However, because she wanted to walk so badly, she reluctantly resorted to asking them and even her neighbour Agnes Evans to assist with her physiotherapy. They helped by raising and lowering her legs and by making her legs move as if she were riding a bicycle. Her mother also became very adept at massaging her legs and back to relieve the muscle spasms Jenny often suffered after exercising.

Jenny had been taught many skills when she trained for the Olympics. One was the ability to go *'past the wall'* – the wall every athlete comes to where they don't think they can go further. She used that skill towards walking again. It took her six months to move her left big toe. She whooped with glee and Russ rushed to her side, thinking she had hurt herself. She finally explained what she had been doing for the past six months without her family's knowledge.

Then the painful physiotherapy began, but she continued to improve week by week. As the feeling in her legs returned – so did the pain, and she was often in tears because of it. She hated taking pain killers, so toughed it out. Every little success was written in a journal. She brought out her journal when she felt emotionally down, feeling sad because she still could not stand and walk without assistance which boosted her spirits until she hit her next low.

Nine

Jenny knew that when she was better, she'd have to face a court case against the driver who had caused her accident. She and her family had learned that when the police investigated the accident site, they were able to determine that the vehicle that hit Jenny's car was travelling well over the speed limit even for bare concrete and was being driven far too fast for the treacherous road conditions. They also noted that even though Jenny had her foot solidly on the brake, her car had been pushed backwards for seventy-five feet.

Three months after her accident, when Jenny was sufficiently healed to testify against the driver, she and her grandmother attended a court hearing. After hearing their testimony, the judge charged the eighteen-year-old driver of the other car with reckless driving. He was given a heavy fine, ordered to pay Jenny's legal fees and his insurance company had to pay for all Jenny's medical expenses now and in the future.

As Jenny sat in the courtroom in her wheelchair, she, Russ, her parents and grandmother were shocked when they heard the judge give the amount of her compensation settlement for her pain and suffering.

'I award to the plaintiff, four thousand dollars as compensation for her pain and suffering.' he announced.

As Jenny sat in the courtroom in her wheelchair, she, Russ and her parents were highly insulted that the judge thought that her injuries and not being able to walk again warranted a settlement of a paltry four thousand dollars. How insulting. They stared unbelievingly at each other and Jenny's lawyer had to restrain Ian from standing up and shouting at the judge. They sat there shaking their heads.

'Court adjourned.' announced the court clerk.

In the hallway outside the court room, Jenny's lawyer explained that because she was employed as a secretary, her injuries would not receive the same settlement as would be awarded to those working in higher-paid positions.

'Can't we appeal?' Ian asked.

'You could, but you would be responsible for all legal and court costs – and you might not win.' was his sad advice.

Jenny, having no other real option, took the money, opened a bank account and put it into a high interest-bearing account in her name. She didn't want to put it into their joint account because she was still concerned that Russ might possibly walk out on her. If her marriage ended, she wanted to have at least this money to fall back on.

Ten

Once when Jenny was practicing her biofeedback, she became aware that Russ was standing in the doorway observing her. 'What are you doing?' he asked, 'You're grunting and groaning as if you're working hard.'

'I'm using biofeedback to try and help with the muscle spasms I have in my back and legs.' she lied.

For six months, Jenny didn't give up even though she did not see or feel any response from the muscles she was trying to move. Her legs were now rather scrawny looking, even though she tried to keep them moving. From time to time she did feel very depressed and was ready to give up, but immediately she gave herself a mental kick in the pants and started practicing again. She was not going to give up!

Soon it was June, six months after her accident. Summer had arrived. and she was enjoying the sunshine, sitting in a lounge chair in their back yard. Russ was puttering with his car in the garage. So, she knew he could not see her as she strained to move her muscles. That morning she concentrated on trying to move the toes on her left foot. As she watched her big toe – she thought she saw it move. 'Nah. That's just wishful thinking.' she told herself and tried it again. Again. it moved – up and down as she concentrated on it.

Jenny was ecstatic. She'd done it! She screamed for Russ, 'Russ come here quick!'

He rushed out from the garage wiping his oily hands on a rag, thinking she had fallen or been hurt somehow and was relieved to see her still sitting where he had left her. He did notice that her face was full of smiles and that she was terribly excited about something. 'What happened?' he asked.

'Watch!' she said as she pointed excitedly at her left foot.

Russ watched, wondering what she was doing. Then he too saw her toe move and looked incredulously at her. 'How did that happen?' he asked in awe.

'I've been practicing biofeedback for almost six months now. It's finally working! Please help me get inside so I can phone Mom and Dad and give them the good news.'

Her parents were beaming when they came to see what she had accomplished. After that breakthrough, Jenny insisted that she receive formal physiotherapy.

When she saw Dr Warren, he was amazed at her progress. He agreed with her and immediately arranged treatment at a local rehabilitation centre where she could receive ongoing treatment as an outpatient. He sent a letter to the other driver's insurance company that her recovery was still in progress and they were still responsible for these additional medical expenses.

Jenny couldn't understand why, but she went into a deep depression. She kept telling herself that she was on the road to recovery – that she had survived a terrible injury and was going to recover. Russ couldn't understand her behaviour and started withdrawing from her again. Her depression continued, until in desperation, she decided to talk to the minister of her church, Reverend Thompson. She asked him why she wasn't more elated over her progress. He explained that he thought she was suffering from Post-Traumatic Stress Disorder (PTSD) – that she had been under tremendous pressure while she was incapacitated but wouldn't allow herself to wallow in it. Now that she was on the road to recovery, she was able to relax, and the immensity of her condition finally hit home in her subconscious.

Reverend Thompson explained that her Post Traumatic Stress Disorder was a natural emotional reaction to a deeply shocking and disturbing experience. Jenny had spent the past six months denying that anything traumatic had happened to her. Instead she had concentrated on making her legs move – against all odds. When they did move, she was boomeranged back to the first day she arrived in the hospital and realised that she would never walk again.

He added that post-traumatic stress following an accident was largely due to the shattering of basic assumptions victims hold about themselves and the world, that the world is kind, caring, compassionate, generous, and giving; and the world is meaningful. He explained that there is growing recognition that PTSD can result from many types of shocking experiences including those who have been involved in traumatic road and plane accidents. He added that sometimes those who are in accidents may think that they are going mad. They are not, as PTSD is an injury, not an illness. Jenny left their session feeling revitalised and back on track now that she understood what was happening to her emotionally.

Suddenly she was energised and again spent more and more hours pushing herself to the limits of her endurance. The physiotherapist often placed Jenny in a heated pool and soon Jenny was swimming on her own with a flotation device around her tummy. Bit by bit she regained the use of first her feet, then her legs. It was a day for celebration when she was finally able to stand and hold her weight.

She was overwhelmed with joy at her progress. However, her gain in movement came with a serious drawback. Her legs and back now had feeling in them and she suffered from intense pain. She used biofeedback to try to relieve the pain but was only marginally successful. When she took pain medication, she felt lethargic so took them as seldom as possible. One morning her pain was so severe she called Dr. Warren to make an appointment to see if he could suggest a remedy. When she learned that he was on holidays and she'd have to wait four weeks for an appointment, she knew she had to do something drastic. She couldn't tolerate the intense pain any longer without relief. In desperation, she called a chiropractor, Dr. Redwood whom Elaine had recommended.

Jenny was apprehensive and wondered if she was doing the right thing, but after her first treatment that afternoon, she was amazed to learn that her pain was greatly relieved. Her pain had lessened to such a degree that it was as if someone had removed an opaque piece of plastic from in front of her eyes. She felt wonderful and almost pain free for the first time in months.

Her excitement lasted until she got up the next morning and she was again in intense pain. Luckily, she had another appointment with Dr. Redwood that day. When she saw him, he explained, 'Everything along your spine has been such a mess for so long, that it will take months of treatment to encourage your back to stay in place for any length of time. Are you willing to keep coming until we're able to stabilise it?'

'Oh yes! Yesterday was wonderful after you put everything in place again. I'll do anything to get it to stay that way permanently.'

Dr. Redwood also recommended that she receive regular massages in addition to her physiotherapy sessions, so her muscles would remain relaxed instead of in spasm. She asked him to send a letter to the insurance company telling them of this additional treatment that had been recommended.

Jenny received regular treatment with Dr. Redwood and had a sports massage every two weeks. Jenny used her wheelchair most of the time, but at home, she occasionally held onto furniture to get around. She was improving.

Eleven

Jenny had not had sex with Russ (she refused to think of it as lovemaking because it wasn't) since before she'd had her car accident. She wondered, '*Will I ever have enough feeling in my lower body for us to have sex again even though I don't enjoy it? Will Russ stay with me if we can't?*'

She needn't have worried, because six weeks after her accident Russ made it clear that he intended to continue having sexual relations with her whether she was capable of participating or not. He didn't consult her about this or even hug or kiss her before entering her. That night he simply climbed over her, parted her legs, lifted her hips and dove into her. Jenny just lay there in shock.

'*He knows I feel nothing, but he still does this.*' she thought as he rammed into her. '*It seems that his own sexual release is far too important to him to allow me to participate in any way.*'

'Would it hurt you too much to at least pretend I'm part of this sex act?' she asked after he was sated.

'What do you mean?' he asked

'You could at least hug me or kiss me to let me be part of your sexual release!' she added.

He could see in the dim light that she was furious and vowed to do better next time. However, most of the time she was asleep when he got home from work, so he neglected following through with his promise. He just climbed aboard her, sometimes even before she was awake and relieved himself.

Many times, the first inkling Jenny had that he was even home was when he groped her and took off her pyjama bottoms. Most of those times, she was too sleepy or didn't have time to get up and insert her diaphragm.

Eighteen months after their marriage, one year after her accident and six months after she'd started recovering movement in her feet. Jenny realized she could be pregnant. Her family doctor, Dr. Sims examined her and confirmed that she was pregnant.

'How will I manage?' she asked apprehensively.

'You're improving so much with your therapy, that you'll manage all right.' He reassured her.

Russ was so excited when she told him that night. You'd have thought he'd performed a miracle. Later Russ marvelled when he first felt their baby move through Jenny's abdomen. Nellie was also enthralled. She'd never felt either of her babies move nor had she felt them externally with her hand. Nellie had been overweight before, during and after her pregnancies so Jenny surmised that the layers of fat had kept her from feeling her babies move.

As Jenny progressed through her pregnancy, she realised that there really wasn't room in their one bedroom rented home for a baby. She secretly checked the paper for a bargain home and found a small two-bedroom home that would need some work but would be fine for their growing family. That evening she told Russ about the home she had found.

'We can't afford to buy a home,' was his simple reply.

'That's where you're wrong.' Jenny said excitedly. 'With the down payment I'm able to put on it, our mortgage payments would be the same as our rent payments are now and it will be a bigger home.'

'What down payment? You know we don't have much in our joint savings account.' he exclaimed.

'Well, I have an account of my own that I opened with the money I received from the settlement from my car accident. There's more than four thousand dollars in that account. We can use that for the down payment.' she said excitedly.

They went to see the home, purchased it and moved in a month later. It was only three blocks away from Russ's parents' home. Sadly, for Nellie, Russ, and Antonio, Frank was diagnosed with pancreatic cancer and died five months later, before his first grandchild was born.

Jenny had an uneventful pregnancy but as she progressed with her accident recovery, she felt more sensations in her lower extremities and back. She suffered with terrible back pain and was often in tears as she fought the pain. This did not stop her from continuing her physiotherapy and she kept gaining extra movement in her feet and legs.

She kept wondering when her baby was going to be born. His birth date was predicted to be in mid-August, but that time came and went. Jenny was so huge she felt like a beached whale and wondered if her baby could be twins rather than just one baby. Finally, on the first day of September, she went into labour. Her first labour pain was at seven-thirty in the evening, and she started timing her contractions. By nine o'clock she realised that they were only five minutes apart and narrowing fast. Russ drove her to the hospital. When Dr. Sims examined her, he explained that it was just one big baby she was carrying, and he expected her to be in labour for some time. Their son Mark was born just before midnight. He was nine pounds six ounces, so was a large baby to have been born after only four and a half hours of labour. Jenny thought how ironic it was that he arrived on what Canadians celebrate as 'Labour Day.'

Dr. Sims delivered the baby and after she was settled in her room he explained, 'Your delivery was likely quicker because you had a large tear at the entrance to your vagina that was never repaired.' he added, 'I've repaired that tear, so you might feel sore for a few days.'

Jenny was too embarrassed to tell her doctor that the tear had happened on her first sexual experience. The nurse arrived with a bundle in her arms. She jokingly said, 'We searched all over the ward for a newborn with your name tag on it – but all we could find was this two-month old beauty.'

It was true. Mark did not resemble most newborns. His flesh was filled out and when he looked at Jenny, she was sure he was focusing his eyes on her. He was a model baby – very happy and contented. She nursed him until he was eight months old then on a regular visit to his paediatrician, he advised her to stop nursing him. Mark was a strapping baby who was thriving well, but Jenny had become a bag of bones because she'd lost so much weight. Her frail frame was unable to take the extra burden of nursing and looking after Mark. She could not carry him around unless she was in her wheelchair.

Disappointed at having to do so, Jenny stopped nursing Mark and the next month started taking birth control pills. It wasn't long before she realised that she'd waited one month too long and found herself pregnant again. Russ was so proud – as if it somehow it proved *his* fertility.

This time, her morning sickness was so severe that Dr. Sims prescribed medication to try to ease her discomfort. One Sunday night, a month later, she was watching television when she learned that babies were being born with deformities and that a new anti-nausea medication called Thalidomide was being taken off the market. Doctors were advising women who had taken the drug to see their doctors and possibly have abortions. Jenny had used up all her medication and had thrown away the container, so didn't know whether that was the medication she'd been prescribed. She hated to bother Dr. Sims at home on a Sunday night, so spent a sleepless night wondering if her baby could be born deformed. She called his office first thing Monday morning and was put through to Dr. Sims right away.

'I was in the process of phoning all the women who had been prescribed anti-nausea medication to let them know that I have never prescribed Thalidomide to my patients. So, your baby is safe.' he announced with a smile.

'Thank goodness. I really had a rough night wondering if the baby would be all right. I understand some women are having abortions because the drug is likely to cause severe deformities.' she queried.

'Yes, sadly that's true, but in your case, it wasn't prescribed.' he said emphatically.

'Thanks Dr. Sims. I feel very relieved.' she added gratefully.

Jenny hadn't phoned Martha about her fears the night before but phoned her right away. 'Oh my God.' she replied. 'You were certainly lucky, weren't you?'

When Jenny first recognised that the flutter she was feeling in her abdomen, was made by her baby, she was very excited and told Russ about it. During her pregnancy with Mark, she had not had enough feeling in her abdomen to feel such a light flutter. After her morning sickness was over, Jenny's pregnancy progressed normally.

Jenny and Russ examined their home and realised that there really wasn't room for two babies in their home as it was now, so Russ started renovating their home. The living room was large, but what would soon be Mark's and the new baby's bedroom was quite small, so he decided to move the living room wall and make that bedroom larger.

Jenny had to be very careful to make sure Mark didn't eat any sawdust off the floor or grab one of Russ's dangerous tools. It was a trying time, because their home was not very large, and there wasn't much room where she could pen Mark up and keep him safe.

Russ was still remodelling their living room but was at work when Jenny heard Mark's sudden terrified scream. She rushed into the bedroom that was being renovated and quickly analysed what had happened. Russ had failed to replace the cover on an electrical outlet and Mark had somehow put his tiny fingers around the socket making an electrical connection. He was getting jolt after jolt of power and his little body jerked every time one surged through his body. Jenny rushed over to Mark, pushed herself out of her wheelchair onto the floor so she wouldn't be near metal and pulled his hand out of the socket.

She and Mark ended up lying on the floor a few feet away from the outlet. Jenny realised that she too had received a terrible shock just by pulling Mark's hand out of the socket. They both lay on the rug sobbing; Mark because he had received several jolts of electricity and she because her son had been hurt and knowing that the shock could have harmed her unborn baby.

As soon as she had comforted Mark, she phoned Martha. 'Mom I need your help. Russ left the cover off an electrical outlet and Mark has received several jolts of electricity. I had to pull his hand out of the socket, so I got a shock too. Can you come and take us to the hospital emergency ward?'

Her mother replied, 'We'll be right there.'

In record time her parents arrived. Ian drove, and Martha held Mark as he continued to cry. In the emergency ward they were taken into two separate curtained rooms and two doctors dealt with their injuries. The paediatrician, Dr. Williams, examined Mark while Ian stayed in the room with him. Dr. Sims attended to Jenny and Martha stayed with her. Jenny kept glancing over towards the curtain around Mark and asking, 'Is he all right? Is he all right?'

Mark had cried the entire drive to the hospital, so she was afraid that he had been injured more than she'd originally thought. The only sign of injury she could find before they left for the hospital was a small burn on his left hand. By now, Jenny knew that Mark was left-handed, so hoped there were no serious injuries to his hand.

'He's going to be fine – just some minor burns on his hand.' said Dr. Williams. 'He's had a terrible fright. There's no damage to his nerves and he seems all right mentally as well. But as a precaution, we'll keep him under observation overnight in case there's something we've missed. But I think he'll be fine.'

Dr. Sims examined Jenny – listening carefully to the baby's heartbeat. 'The baby's heartbeat is a little fast, but that's understandable after the shock it's received. Your heartbeat is fast too, but that too is understandable after the shock you've received and the worry it's caused. We won't know whether there's been any serious damage to the baby until it's born, but it's likely the baby will be fine. We'll monitor your pregnancy every week from now on.'

'So, we won't know for six weeks or so whether the baby has been damaged by the shock I received?' she said with concern.

'Unfortunately, no we won't. But it's likely the baby will be fine. We'd also like to keep you in for observation overnight, but I expect to release you tomorrow morning.'

Russ had forbidden Jenny to call him at work, so Martha promised to leave a note on the door of their home so Russ would know where they were.

'I'll be back early tomorrow morning to see how you're doing.' Martha said as she left Jenny's ward.

Mark was sent to the paediatric ward and Jenny to the maternity ward, so they didn't see each other until morning. In the morning, when Dr. Sims asked her how she felt, Jenny smiled and replied, 'I feel fine. I'm surprised that I do, but I feel fine.'

'You can go home, but if you have any further symptoms don't hesitate to call me right away.' he said as he signed her discharge papers. Jenny dressed and wheeled herself to Mark's ward to see how he was doing. The ward nurse stated, 'Dr. Williams says he can be released this morning. He's smiling and waiting for his mommy to come. He'll be glad to see you.'

Jenny cuddled Mark, signed his discharge papers and took him for a ride in her wheelchair back to her ward. Soon Martha arrived and drove them home. When they arrived, Russ was still in bed, but as soon as he heard them in the kitchen he got up.

'How could you do something so careless?' Jenny asked as she pointed to the electrical outlet that now had its proper cover on it. 'How could you be so careless! All of us could have died!'

'I'm sorry. I was in a rush to get to work. I guess I forgot to put it on.' he replied quietly.

Jenny just gave him a scathing look and made coffee for the three of them. Martha had not said a word, but her hostile glance echoed Jenny's comments. She was furious with Russ, didn't trust herself to say a word to him and left shortly after finishing her coffee.

Twelve

Three days later, when Russ was doing their weekly shopping, Jenny's water broke and a few minutes later she had her first labour pain. She called Dr Sims who advised her to come directly to the hospital to ward off infection. Jenny promised to do so as soon as Russ returned.

She packed a bag for herself and two for Mark then phoned Martha to ask if she could look after Mark. Martha had already agreed to look after Mark during Jenny's confinement, but this was six weeks earlier than she expected. She agreed, and they dropped Mark off on their way to the hospital.

Jenny's labour was long and arduous – far different than when she'd delivered Mark. After thirty-four hours of hard, painful labour, their son Bruce was born. He weighed only five pounds but was considered a big baby seeing he was born six weeks prematurely. Dr. Sims said he would likely have been close to ten pounds if he'd been born full term.

Because he was a preemie and was having breathing problems he was whisked away and placed in an incubator. Jenny was taken to her room and when she felt a bit rested asked the nurse if she go to the nursery to see her new son.

'We'd like to hold off on that for a while.' said the nurse.

Immediately Jenny began to panic. 'Why won't you let me see my baby? Is something the matter with him?' she asked. Pictures of Thalidomide babies flashed in front of her eyes.

'Oh no – he's fine. Because your water broke, we took the precaution of taking a blood sample to see if you had picked up any infection. Well it appears that you do have an infection and by the look of your left eye,' she said as she examined it, 'You're heading for a bout of conjunctivitis.'

Jenny gave her a questioning look. 'The popular name for that is 'pink eye' and it's highly infectious. You'll have to be in isolation yourself and until we know for sure, we don't want you to go near your baby in case you pass it on to him.'

When Russ visited her that afternoon before going to work, he had to wear a mask. They discussed names for the new baby and decided they would call him Bruce.

Jenny did have conjunctivitis, so was not able to go near Bruce. She was dripping milk, but they couldn't give it to Bruce in case it passed her infection to him. But they did pump her breasts, so she would continue producing milk. She normally would have gone home the next day, but they were worried that she would pass the conjunctivitis onto her family at home.

By the time Jenny was discharged from the hospital four days after her delivery, she had almost stopped producing milk. She was told that Bruce would have to remain in his incubator until his weight returned to five pounds and his breathing improved, so she wouldn't have been able to nurse him anyway.

Russ picked Jenny up at the hospital then retrieved Mark at her parent's home. Finally, when Bruce was three weeks old, Jenny received word that she could bring Bruce home from the hospital. He looked so tiny next to Mark. Mark patted the little bundle and said, 'Baby. Baby.'

'Yes Mark. That's your little brother Bruce. Can you say Bruce?' she enquired.

'Brut.' he said. Mark had been saying words for months and seemed to pick up words very easily. He was also toilet trained and did not wear diapers any more. Jenny thanked her lucky stars that she only had one baby in diapers.

Jenny was dismayed that she hadn't been able to bond with Bruce until he was three weeks old. He was a baby who was not comfortable being cuddled and often cried if someone picked him up. Jenny also wondered if the electrical shock had affected him in some way. Dr Sims said it was too early to determine whether he had any permanent brain damage from the shock but would test him when he got older. Jenny was very sad to realise that she did not feel the closeness with Bruce that she'd always felt with Mark and of course could not breast feed him and have that special bond either.

Bruce was a fussy baby but loved his food. Jenny soon learned that when he awoke from his naps, he wanted food – now! One day when she was preparing a meal and Russ and Mark were out in the back yard, she thought she heard Bruce stir in the bedroom. Instead of heating his bottle as she usually did, she went directly to his dimly lit bedroom. He was silent. She looked closer and was alarmed by what she observed. His little face was blue, and his eyes stared at her. She put down the crib side, snatched him up and took him into the living room where there was better light. He wasn't breathing. '*Crib death!*' she thought in terror.

She screamed for Russ, and began infant resuscitation knowing that she had to be careful not to blow too hard into his little lungs. She also knew that she should cover both his nose and mouth with her mouth. After she had given her first puff of air, she looked at Bruce. He was still not breathing. She did it again. He was still not breathing. By that time Russ and Mark were standing at her side watching what she was doing.

'I've called an ambulance.' Russ said. Their car was in the shop getting repaired, so they had no way of getting him to the hospital.

Thankfully, after her third puff of air, Bruce began breathing and let out a little mewing sound. His face had a puzzled look then he took a big breath and bellowed his rage.

Soon a police car pulled up at the door, lights flashing. The officer said, 'All the ambulances are out right now. We're to take your son to the hospital. How is he?'

Jenny was able to tell the officer that she had done pulmonary resuscitation on Bruce and that he was now breathing all right. The officer peered into Bruce's face and nodded. 'We still should get him to the hospital to see what happened to him.'

When Bruce was admitted, the doctor on call that day said they were lucky - that Bruce would likely have died if Jenny hadn't immediately resuscitated him. 'It could have been a case of SIDS.' he said as he gazed at the parents.

Russ's puzzled look confirmed that he did not know what SIDS was, so he explained, 'Sudden Infant Death Syndrome'. We have no idea what causes some babies to die suddenly and unexplainably. From what you've said, he's a robust, healthy baby. But we'll have to put him into the hospital on a monitor in case the same thing happens again.'

The next day, Bruce's nose was running like a tap. He'd been in the early stages of a bad cold. The doctor said that the cause of his breathing problems was likely a plug of mucus that had settled in his throat as he slept. He advised Jenny to place him on his side when he slept to ensure he didn't have the same problem again. He did however want to keep Bruce in the hospital for two more days on the monitor in case he stopped breathing again.

Bruce went home on the fourth day and was fine except for his runny nose. He never had another episode like that again.

Thirteen

When Bruce was eighteen months old Russ purchased a piece of property on the waterfront at Sunset Beach, fifty miles from Winnipeg. It was close to Grand Beach where Jenny had spent most of her childhood summers. Jenny didn't know until later that Russ had the property and the cottage, listed in his name only. The property was lakefront, but when they first saw it, it was covered by trees and brush.

By now, Jenny was out of her wheel chair, used a cane to walk and was able to drive a car. Her balance was still not perfect, but she managed quite well without her wheelchair. She was able to go for longer periods of time between visits to the Chiropractor.

Russ and Jenny spent every weekend clearing the lot by hand while Jenny's sister Susan babysat the boys.

'Where are we going to find the money to buy roof rafters and trusses, shingles, nails and other things I don't have?' Russ asked Jenny.

'We don't have much in our savings account, do we?' she replied.

'Could we borrow some money from your parents? I'll get my Christmas bonus in December, so we could pay them back then.' suggested Russ.

'I can ask them, but they may say 'no'.' Jenny said cautiously.

Jenny spoke with Ian and Martha who agreed to lend them the fifteen hundred dollars Russ estimated they would need to start building their cottage. When Russ got his Christmas bonus, he spent it on more material to add inside walls to the cottage but never repaid her parents for the money that was borrowed.

After two years, the cottage was completed sufficiently enough that they spent many happy weekends and summers there. The boys enjoyed playing on the beach in front of their cottage. They built sandcastles and swam in the water and thoroughly enjoyed the short Canadian summers. They frequently saw white pelicans that roosted on a nearby island. Russ built a dock in front of their cottage and bought a small rowboat, so they could enjoy the occasional boat ride.

Because of her lifeguard training Jenny insisted that they all wear life jackets when they were in any boat. She remembered the story she'd been told when she took her lifeguard training about a man who had taken his twelve-year-old son and eight-year-old daughter on a boat trip. Both children wore life jackets, but the father did not. They hit a log and the father was thrown from the boat. He hid his head and was unconscious and started sinking. His son tried to save him but couldn't go down to save his father because of his life jacket, so he took it off and dove down after his father. He never surfaced. The eight-year-old daughter was left alone in the boat for over an hour before another boat came along and rescued her. She was traumatized for months. Because of that Jenny insisted that all people in a boat wear life jackets - whether they were adults or children.

They were able to purchase an old wood-burning stove for the cottage from a farmer. This had been Russ's reason for cutting up all the timber he found on the property when he was clearing it. The stove had a big water container on the side that provided plenty of hot water needed for bathing or washing up and a warming rack where food could be kept warm while the rest of the meal was cooking. It was also instrumental in keeping the cottage warm on cooler days.

Everyone agreed that food cooked on it seemed to taste better somehow than those cooked on the electric stove at home. The smell of Jenny cooking bacon and eggs on the stove with toast being kept warm on the warming shelf would be the family's occasional welcome to the day. One of their favourite treats was when one of the local fishermen came to the door selling fresh pickerel that tasted especially good when fried in butter over the wood stove. They enjoyed many evenings gathered around the old wooden table. The boys made puzzles while their parents did their evening chores.

Russ often suffered from poison ivy that would leave him with ugly watery sores on his body that itched terribly. One weekend when he was having a bout of it, he was working inside the cabin installing a large plate glass picture window in the front of their cottage that overlooked the lake. He had just secured the window with several huge spikes per side when they heard a radio announcer say there was a storm coming their way across the lake. Lake Winnipeg could be a dangerous lake and had been for thousands of years. Sailors knew they had to carefully check the weather patterns before venturing out any distance from shore. Winds and squalls could materialise in minutes and make it a bubbling cauldron. The announcer warned people living on their side of the lake that the storm would likely push large amounts of water their way and to expect some flooding in low-lying areas. That meant the storm was heading right towards them.

They looked outside and saw nothing but a beautiful sunny day. However, they knew from stories they'd heard about the lake that they needed to heed such warnings.

Because Russ was suffering from poison ivy and dared not get wet, they decided that he should concentrate on securing the picture window, so it would withstand the storm.

'I'd better let our neighbours know that the storm is coming,' said Jenny as she headed out the door. After warning their neighbours, Jenny and the boys put anything outside that could possibly blow or be swept away into a little shed at the side of their cottage. When Jenny glanced around the yard to make sure she'd removed everything, she spotted their car parked at the end of their property. Making sure the boys were safe in the cabin, she grabbed the keys and moved their car to a road two blocks away on higher ground. By the time she walked back to the cottage, ugly storm clouds had formed over the lake and it was obvious that the storm was heading their way.

She and Russ watched in horror through the temporarily secured picture window, as a dark line formed across the lake. The line kept coming towards their cottage. As it got closer and closer, they realised that it was a huge wall of water and it was obviously going to hit their cottage. Their cottage was built about one hundred yards from the water, but a slope raised it about ten feet above the waterline. The cottage sat on twenty-four piers that were made of four eighteen-inch square hollow concrete blocks, piled one on top of the other. In the middle of those blocks were pieces of telephone poles that had been driven into the ground that kept the blocks from moving.

Jenny quickly handed out life jackets and helped the boys secure theirs. When the wave hit the cottage, it was high enough that it hit the bottom of the newly placed front window and water gushed in around the sides, soaking everything in the area.

They scurried back from the window praying that the big spikes would hold the huge piece of glass against the onslaught. Suddenly they heard a terrible thumping and banging under their cottage and wondered if it was going to collapse into the water and possibly float away with them in it. They huddled together at the back of the cottage; the boys wide-eyed with wonder as the big wave hit their cottage. They peered out the window in the back door and saw that the wave had gone as far as the road and a bit beyond. Their car could possibly have floated away if Jenny had not moved it.

Soon the banging stopped, and they were relieved to see that their cottage remained upright. The water receded, taking with it anything that was not secured – bushes, small trees, sand and mud. The area around the cottage was a sea of mud and debris. Their dock had disappeared except for the occasional big rock that had been under it.

When the storm passed, Russ went out to survey the area under the cottage. He saw that the banging they'd heard had been caused by a full-length telephone pole that had banged again and again against some of the piers. After the storm, the pole was half submerged under the cottage in sand and mud and nine of the twenty-four piers were damaged or gone. Thankfully, the missing piers were scattered, so the cottage was not in danger of collapsing. What a mess!

It took Russ two of his weekends to remove portions of the telephone pole with a chain saw. First, he had to dig around it, prop the huge telephone pole up with bricks then use a chain saw to cut it into moveable pieces. With little more than three feet to work under the floorboards of the cabin, it was dangerous work. Then he tackled the repair of the concrete piers. He and Hugh Mackenzie rented huge house jacks that held the cottage up while they replaced the damaged piers. Those weekends Jenny and the boys stayed home because the dangerous job they were doing required that the cottage be vacant. He then cleared the lot of debris and replaced their boat dock.

Fourteen

Eighteen months after Bruce's birth Jenny became pregnant again –
this time they hoped it would be a girl. Now they really needed a
newer home and began searching for a bargain. They were able to
find a lovely bungalow that had three bedrooms and an unfinished
basement.

Russ got busy refinishing the basement. He divided it into a rumpus
room, a workroom and a laundry room. When the walls were
completed, Russ built a huge train set layout in the rumpus room.
Russ bought expensive train sets and built an elaborate setup
including towns, mountains and lakes. It kept the boys entertained,
but they weren't allowed to touch the set – only Russ could do that.
Over the next few years, Russ added more train track to the already
huge train extravaganza.

Jenny's pregnancy was normal, no morning sickness this time, and
she felt very healthy. Then suddenly, in early November, when she
was seven and a half months pregnant, her water broke, and she was
rushed to the hospital. This labour lasted thirty-eight hours and Jenny
cried when she was told that her baby – a boy had died shortly after
his birth. Jenny went home from the hospital with empty arms and
for weeks suffered from post-partum depression. She cried and cried
but had two toddlers to care for so forced herself to get through the
days. Russ was no help and simply told her to 'get over it.' At no
time was she offered counselling or treatment for her depression
except to be given Valium which made her head spin and she refused
to use it.

She was still bleeding quite heavily when she went for her six-week
check-up with Dr. Sims. When she explained about the bleeding, he
frowned and pressed her abdomen then said, 'I want to do an internal
examination.'

After he examined her, he stated, 'I want you to have an X-ray taken
of your abdomen. I can feel a mass near your left ovary and need to
check to see what it is.'

He sent her to an X-ray clinic where she had several X-rays taken.
She was dismayed to learn that she would not have the results until
the next day when she was to see Dr. Sims again. She sat shaking as
she waited for the results.

'You have a mass attached to your left ovary. We think it could have
been growing throughout your pregnancy. We'll have to remove it,

73

but because you're still haemorrhaging, I want you to be in better physical health before we can remove it. I will book the surgery for mid-January. In the meantime, I want you to take it easy and try to gain some weight. You're far too thin right now, and I want you to eat lots during the Christmas holidays.'

'How big is the lump and what do you think the lump is?' she asked fearfully.

'The lump is the size of a grapefruit. We're not sure what it is because we don't know how long it's been growing inside you. It could be a benign cyst or tumour. The worst-case scenario is that it's malignant. However, I doubt that it is.'

Jenny left his office feeling defeated, depressed and worried about the next crisis she'd have to face. Hadn't she had enough problems in her life? Life wasn't fair. When she got home, she wondered how she could prepare for the fact that she could possibly be dying - dying of cancer. She'd learned that ovarian cancer was one of the deadliest cancers - and she possibly had it.

What steps did one take to prepare for such an eventuality? Should she prepare for a burial plot? Should she make out a will? Should she clean out all the unnecessary stuff she had accumulated, but didn't need? What was one expected to do when one could possibly have a limited time to live? In the end, she did nothing as she slipped into an even deeper depression.

When she told her parents, they were naturally concerned. Martha helped with Mark and Bruce as much as she could, and Russ made stabs at doing some of the housework. They were all worried because Jenny spent much of her time moping about, just staring into space or reading a book. It was a terrible Christmas for everyone as they contemplated whether Jenny did or did not have cancer. Jenny lost even more weight. Although she tried, she couldn't seem to gain weight and looked very haggard and pale in pictures taken during the holiday season.

She entered the hospital the afternoon of January 15th and the surgery was performed the next day. The morning of the surgery, her parents came to see her before she was wheeled into surgery. Russ was at home with the boys.

'Mom, if it is cancer – who will look after the boys? You know Russ is hopeless with them. And if I die, how will they be brought up?'

'I want you to go into your surgery thinking positively. Tell yourself – you do *not* have cancer. If the worst happens, you know we'll always be around to help out.' Martha said as Jenny was wheeled into an elevator. Jenny waved then laid back on the stretcher, tears streaming down her face.

Martha and Ian sat waiting for their daughter to return from surgery. Both were terrified that Jenny's concerns could in fact be true. What would Russ do if Jenny died? Would he ignore his sons as he did now? Would he realise that he couldn't manage them and let them bring up the children? Would he give the children up for adoption? Martha felt sick thinking of what might happen to her lovely grandsons.

Jenny awoke from surgery with a scar eight inches long that started from her mid abdomen downward. Dr. Sims had good news for her, 'The lump was a benign cyst, but we had to remove your left ovary.'

They all breathed a sigh of relief. However, it took Jenny several months to recover from losing her baby and from her surgery. One of the reasons she found it so difficult to recover, was Russ's attitude when he saw how deeply depressed, she felt.

'Stop feeling sorry for yourself and get on with life!' were his comments. More and more, Jenny realised that Russ did not seem capable of showing empathy for her or anyone else, nor did he give her the sympathy and support she needed so desperately.

She had just recovered from her surgery when three months later, on April Fool's Day, Jenny heard Russ as he came home from work. He was making a lot of thumping noises and when she looked at her bedside clock, saw it was three o'clock. Her immediate thought was that Russ had been drinking but when she investigated, she learned that the noise was caused by the crutches he was using.

'What happened?' she asked as she tied a housecoat around her.

'I injured my knee at work. They took me to the emergency department for X-rays and the doctor has booked me to have my cartilage removed in two days.' he replied as he sat down carefully on a kitchen chair – his damaged leg straight out in front of him.

There was no such thing in those days as keyhole surgery - so he had major surgery. At the hospital, before he underwent surgery, he reached for Jenny's hand and she became aware that he was terrified and needed her support. He explained that the only time he'd been in the hospital was when he'd had his tonsils out when he was a child, and he was afraid he would die on the operating table. Jenny couldn't help but wonder why he didn't understand the kind of terror she'd felt when she was going through the trauma or her car accident and during her disastrous pregnancies. Could he not equate his terror with what she'd already endured in her short life?

Russ came through the surgery well and was on crutches but unable to work for six weeks. It had been seven years since she'd had her accident, and thankfully she could now walk without a cane or assistance. Jenny cared for him and her sons and tried to recover mentally herself.

Fifteen

Russ had just returned to work after his knee surgery when Russ's mother, Nellie phoned to ask if she could come over to speak with Jenny. Nellie lived with Antonio in the home she'd shared with Frank before his death. Jenny wondered what her mother-in-law wanted to discuss. When Nellie arrived, she took Jenny into her bedroom and said, 'I have something I need to discuss with you. I can't talk to Antonio or Russ, because they likely wouldn't know what to advise me.'

Jenny nodded, 'Please tell me what's concerning you.'

'I have a rash on my left breast that I want you to look at. I've had it for three weeks and it's just getting worse. It's so tender and itchy and I can't seem to stop scratching it.' she said worriedly.

Jenny watched as her mother-in-law shyly exposed her breasts. The woman was so shy that Jenny knew that this must be an ordeal for her. Jenny peered carefully at the rash. It was very red and inflamed and when she touched the skin it felt very hot and looked swollen.

'I also have a lump under that arm.' Nellie added almost as an afterthought.

'This is definitely something that your doctor should examine. Why don't you phone and see whether he can see you today?' suggested Jenny.

Nellie phoned and was able to see her general practitioner, Dr. McNeil that afternoon. Because Nellie couldn't drive and didn't have a car, Jenny drove her in her old car. Nellie's doctor sent her to a clinic that was down the hall from his office to have a mammogram.

'Please return to Dr. McNeil's office and I'll send him the results.' advised the X-ray technician after she'd completed the mammogram.

When Dr. McNeil beckoned Nellie to come into her office, Nellie asked Jenny if she would come with her. Dr. McNeil looked grim.

'I have bad news. We've detected a large lump in your left breast and another under your left arm. We'll have to surgically remove them. We're almost sure that they're malignant but won't know for sure until we do a biopsy during the surgery. In any case the lumps must be removed. Whether we do a lumpectomy, or a mastectomy depends on what the biopsy shows when we operate.'

Nellie reached for Jenny's hand, became very pale and looked as if she were going to pass out. Dr. McNeil gave her a glass of water and she seemed to rally. 'When do you want to do the operation?' she finally gasped out.

'I'll see what I can arrange. It's possible that what you have could be inflammatory breast disease. It's a fast-moving malignancy, so I want to deal with this as soon as possible. Wait here while I contact the hospital.'

Jenny knelt on the carpet at Nellie's feet and gave her a big hug. Nellie finally allowed herself to cry – sobbing almost as if she were in pain and finally took a large breath to enable her to retain her control. 'I'm so afraid, so afraid.' she gasped.

'I know you are,' consoled Jenny, 'but Russ, Antonio and I will help you through this.'

Dr McNeil returned and said, 'I was able to schedule your surgery for a week tomorrow. You'll be admitted to the hospital late Tuesday afternoon and the surgery will be done early Wednesday morning.'

Jenny drove her home. Antonio was now home from work and immediately noticed how upset Nellie was. He asked, 'What's wrong Mom?'

Nelly and Jenny explained what had happened. Antonio just sat there with an agonised look on his face. His mother had always been so healthy. This was the first time he could recall her having anything more than a cold or the flu. When Jenny told Russ the news, he was just as stunned and surprised as his brother. They'd both lost their father to cancer, and now their mother could possibly die of the same horrible illness.

That next week Nellie had her operation. Mid-way through the operation, they had to wait for the pathology department to analyse the biopsy they'd taken. Dr. McNeil shook his head at the terrible analysis that it was indeed a malignant tumour and proceeded to perform a mastectomy and removed the lymph glands under her left arm.

Jenny was at home with the children when Dr McNeil called her to tell her that it was cancer and that he'd had to remove her breast and lymph glands. He also explained that Nellie was coming out of the anaesthetic but kept insisting that she had to go home to cook supper for her husband. She was delirious and was in danger of ripping her stitches as she kept trying to pull herself up in her bed and climb over the bed railings. He asked Jenny if she could possibly come and try to calm her down.

Jenny dropped the boys at Martha's and rushed to the ICU ward. When she arrived, she saw that the hospital had put restraining ties on her mother-in-law's wrists, so she couldn't climb out of her bed. Nellie seemed to be awake but had a wild look in her eyes. Jenny went over to her and said in as calm a voice as she could, 'Hi Mom. It's Jenny. How are you feeling?'

'Got to make Frank's dinner!' she shouted.

'No Mom. You're in the hospital. You've just had an operation. Do you remember?' she asked anxiously.

Nellie looked at her and the veil of memory loss lifted 'Yes. Hi Jenny. How long have you been there?'

'I just arrived, Mom. The hospital called me because you were trying to climb over the railings. You insisted that you had to go home to make dinner for Frank.' she explained.

'I must have been out of it then.' she said as she glanced at the restraints. 'You can remove these now.'

Jenny nodded to the nurse who removed the restraints.

'Mom, the best thing for you to do now, is to sleep. You've just come out of the anaesthetic so need to rest so you can recover.' Jenny advised.

'Yes, I do feel tired.' Nellie admitted as she smiled at Jenny. 'Thanks for coming. Where are the children?'

'They're at my Mom's place.'

'Well you go to them. I'll be fine now. Antonio will be up to see me as soon as he finishes work. You go home now.' she said as she drifted off.

Nellie had not asked Jenny whether it was cancer or not, so she was glad she didn't have to be the one to tell her.

A week later, when Nellie was well enough to be discharged from the hospital it was obvious that she couldn't go to her own home. Antonio would be at work all day and Nellie was not well enough to look after herself. So, Russ and Jenny took her to their home and made her comfortable.

One of the hardest things Jenny had to do while she cared for Nellie was to bathe her. Nellie insisted that she wanted to take a tub bath. She was a short but large woman and had difficulty getting in and out of their bathtub without assistance. Because her surgery included removal of the lymph nodes under her left breast, Jenny couldn't help her in and out by lifting that arm. Besides with her own weak back, she couldn't even contemplate lifting the woman. So, with much physical effort, Nellie was finally able to hoist herself out of the tub. Jenny vowed not to let her have another tub bath again until her surgical area was healed.

Nellie had been there a week when she asked, 'Jenny, would you look at this for me?' and pointed to a small lump on her left arm between her elbow and shoulder.

'I think it's something your doctor should see.' replied Jenny. 'Do you want me to phone him and see if he can see you?'

'Yes, I guess I should see about it in case it is infection caused by my surgery.'

Russ was at home and was able to drive Nellie to see her doctor just after lunch. He was very upset when he phoned Jenny a short time later. 'I had just taken Mom into the doctor's office when she had a heart attack! The doctor revived her, and she's been taken to the hospital in an ambulance. I'm there now and will go directly to work from here.'

Three days later, shortly before Christmas, Nellie had a massive stroke and lapsed into a coma. Jenny, Russ and Antonio went up to see her. They stared down at her knowing how seriously ill she was.

'What if she dies?' asked Antonio.

'Has she bought a funeral plot next to Dad's?' Russ asked.

Jenny looked at them and pointed to the hallway. When they were outside the door she said, 'You do realise don't you, that even though your mother's in a coma, she might still be able to hear everything you say? So, watch what you say when you're near her.'

The men were obviously not aware of this and felt terrible that they'd said something like that in her presence. They decided they would go to the hospital cafeteria to have a cup of coffee. Jenny returned to her mother-in-law's room. She was sitting beside Nellie when she noticed that the woman was pulling away at her covers with her hands. Jenny, an avid reader of body language thought she understood what Nellie was trying to tell her. 'Mom, it's Jenny. Do you want a bedpan?'

The woman's hands stopped pulling at the covers.

'Hold on a minute Mom. I'll get a nurse to help you.'

Jenny went to get a nurse, and both helped put Nellie onto a bedpan. Nellie passed her water even though she was still mainly in a coma.

Unfortunately, the next day Nellie had another massive stroke and passed away in December 1965. She was buried in the plot next to Frank.

I can do it! The sky's the limit!

Sixteen

Two years after she delivered and lost her baby boy, she and Russ decided to try again to have the daughter they wanted. Jenny didn't know whether she could conceive with only one ovary but tried anyway. When she did conceive, her pregnancy progressed normally.

As they did every year, she and the children went to their cottage at the lake for the summer. Russ came down on his days off, but otherwise she was there alone with the children. Mark was six and Bruce was four and a half that summer and Jenny was five months pregnant. The boys were playing on the beach and Jenny was washing some vegetables in a bucket of rainwater at the front of the cottage when she heard Mark shouting to her. 'Mom come quick - hurry. Bruce fell off the dock and he's stuck under it. Come quick!'

Jenny had forbidden them to go on the dock and was dismayed that they had done so. She ran down the dock as quickly as she could manage and could hear Bruce's voice calling for her under her feet. She jumped into the shallow water beside the dock and swam back a few feet until she could see Bruce's face through the girders. There were high waves that day and he was being swamped by wave after wave that was pushing him closer to shore leaving him less room to breathe under the dock. She poked her hand through the wooden girders at the side of the dock and grabbed Bruce's hand. 'Take a breath honey – here comes another wave.' she shouted.

He did what he was told then as she held one of his arms, she told him to move along towards the far end of the dock. Mark patrolled the dock, encouraging them along. Bit by bit, between huge mouthfuls of air as the waves battered him, Bruce moved towards the area where he could escape from under the dock. It seemed to take an eternity but must have been only about ten minutes. Finally, Jenny was able to find a break in the boards at the side of the dock. She scooped Bruce's other hand, lifted him up and cuddled him against her shoulder. He was safe. She could feel his little heart thumping almost as hard as was her own. He held on tight as she walked with him back to the shore and dried him with a towel.

In November, two months later, as had happened twice in her pregnancies before, Jenny's water broke, and she went into early labour. With one and a half months left in her pregnancy, she had hopes that the baby would live. Her labour went on and on and after thirty-eight hours of labour, Dr. Sims finally did an internal examination and announced that the baby was presenting buttocks first – was a breach baby. He turned the baby, and the baby was born shortly after. Jenny was very excited when she knew she finally had her long-awaited daughter. They would call her Darla.

Because she was a premature baby, Darla was placed in an incubator and when Jenny went to the nursery to see her, she was dismayed to see all the tubes and things attached to her little body. She seemed to struggle for every breath.

Tragedy struck again, and Darla survived for only a few hours.

The hardest thing for Jenny to accept was the knowledge that Darla would likely have survived, had the hospital staff identified that hers was a breach birth. Again, Jenny went home without a baby. Because it was a live birth, they had a funeral and buried Darla in a small casket beside her Grandmother.

Jenny didn't know until he was an adult and he talked to her about it, that Bruce believed he had been responsible for the loss of that baby. How sad that he spent all those years worrying that he was the cause of his sister's death.

Jenny fell into another deep depression, but after a short mourning period, she and Russ realised that they couldn't go through the trauma of another pregnancy. Because Jenny still ached for a daughter, they decided to adopt a baby girl. In mid-December, just six weeks after she had lost her last baby, they completed the paperwork to put their name on the list of many parents wanting to adopt a baby. They expected it to be a couple of years before a baby would be available.

Both were thrilled, excited and overwhelmed when in mid-February, only two months after signing the papers, they were presented with their beautiful eleven-day-old adopted daughter they named Debbie. Her parents were university students who knew it would be better for Debbie if they gave her up. When Jenny first saw Debbie, she couldn't believe that her parents had agreed to give her up, especially if they had seen her before doing so. Debbie was a beautiful baby, with big brown eyes, adorable cupid-bow lips and tiny nose. Jenny was content. Her family was complete.

Throughout the years, Debbie continued to be beautiful, but the best thing about her beauty was that she didn't seem to know how attractive she was. She remained self-conscious, never realising the affect she had on any red-blooded male who saw her. When she was a teenager, she was stunningly beautiful and turned heads wherever she went.

Jenny enrolled her in modelling classes and could barely recognize the calm young woman who walked down the catwalk. She complimented Debbie about how professional she looked, but Debbie replied, 'Mom, I was terrified. I was shaking so badly I was sure everyone could tell. I'll never do that again.' And she didn't, but she did some poses for still photography.

Seventeen

Jenny was often puzzled by Russ's behaviour and wondered why he wouldn't discuss his feelings with her. She tried many times to talk to him about what he was feeling and concluded that he simply didn't trust her with that level of openness. This kept Russ and Jenny apart because of his inability to be intimate with her. Jenny concluded that it was likely caused by his upbringing by his Italian father who taught him to keep emotionally detached and separate and to suppress his softer emotions.

When he was upset, Russ often responded as if he was angry. He seemed able to show happiness and anger, but not feelings between those two emotions. When he felt anxious, disappointed, jealous, sad, hurt, rejected, stupid, intimidated, insecure, ashamed or ignored, his outward appearance showed only anger.

One time when Russ came storming home from work in a rage and woke the entire family, Jenny said, 'I can see you're distressed about something and understand that you don't want to talk to me about it now, but I can't stand by and condone your destructive behaviour. We have to talk about this because of the spin-off problems it's causing, not only for me, but for our children.'

He got her message, but still refused to talk about what had caused his rage.

Russ didn't seem to have empathy towards others. She recalled how Russ had failed to react when another man abused his wife in their presence. On one of their few evenings out, they'd gone to Russ's favourite tavern. That night, they met up with Russ's friend Grant Davidson who was there without his wife. 'Where's Betty?' Jenny asked.

'She's at home with the kids.' They had three children and were expecting a fourth even though Betty was just twenty-three. That evening Grant became so drunk, that Russ grabbed the keys out of his hand and drove him home while Jenny followed in their car. When they arrived, Russ helped Grant to his front door and beckoned to Jenny when Grant insisted that they come in for a cup of coffee. Grant gestured for them to sit at the kitchen table then staggered into the bedroom.

They heard him as he nudged Betty, 'Come on. Get up and make us some coffee.'

'Grant. Don't wake her up. We're going now.' Jenny said as she stood at the kitchen door.

'Oh no. She's getting up and will make us coffee.' Grant roared. Jenny took Russ's arm and tried to get him to leave. He gave her a dirty look and shook off her arm.

It was obvious that Betty had been deeply asleep and resisted having to get up. 'Put this on.' he said roughly as he handed her a housecoat.

Grant had Betty by the arm and pulled her roughly down the hallway then shoved her against the doorway into the kitchen. Betty was five months pregnant and winced when he again roughly shoved her against the kitchen wall.

'Make us some coffee.' he demanded.

Jenny looked at Russ to see what he was going to do about this violent behaviour; but he did nothing. She stepped in front of Betty and facing Grant said 'Grant, leave her alone. She's tired and Russ and I are leaving.'

Grant turned and stumbled into the bedroom. Jenny looked at Betty and asked, 'Are you going to be okay?'

Betty nodded, 'He'll be asleep in about five minutes.'

'Okay. We're going, as long as you think you'll be okay.' she added.

Betty nodded again and gave Jenny a quick hug as she left.

When Russ and Jenny got to their car Russ asked, 'Why did you do that?'

'Didn't you see him shove her against the wall?' she asked angrily.

'Yeah. But that's none of our business.' he stated.

'Don't you realise that she's five months pregnant and that shoving her like that could harm the baby? That's wife and child abuse!'

Russ just grunted and continued driving them home. It was several days before they had a normal conversation and even longer before Jenny spoke civilly to Grant. She phoned Betty the next morning to be sure she was all right and was assured that she was fine, and Betty thanked Jenny for her intervention.

Russ did not protect Jenny from other men's attention. A neighbour, Barry Fellows, who was twice Jenny's age, sometimes came to the tavern with them. Barry was forever making sexual advances towards Jenny; sitting beside her and running his hand up and down her thigh. Jenny kept moving away from him to another seat, but he eventually would find some way to sit beside her again. Russ was aware of this, but just smiled and did nothing. It was almost as if he was proud of the way Jenny turned on this older man.

When Jenny was in her back yard playing with the children, she often caught Barry spying on her from his upstairs window two doors away. The most disturbing situation relating to Barry's actions came one night after they'd been at the tavern. Jenny just wanted to get home and go to bed but Russ went to Barry's place to drink more beer. About an hour later, Russ staggered home and woke Jenny saying that Barry had offered him a hundred dollars to spend the night with her. He seemed to be pleased at the man's comments - instead of defending her against such lewd suggestions. From then on, Jenny refused to go out if Barry was going to go with them. Several times Russ went alone when she refused to do so.

Russ repeatedly let her down and she realised later in her marriage that he had abused both her and their children emotionally, mentally and physically. His lack of support during her efforts to walk again, and his disregard for her during their sexual relations left Jenny wondering what she had done to deserve his terrible treatment. Even when Jenny was paralysed from the waist down and did not have the ability to insert her diaphragm for birth control, Russ still climbed over her to relieve his own sexual tensions. He refused to use a condom. Again, and again he made her pregnant with disastrous results and she'd lost two almost full-term babies.

It was after Jenny had completely recovered from her accident that she looked seriously at the life she shared with Russ. She realised she would have to do something to get their relationship back on track. Jenny craved adult conversation and with Russ on a four-to-twelve shift with Wednesdays and Thursdays off, she spent five evenings alone and two of those evenings were over the weekend when all her friends were out socialising.

Jenny was very lonely and felt as if she was just putting in time. Her house was spotless, her children were happy, but a void was always there. She began asking herself, *'Is this all there is? If it is, I don't want it. I want a husband that I can communicate with, who will do more for his family than bring in his paycheque.'*

Jenny tried to talk to Russ about it, but he scoffed at her. 'I just wish I had it as easy a life as you have.' was all he said.

Eighteen

Jenny had a chance to think about her life and realised that there was something drastically missing in it. Often, she felt alone and so lonely she felt like weeping. She became so depressed that at one point she contemplated suicide.

Did she love Russ? Had she ever loved Russ, or had it been a girlhood fantasy that she was in love with him? Would she have chosen Russ as a husband if she had not been so young and naïve? Now that she was twenty-eight, would she have chosen him as a husband?

What did love mean? What did it involve? Shouldn't love mean that you felt so close to another person that you'd do everything in your power to make your life with them a good one? Did Russ do that for her? Did she do that for him? Jenny felt in her heart that she had done her part in the marriage, but had Russ done his?

What she missed the most was the emotional and mental stimulation of having adult conversations with others. Russ was hopeless in this area – often eating his dinner in silence. He would then go down to his workshop or train set and putter around. Or he'd go out to the yard and spend time there – anything it seemed but spend time with his family.

She also knew that what Russ did almost every night when he finished his four-to-twelve shift could not be considered lovemaking. Lovemaking included foreplay and loving actions – and there was none of that. It was pure lust and sex – done so he alone could release his own sexual tensions. It didn't seem to matter to him that Jenny was normally fast asleep when he got home from work. He just climbed aboard and had sex with her.

At first Jenny would lie awake after he'd finished rutting, not realising why she couldn't sleep. After reading books on the topic she realised that she was sexually frustrated. Russ would start to wake her up sexually, ejaculate then turn over, leaving her turned on, with no sexual release. Sex with Russ took as long as it took her to clean her teeth, but he gave nothing to her in return. Slowly but surely, she developed a mental switch that she used to keep herself from becoming aroused.

How annoyed and frustrated she felt when Russ accused her of being frigid. After that cruel comment they had another long-drawn out argument about how uncaring he was. Nothing changed.

Russ would often make lewd advances to Jenny in the presence of their children - running his hands over her breasts or surprising her when she was cooking by coming up behind her and putting his hands around her to grab her by the crotch. He knew this annoyed her but became angry when she shunned his advances. He didn't seem to understand that he repelled her rather than turned her on with these actions.

Russ had bad body odour and breath. Although he worked at a labouring job, he would only have one or two baths per week. He insisted on having baths instead of showers, because he expected Jenny to stop whatever she was doing to scrub his back. Instead of complying with his request, she sent one of the boys to do this chore. Russ seemed to believe this action would turn her on sexually, but it simply turned her off. He neglected his teeth and didn't clean them regularly, so he had bad breath. Even kissing him was distasteful. Besides - he smelled.

Being an efficient housekeeper, her household chores were often completed by noon, and she had the rest of the afternoon to put in time. She approached Russ about returning to work, but he made it abundantly clear that if she decided to go back to work, she'd still have to do all the work she normally did in their home. She attempted to work part-time for a while, but with small children to care for and all the work that had to be done around the home she gave up on the idea. Instead, she offered dressmaking out of her home and although it gave her exposure to others, she found that it didn't make enough money to warrant the time she spent on it.

To keep herself occupied and stimulated, she started learning different kinds of crafts. Macramé was all the rage, so she learned all the knots, found the hardest pattern she could find, did it well, but she soon became bored with it. When she noticed that an old sofa set in her basement required recovering, she tackled the job head-on. After carefully removing the original covering, she made it into a pattern, and did an excellent job of re-upholstering the sofa. Her next project was refinishing their wooden dining room table. This involved seven weeks of hand-sanding the dowelled legs of the chairs and table then refinishing them with two coats of clear acrylic varnish. Again, she was bored and looked around for anything else that would keep her mind occupied.

Jenny loved to read and became a voracious reader. However, she soon learned that Russ hated seeing her doing so when he was around. He seldom read anything and thought she was wasting her time when she did. When he spied her reading, he would ask her to put down her book and sit beside him on the sofa while he watched his sports programs. She wasn't into sports, so this was torture for her. She often left the living room and did ironing or some other chore, so she wouldn't have to waste her time watching sports. Jenny finally defied his wishes and read even though she knew it annoyed him.

But things were no better between Russ and Jenny. At home, she still spent most of her time alone with the children and knew she could no longer tolerate Russ's non-participation in both her and their children's lives. One Friday night after Russ had literally ignored Jenny and the children during his days off, she sat thinking about how sad her life had become. She couldn't remember the last time she'd laughed when Russ was around and acknowledged that she didn't even laugh when she watched funny television shows any more. The only time she remembered laughing was when she watched the antics of her children. Yes, she'd certainly lost her sense of humour and she wanted it back!

So, what was she going to do? 'I've had enough of living this half-life,' she decided, 'and I'm going to do something about it!'

When she phoned her brother Jeff and his wife Marion to ask if she and the children could stay with them for a few days, Jeff replied 'It will be an awfully tight fit, but sure come on over!' She hoped that Russ would finally understand that she was serious and take some steps to improve their family situation.

After two days, as Jenny had hoped, Russ came to beg her to return home with the children. 'Please come home. I miss you and the kids.' he said as he sat on the sofa at Jeff's home.

'Russ, I'm serious this time. Unless things change drastically, I don't want to live with you any more.' she said emphatically.

'What do you want me to do?' he asked sheepishly.

'I want us to go to a marriage counsellor and see whether we can turn things around.' she said insistently.

'Why do we have to bring in an outsider? Can't we settle this between us?' he questioned.

'No, I've tried for years to get you to listen to me but time after time you've ignored me completely. I refuse to let that happen this time. Now will you agree to see a marriage counsellor?'

'All right. But please come home now.' he pleaded.

The next day Jenny made an appointment with a marriage counsellor. When they arrived at his office, the counsellor talked to them together, then separately. Then he asked them both back into his office to ask more questions and give his recommendations.

'Russ, are you happy with how Jenny is managing your home and the children?'

'Oh yes, she does a great job.'

'Why do you think she's unhappy?'

'I think it's because I spend so much time working and don't spend enough time with her and the children.'

'How about your social life? Do you do things together that you both like?'

'We go to the tavern about every two weeks.'

'Does Jenny like going to the tavern on your nights out?'

'No, not really. I guess she doesn't.'

'Do you ever go where she wants to go?'

'She always wants us to go to a restaurant or a dinner theatre. That costs too much money, so we don't go there.'

'Do you think that's fair to Jenny if you never go where she wants to go?'

'I guess not.'

'When's the last time the two of you were away from the children to enjoy a weekend together.' he said as he glanced from Russ to Jenny.

'We've never been away from the kids for more than an evening out since Mark was born.' replied Jenny.

'Well, I think it's time you planned on a 'wicked weekend' so you can get the spark back into your life. And Russ, I also think that you should change working your four-to-twelve shift and have normal weekends. You mentioned that your company was willing to have you do this. Why have you continued with the shift-work now that you have a wife and children that want and need you home in the evenings and weekends?'

'I like working that shift.' Russ said stiffly. 'I hate driving in rush hour traffic and that's what I'd face coming and going to work if I worked the day shift. With this shift, I travel before the rush hour and there's hardly any traffic when I drive home after midnight.'

'Well, will you at least think about what it would mean to your family if you were at home with them more?'

'Okay, I'll think about it.' Russ reluctantly agreed.

'So, when do you think the two of you can get away for that 'wicked weekend?' he asked.

'First we will have to decide where we will go. Then I'll have to see if I can find someone to look after the children for the days we're away.' Jenny replied.

When they returned home, Jenny and Russ discussed where they would go for their 'wicked weekend.' Russ wanted to go to their cottage at the lake, but Jenny felt they could go there anytime. She wanted to go somewhere special – some place that was more romantic. They finally agreed they would drive to Thunder Bay and stay in a motel that had a swimming pool for a few days. Because Ian and Martha were now living in Victoria, she spoke to her mother's friend Evelyn Jenkins who offered to come over and care for the children while they were away.

Jenny looked forward to leaving the next Wednesday morning. They would have all day Wednesday, Thursday and part of Friday to enjoy each other's company until Russ had to return to work on Friday at four o'clock. Jenny was more than a bit upset that he still hadn't spoken with his boss about changing his work schedule, so she hoped she'd be able to discuss that further with him during their short holiday.

The Sunday before they were to leave, Russ had just finished his breakfast and was having a cup of coffee when he said, 'The boss told me last night that I have to work on Wednesday and Thursday evenings. So, we can't go away this week.'

Jenny looked incredulously at him and thought, '*You're the one who decided to work those extra nights – not your boss.*'

Instead, she said, 'How could you do this Russ? Our marriage is at stake here! Don't you realise how important it is for us to get away.'

Russ just shrugged his shoulders and said, 'We'll go away another time.'

'When? Give me a date!' she almost shouted at him.

'Quit pushing me!' he bellowed as he got up from the table so abruptly that his chair crashed to the floor. 'I don't want to hear about this again!'

Jenny realised that he was not going to change. She knew he had not tried to change his shifts, so he was completely ignoring the advice of the family counsellor. He would not change – that was obvious. So, was she willing to stay with him? She began seriously thinking that the only solution would be for them to separate for good.

Nineteen

Jenny was tired of living a half-life. So, she began thinking seriously about obtaining a divorce. She held off for a while because shortly after speaking with the counsellor, Jenny became ill. The children had been home with the flu, but her illness seemed to go on far too long. She wondered if she had the flu or if her illness was due to the tension and stress she lived under. She sat lethargically in Dr. Sims office. After his examination, Dr. Sims smiled as he dropped the bombshell, 'Congratulations, you're pregnant.'

'This can't be happening!' she said. It was the last thing she'd anticipated. She'd faithfully taken birth control pills since her last pregnancy, so she and Russ believed they were safe from pregnancy the few times they'd had sex lately.

'I can't go through this again!' she groaned.

Dr Sims pointed out that she did have options, 'You realise, that with your gestation history, you have the option of terminating your pregnancy. Should you choose to continue your pregnancy, it will be imperative that you obtain help at home and become almost bedridden during your third trimester.'

For the first time in her life, she contemplated the distasteful idea of having an abortion. Memories of her past two lost pregnancies crowded her mind.

And now that she felt her family was complete – to be told she was pregnant again – well things were different this time. Losing two almost full-term babies was bad enough – but trying again – that was another thing to consider. The possibility was high that she would deliver another premature baby, so she'd have to consider carefully the option of continuing her pregnancy. Jenny loved children, and her feelings about ending a life were very strong, but what was best for her family?

A new baby had been started. Like every newly pregnant woman she felt the excitement of having started a new life. What would it be – a boy or a girl? Would it be healthy – have all its fingers and toes? Or would she go into early labour again and be tossed into the tornado of feelings involved with losing another baby. Would she suffer the heart-wrenching emptiness she remembered from the other two times her babies had died? Could she withstand the long period of time it would take her to start to function normally again? Would she suffer from weeks of depression as she had those other times? Would it be worth taking the chance again of having to live through such a nightmare? Or would the baby be fine this time?

Then she remembered her other pregnancies when the first flutter of the butterfly in her lower abdomen announced to her that a new life was making itself felt. She remembered touching her abdomen just over the fluttering feeling, her face full of wonderment. Later in her pregnancies she recalled feeling the thumps from an arm or leg stretch of the developing baby. And in Mark's case the battering she'd had to her rib cage given by her big beautiful boy?

Could she cut off the life of a baby just because she and Russ had been careless? Didn't this child deserve a chance to live like any other baby? It wasn't as if they couldn't afford another baby. Oh, sometimes the budget was strained, but they could afford this baby. So, what was she going to tell the doctor? Or should she abort the baby and follow through with leaving Russ? What a decision to have to make!

She knew she'd have to consult Russ about it even though she and Russ hadn't been getting along very well since he'd ignored the marriage counsellor's advice. That's why they hadn't had sex very often. Their most recent battle still revolved around the hours he worked. He still refused to accept the day shift with weekends off that was open to him and didn't seem to understand why she was so angry with him. 'I bring in the paycheque – what more do you want from me?' he asked.

Jenny knew that until that issue was settled, the cold war would continue. And yet when she had gone to Jeff's for those few days, he had told her how much he missed her and the children. It didn't make sense to her.

Did he or didn't he love her?

She brought her mind back to her current situation – finding herself pregnant again. She'd have to find the right moment to speak to him. Several times she prepared herself to tell him she was pregnant, so they could discuss their options, but couldn't find the right moment to do so. Time passed, and soon it was too late to safely end her pregnancy. In hindsight she realised that she would never have seriously considered aborting her baby.

She was over four months along when she decided to give Russ a baby card that congratulated prospective parents. On it she had written, 'Congratulations – You're going to be a Daddy!'

He gave a questioning look at her abdomen and asked, 'Why didn't you tell me earlier?'

'We certainly weren't getting along very well when I learned about the pregnancy, and I couldn't find an ideal time to tell you. Besides with my history there'll be less time friends and family will have to wonder whether I can carry the pregnancy to full term.'

They didn't discuss the situation further. Her pregnancy progressed normally, but Jenny remembered Dr. Sim's caution that she absolutely must obtain help during the last trimester of her pregnancy. Her baby was due in early January, so in September, she started discussing the need to obtain housekeeping and childcare help for her. When the time came to get help, Russ's answer was, 'We can't afford it. We'll just have to manage somehow. I'll do what I can, and the boys can help more. There's no reason why they can't do the laundry and wash floors!'

This made sense, but who would run around after their two-year-old daughter Debbie, provide meals, do the shopping and the thousands of other duties when he was at work?

Jenny knew Russ wouldn't help much himself and rather than start another argument, decided to make the best of things. She tried to rest more but found it almost impossible with three children and one of them a toddler. Just keeping track of what two-year-old Debbie was doing was a monumental task. Jenny felt lucky that she was an easy child to care for, had a sweet disposition and was able to amuse herself for a much longer time than the boys had be able to do at her age. The boys did their best and helped as much as they could. Mark took over the laundry and helped care for Debbie. Bruce became very proficient at washing floors, doing dishes and generally cleaning up. They did an admirable job and she was amazed at how much help a nine- and seven-year-old could be.

I can do it! The sky's the limit!

Twenty

Her pregnancy continued to be uneventful and she began to hope things would be different this time. At least that is until the first morning of November when she had just entered her seventh month of pregnancy. Everything appeared normal when she got up that morning, but when she went to the bathroom, she noticed that she was spotting lightly. Her heart raced, and she realised the signs. The thought, '*Here we go again! – I'm in trouble again.*' entered her mind. Russ was home and she told him what had happened. She also phoned Dr. Sims, who told her she must have full bed rest from then on.

Russ looked after the children, gave them lunch, put Debbie down for her afternoon nap then started packing his lunch box.

'What are you doing?' Jenny asked.

'Making my lunch for work.' he replied.

'Are you going to work?' Jenny asked incredulously.

'Yes, I am.' was his simple reply.

'And what about the bed rest I'm supposed to get?' Jenny was getting madder and madder.

'Just tell the boys what you need done. Or why don't you phone one of your friends to come and look after you?'

'It's up to you to make some arrangements. When are you going to start helping me for a change?' she said as she waited for his answer.

'You'll do fine. The boys have been doing a great job. By the way, I hope you haven't forgotten that I'm going hunting with a few of my co-workers after work tonight. I won't be back until tomorrow some time.'

Jenny simply couldn't believe Russ could be so thoughtless. At that moment she really hated him. She just glared at him and didn't speak a word to him before he left for work. That night the boys pitched in and were able to make sandwiches for dinner. Debbie climbed into bed with Jenny and they spent an enjoyable evening reading their books. The boys also joined her, then Mark helped Debbie get ready for bed. Before Mark went to bed himself, he asked Jenny if she needed anything else. 'I'd love a cup of tea. You know how to make it don't you?'

'Sure Mom. I'll be right with you.' Mark replied.

He arrived shortly after with a steaming cup of tea with just a bit of milk and sugar the way she liked it. She gave him a hug and said, 'Thanks Mark for helping me out so much. Good night. See you in the morning.'

That night Russ did not come home after work, so she knew he'd gone hunting with his buddies as planned. Why they would go hunting at night she couldn't figure. It was hunting season but didn't think people could shoot at animals at night.

Late the next morning Russ came home – without his rifle. He and his buddies had been caught 'spotlighting' for deer with a powerful light and had bagged an adult male. The Royal Canadian Mounted Police had heard the shots and had caught them loading the deer into the back of their vehicle. All their rifles were confiscated for three months and later they paid hefty fines for the offence. That money could have been used to hire help for Jenny.

Jenny just listened while he told his tale. She was still furious with him and made it plain to him with her silence and dirty looks. She was still trying to stay in bed, but more and more it became obvious that the boys couldn't be expected to look after their two-year-old sister forever. They wanted to go outside to play, so Jenny sent them off and got up to sit on the living room sofa. Debbie played quietly with her toys but needed Jenny to get up occasionally to get her a drink, a tissue to wipe her nose and other necessities. Russ carried on as normal ignoring the danger he was putting Jenny in by not providing her with the care she desperately needed.

One week after she started spotting, her water broke. Jenny wasn't overly surprised and after she had cleaned herself up and changed her clothing, she phoned Dr. Sims. He instructed her to go directly to the hospital stating, 'We'll have to try everything we can to discourage you from going into full labour.'

After she hung up, she thought, 'How am I going to get there and who will look after the children?' Russ was on an errand, so she sent Mark next door to get help. Agnes Evans' daughter Denise agreed to look after the children while Agnes drove Jenny to the hospital.

Before getting into Agnes's car, Jenny placed a thick bath towel on the seat. On the way to the hospital, Jenny couldn't help thinking,

'Time, I need more time! This baby won't survive unless I can hold off delivery. If only I can hold on for another two or three weeks, we'll probably make it. Maybe if I'm in the hospital I can finally get the bed rest I'm supposed to have.'

When she arrived at the hospital she was soaked again from the amniotic fluid and was glad she'd remembered to take the large towel with her. Thankfully she had not felt any labour pains. When Dr. Sims examined her, he told her this was a good sign.

After she was settled in her room, her nurse attached a foetal monitor to her abdomen. Jenny's eyes widened when she heard the steady, but very fast, heartbeat of her unborn child and watched the screen showing the blip, blip, blip that showed proof of her child's healthy existence. After an hour, the nurse had to disconnect the machine for another woman who was having a difficult delivery.

Jenny wondered what was keeping Russ. He finally arrived at three o'clock explaining that Denise Evans from next door would continue looking after the children until he came home from work at midnight.

'You're going to work, knowing that I might lose another baby tonight?'

'Well, what do you expect me to do?' he asked quizzically.

'You could stay with me and at least pretend that you care what happens to me and our child!' she almost screamed at him.

They had another heated argument and by the time Russ stormed out of the hospital, Jenny realised that she was on her own - again. She also realised that she had a raging headache. Jenny couldn't remember when she'd last had a headache. It soon became unbearable, so she rang for the nurse and asked if she could have something to ease the pain. The nurse left to contact Dr. Sims.

While she was gone, everything seemed to go wrong for Jenny. Although there was another bed in her room, it wasn't occupied, so she didn't have anyone else to recognise her difficulties. She was holding her forehead, when she suddenly felt her first wrenching labour pain. This contraction was far stronger than those that normally accompanied the onset of labour. It was more like the kind of pain she would expect to have in the later stages of labour. In addition, Jenny realised that she felt icy cold, was perspiring heavily and began to shiver so violently that her shaking body moved the bed.

'This isn't right!' she moaned. 'This has never happened before! What's happening to me?' She searched for the bell and couldn't find it and wondered whether she was going to pass out before she could summon help.

Thankfully, a nurse appeared, took her temperature, and rushed out of the room. She returned with and applied several warm, flannelette sheets and a blanket that felt as if they had just come out of a dryer. How soothing they felt. Soon Jenny stopped shivering and recognised that her labour pains had stopped as well. By five o'clock she felt almost normal and wondered what had happened to her.

'We've called Dr. Sims to let him know about your fever, and that you had several strong labour pains. I've checked you and it appears that you haven't started dilating, so we may still be in luck and can hold off delivery for a while.'

While Jenny waited for Dr. Sims arrival, she tried to remain calm. It felt very soothing to lie under the warm blankets, and she was pleased to note that she had stopped perspiring and shivering. She felt so comfortable that she removed the top blanket, sat up and read a magazine for half an hour. While she read, she found herself running her hand over her swollen abdomen.

Her calmness ended when she recognised that something was dreadfully wrong. Her normally very active baby was suddenly very still. Then came the realisation that since her fever episode, she couldn't remember feeling the baby move. Her hand reached for the bell.

'I haven't felt my baby move since I had the fever and I'm really worried. Could you hook up that foetal monitor again, so I know the baby's okay?' she asked.

As the nurse checked her abdomen with a stethoscope, her frown confirmed that Jenny's concern was warranted. 'I'll see what's keeping your doctor.' she stated as she swiftly left the room.

Twenty minutes later, Dr. Sims arrived, listened to the baby's heartbeat, and declared. 'Your baby's in trouble. I don't think we have any recourse but to do an immediate caesarean. I'll see if I can find a specialist to do it.'

'Has the hospital contacted my husband since I started having trouble?' she asked.

'Yes, we have, and I thought he'd be here by now. I'll make the arrangements for the surgery to be done. In the meantime, I'll be starting you on antibiotics to fight the infection.' he added as he left the room.

Jenny knew her caesarean would have to be done right away, so became more and more frantic as time raced on. Two hours passed before Dr. Sims returned with the obstetrician Dr. Miller, who would do the surgery. Dr. Miller carefully listened to the baby's heartbeat, shook his head and said the simple distressing words, 'It's too late – the baby's dead.'

He patted Jenny's arm as he continued speaking to Dr. Sims, 'We might as well wait until she goes into labour naturally. Because she's had that 105° temperature earlier, the longer we can hold off delivery, the better. In the meantime, I want her to have something to help her sleep and keep her muscles relaxed. The longer we have to fight the infection before she goes into labour, the better it will be for her.'

He looked directly at Jenny and patted her again. 'I'm sorry this happened. I wish I'd been called earlier in your pregnancy – we may have been able to save your baby.'

'What caused the infection Doctor?' she asked quietly.

'When your water broke, it left you very vulnerable to infection.'

The doctors left the room, but Jenny could still hear what they said as they stood outside her closed door. 'She may not make it through the night unless her fever goes down. Let's hope and pray that she rallies and doesn't go back into labour until tomorrow or later.'

Their voices faded away as they walked down the hall, so Jenny couldn't hear more. The knowledge that her own life was in danger crowded her thoughts and she wondered whether she was going to die. Then her thoughts turned to the plight of her unborn child. 'You poor little waif,' she crooned as she ran her hand over her distended abdomen. 'You didn't stand a chance, did you? Maybe I'll be joining you soon.'

A nurse arrived with more antibiotics and something to help her sleep. Jenny wondered where Russ was and when he would arrive.

The medication helped her drift off, but she awoke when Russ opened the door to her room. She felt the cold air coming from his jacket as he stood by her bed. She squinted at the clock and had to work to overcome her double vision. It was nine o'clock, five hours after he had first been told she was in trouble. 'What happened?' he asked.

She was still light-headed from the medication as she unemotionally told him about the baby being dead and the danger she would be in if she went into labour. He sat at her side silently but didn't offer any kind of sympathy or words of comfort. She noticed that he had not touched her since he came into the room nor uttered any words of sympathy about what she was going through. He finally suggested, 'Why don't you try to go back to sleep?'

'So much for sympathy and support,' she thought sadly as she drifted off again.

The clock showed it was just after midnight when she awoke again. The hospital was as quiet as a tomb. She was dreadfully thirsty and looked around to ask Russ to get her some water. He wasn't there, so she rang for the nurse. She asked for a glass of water and asked about her husband. 'He went home shortly after you went to sleep and said he'd be back in the morning.'

There's always a final straw that breaks a relationship. Thoughts raged through her mind, *'He left me here alone – knowing I might die during the night! How could he care so little about me, that he'd leave me to face this all alone?'* She realised then, that Russ had never been there when she really needed him. During every crisis in their marriage, she'd had to face things alone.

That horrible night she made two stunning discoveries. The first was the confirmation that she'd have to deliver her dead baby alone - and secondly - that her marriage was over; this time for good. Thoughts of death permeated her thoughts and she was filled with sadness and despair. How could she survive this night alone? Who could she call to ask if they would come and stay with her? Calling any of her friends was out of the question because it was the middle of the night and she was so ashamed of Russ's desertion. She considered calling her mother but realised that by the time she would arrive from Victoria, the crisis would be over. How she craved having someone's sympathetic and supportive shoulder to cry on. How alone and empty she felt!

The nurse returned and hooked up more antibiotics to her intravenous line and gave her more medication to help her sleep. Jenny drifted off, but in what seemed like seconds, was rudely awakened by a labour pain so severe, that she cried out in pain.

When she realised that she was perspiring badly and shivering uncontrollably, she moaned, *'Oh God, here we go again.'*

Her teeth chattered, and she rolled herself into a ball trying to minimise the pain. The contraction ended, and she searched for the bell. She found herself hesitating as thoughts swirled in her head. *"All I have to do, is let this happen. If I don't press this bell, I can let myself die."*

As soon as this idea surfaced, the image of three little faces flashed before her eyes and she pushed the thoughts out of her mind. She knew that Russ would make a terrible single parent to their three children.

'No, I'm not going to let that happen. My children depend on me too much.' She pushed the bell and within seconds, the nurse arrived stripped off her blankets and put another set of warmed ones on her. Again, as if a miracle had happened, she stopped shivering. Unfortunately, her labour pains didn't stop, and she gradually went through the stages of labour.

Between contractions, the medication made her feel as if she were detached from her body, but the wracking pains soon brought her back to reality. By five thirty that morning, she realised that she was beginning to feel an urge to bear down, so called the nurse. The nurse checked her, but said, 'You still have a while to go. I'll check you again in fifteen minutes.' she said as she left the room.

Ten minutes later Jenny delivered her dead baby - in her bed – all alone in her hospital room.

She lay spent for a few moments then sat up and examined her dead baby. It had been another boy. She patted him gently, and with an eerie calmness, rang for the nurse. It was bedlam after that. The nurse was in tears and kept apologising for not being there when Jenny needed her. Dr. Sims arrived to help deliver the afterbirth and motioned for the nurse to leave the room with the baby.

Jenny and her bed were freshened, and a new antibiotic started. In a few minutes, her door opened and the nurse who'd been sobbing earlier, entered with a flannelette bundle and cautiously asked, 'Would you like to see your baby now that he's been cleaned up?'

Jenny extended her arms and tenderly unwrapped the layers of flannelette until the tiny naked body was fully exposed. She examined his little hands and feet and marvelled at the beautiful child her body had created.

'He certainly was perfect - wasn't he?' Jenny said through her tears. 'What a shame that circumstances beyond his and my control snuffed out his little life. What kind of God lets that happen?'

She carefully re-wrapped the body and handed him back to the nurse who left the room. Jenny had never felt so alone in her life. She cried for hours and finally drained herself of tears.

Twenty-one

It was three o'clock that afternoon before Russ arrived and he wasn't alone. Martha's plane had just arrived from Victoria half an hour before. Jenny brushed Russ away and reached for the solace of her mother's arms.

'I was so alone, Mom – I wish you could have been here to hold me and help me through this.' Martha held her daughter and they cried together. As Martha straightened up, she sent a scathing look in Russ's direction knowing that he had not stayed with Jenny. She'd never forgive Russ for his desertion of her daughter that night.

'I'll stay with you as long as you need me.' her mother promised. She was staying with her son Jeff and his family because there was no place for her to sleep at Jenny's home now that Debbie had the spare room.

Dr. Sims kept Jenny in the hospital for another twenty-four hours to fight the infection, but early the next day, he agreed to discharge her. Jenny's arms and mind felt so empty – again no baby to take home.

She wondered how she could go on being a mother to her children knowing that she hated their father and didn't want to live with him. Because it was his day off, she called Russ to pick her up.

'Okay, I'll be there in about half an hour.' he replied.

Jenny went to the closet in her room to change into her clothing and realised that she didn't have any clean clothes – just the soiled ones she'd been admitted in. She hadn't reminded Russ to bring fresh ones, but surely, he would know that she couldn't come home wearing the garments she wore when she arrived at the hospital? They had been put into a plastic bag and were still wet and stinky from when her water broke.

She sighed and sat in her housecoat waiting for Russ to come. When he arrived, she asked him for her change of clothing. He shrugged his shoulders and said, 'You didn't ask for any.'

'Did you really expect me to come home in these?' she asked as she threw the plastic bag of wet clothing at him. She decided that her only choice was to wear her bras, the top she had been wearing when she was admitted and her housecoat.

When they arrived at their home her spirits rose when Martha and her children greeted her with hugs. She reminded herself why she had decided to live instead of giving in to the overwhelming grief she'd felt when she knew that Russ had deserted her again. It was hard for her to retain any semblance of normal life after her traumatic experience, but she knew she had to do so for her self-preservation and for her children.

After Jenny returned home from the hospital, she and Martha had many long talks. Jenny withheld nothing from her. They talked for hours.

'You know you're welcome to come to Victoria. We can find a rental place for you and the kids that's near our place.'

'Mom I've been through such turmoil; I think I want to wait a few months to regain my health and emotional well-being before I take the drastic step of leaving Russ. I'm in no condition physically, emotionally or mentally to fight him if he asked for custody of the children.'

'I can only stay with you another week – I have to get back to your father. Is there anyone else who can help you through this emotional minefield?'

'I guess I could go back to the family counsellor, but that costs money and I'm going to have to start saving my pennies for when we leave.'

'How about Reverend Thompson? He's the one who married you and buried your babies. Possibly he can help you deal with the break-up as well.'

Jenny had always respected Reverend Thompson. He was a kind, compassionate man who must have had several psychology degrees, because he was so good at understanding people's problems. He had conducted the funerals for her babies and had officiated at Nellie's funeral. 'Yes, maybe that's what I should do. I'll talk to him.'

Jenny phoned and made an appointment. He was able to see her the next day. Martha was relieved that Jenny would have another support person to replace her when she returned to Victoria.

Reverend Thompson greeted Jenny warmly, 'I'm so sorry you lost another baby. You must be devastated.' Because the baby was stillborn, they did not have a funeral for the infant.

'Yes, I am, but I didn't just lose a baby this time. My marriage is over as well.' Jenny said despondently.

Jenny told him everything that had happened, not only about the most recent problems with Russ but how lonely and sad she'd been through most of her marriage. She made it clear that the only thing she thought Russ had contributed to their marriage was his sperm and his paycheque. It was two hours later when she finally finished revealing everything to him.

'I'm sorry Reverend, I'm probably keeping you from doing other more important things.' she said as she realised how long they had been talking.

'Right now – you are the most important thing! Now, what are your plans for the future?' he enquired.

'I plan on leaving Russ, but realise that I'm far too fragile emotionally, mentally and physically now to go through the trauma of another crisis. I think I need several months to get my strength back and get emotionally back on track. Right now, I'm a wreck.'

'I have to agree with your plans. I advise people not to waste their time on others who won't support them in their time of need. It appears that many times Russ has not supported you during your time of need.' he added, then continued, 'How do you think you can regain your strength?'

'I plan on doing things *I* want to do for a change. I need to get out more – to get more involved in doing things for *me* instead of for everybody else. I think that's the most important thing I need to do, to get feeling better about myself.'

'I agree wholeheartedly. How do you intend to do that?' he enquired.

Jenny thought for a moment. 'I've always loved swimming – I want to get back into that. Possibly get a teaching licence and teach swimming.'

'Sounds like a good plan to me.' he said as he nodded his head.

'I'll play it by ear for a while and fit in other things as I think of them.'

'Would you like to continue having talks with me – possibly once a week – even if it's just on the telephone?' he enquired.

'That would be great. I don't have anyone else I can talk to – my parents live in Victoria and they're getting on in years. They've been very supportive, but I hate to keep bothering them all the time. They feel too helpless living so far away.'

'Okay, that sounds good to me.' he agreed, 'now, do you feel a bit better about your future?'

'Yes. You've been wonderful – I feel as if a huge load has been taken off my shoulders. I really want to do what is best for all of us – not just me.'

'Shall we set up an appointment for next week – say the same day and the same time?' he asked.

'That will be fine. And thank you so much for being there for me.' she said gratefully.

As Jenny drove home from the church, she felt so much better. When she got home Martha immediately recognised the difference in her demeanour by observing the spring in her step and the gleam in her eye. She'd really been worried about Jenny. She'd never seen her as far down and beaten as she appeared since losing her last baby.

Jenny told her mother about what had transpired at her meeting with Reverend Thompson. Martha felt content that it was safe to return to Victoria knowing that Jenny's welfare would be well taken care of by the kindly Reverend Thompson.

Three weeks after Jenny's baby was born and Martha had gone home, Russ's brother Antonio's wife Jean gave birth to their first child—a little girl they named Kathryn. Jenny knew she should go over to see the new baby but kept putting it off. She realised that she was jealous of Jean, that she had a live baby.

'This is foolishness.' she said to herself one morning. 'I'm going over to see that baby.'

It was one of the hardest things Jenny had ever forced herself to do. The boys were in school, but she took Debbie with her.

When Jenny saw the baby, she just stared at her in shock. Kathryn was wearing the little sweater, bonnet and bootie outfit she'd knit for her own baby. Jenny's face was as white as a sheet and Jean recognised that she should not have put on that outfit—especially since Jenny was still raw from losing her baby.

'How did you get that outfit?' whispered Jenny.

'Russ brought it and a box of baby things last week. Didn't he tell you he was giving them to me?' Jean asked.

Jenny simply answered, 'No.'

'How could Russ have done this to me?' Jenny wondered. 'What kind of monster would torture his wife this way?'

Now she hated Russ even more. Jean made a cup of coffee while Kathryn slept in her little cot. Jenny, who normally would have asked to hold the baby, found she was repelled by the idea.

On her way home, she phoned Reverend Thompson to see if he had time to see her that afternoon. He was available and had his secretary stayed with Debbie while he talked to Jenny.

Jenny poured her heart out to him, sobbing with great wracking waves of sorrow. She'd just begun to feel better but had been thrown back into her pit of despair by Russ's latest callous act.

Reverend Thompson soothed her and reminded her about the things she had decided to do to boost herself mentally and emotionally. She wiped her face and took some deep breaths.

I'd like to teach you some relaxation techniques you can use whenever you feel the pressure building up.' he suggested.

He walked her through the process and by the time Jenny left his office, she felt rejuvenated and vowed not to let Russ ruin her life for much longer.

I can do it! The sky's the limit!

Twenty-two

When Jenny enquired about training as a swimming instructor, she learned that before she could become one, she would first have to renew her Bronze Medallion qualification to meet the requirements. It had been many years since she'd been qualified and knew that the lifesaving procedures had changed drastically. So that's where she started. She was pleased to learn that her Bronze Medallion lessons were available on Thursday nights, so Russ would be home from work and could take care of the children.

'Russ, I need you to look after the kids while I take some swimming lessons every Thursday night.' she said.

'What do you need to take lessons for? You already know how to swim.' he said in surprise.

'It's to get my Bronze Medallion that will qualify me as a lifeguard.'

'What do you want to be a lifeguard for?' he enquired.

'That's not why I'm taking it. I have to have that qualification before I can obtain a swimming teaching licence.' she said calmly. She had the feeling that he was going to try to stop her from doing this.

'Why would you want to do that?' he asked angrily.

'I think it's about time I started living again and doing things that *I* like to do for a change.' she replied.

Russ thought it was a stupid idea and didn't support her in any way and said, 'Don't expect me to look after the kids every Thursday night while you're pursuing this stupid idea.'

Later, when she analysed his comments, she realised that he was threatened by the fact that she would do something without consulting him first. Three times during the ten-week course Russ let her know at the last minute that he was going out that Thursday night. She had prepared for this eventuality and had earlier confirmed that Denise Evans from next door would be available on Thursday nights should she need her.

At her first lesson, Jenny and another woman began talking and hit it off right away. Little did Jenny know that this woman would eventually become her closest, lifelong friend. Marjorie Stewart's husband Darren had taught her boys hockey, so Jenny had met him many times, but had never met his wife Marjorie. They were pleased to learn that they both wanted to eventually become swimming instructors.

On the Monday, three days before Jenny was to challenge her Bronze Medallion swim test, she was shovelling the sidewalk at the side of her home when she fell heavily on the icy concrete. She felt something crack in her lower back and was in agony. She was terrified that she might again be paralysed, but upon checking her legs she realised that she still had feeling in them. But she winced at the sharp pain she felt in her lower back.

She glanced up at the living room picture window and could see that four-year-old Debbie had seen her fall. Jenny was concerned that she might come outside without her snowsuit.

Jenny rolled over and slowly and painfully crawled up the four stairs to the front door. Debbie's little face was full of concern.

'Mommy's okay sweetie.' Jenny said as she tried to reassure her.

'Why are you crawling, Mommy?' Debbie asked.

'My back is just very sore,' she said, and she kept crawling until she reached a telephone. She lay on her side as she spoke to Dr. Sims. He was able to see her right away. Although it was extremely painful, Jenny dressed Debbie and drove to the doctor's office.

After examining her Dr. Sims announced, 'You've fractured your tail bone.'

'How is that kind of fracture dealt with?' she asked.

'Well, we don't put you in a body cast or anything like that. There's nothing we can do but give you pain relief. It will be very painful for you to sit and lie on your back, so go to the pharmacy and buy a donut; that's a rubber disc that you blow up. Put it into a pillowcase and use it to sit on. You will also find that you'll have to lie on your side when you sleep.'

'I have a swimming test Thursday night. Will it harm me if I have to get in the pool and rescue a victim?' she asked cautiously.

'No, you won't damage it any more than it is. But it will likely be too painful for you to do everything that's necessary to pass your exams. I'll give you a note explaining what happened, so maybe you can challenge the exam later.'

She walked next door to the pharmacy, filled the prescription and bought the donut. Before settling herself carefully in her car, she blew up the donut. It helped tremendously because it kept her sore tailbone from touching anything solid. It became her constant companion even in bed, and she carried it with her everywhere until the fracture was less painful.

It was so painful in bed that she decided she had better sleep alone rather than take the chance that Russ would bump her in any way. So, she slept down in the rumpus room on a long sofa for the next three nights.

That Wednesday afternoon, she decided to go to the pool for a swim to see whether she'd be able to challenge the Thursday exam. She felt considerable pain but realised that she could do most of the things she had to do for her exam. She stubbornly didn't want to miss taking the test because she didn't want Russ to tell her 'I told you so.'

On Thursday night Russ looked incredulously at her when he saw her come into the kitchen carrying her swimming bag. 'You aren't going to do that test tonight are you?'

'I can't pass the test unless I try. So yes, I'm going to take the test.'

He just shook his head and she left for the pool. During the test she groaned when she saw that the supposedly 'unconscious' person she was chosen to save from the bottom of the deep end of the pool was the biggest man in the group. He was well over six feet tall and built like a football player. After retrieving him from the bottom of the pool, she would then tow him to the shallow end, somehow get him out of the water and give simulated mouth-to-mouth resuscitation. She wondered if she should back out of taking that part of the test but decided to at least try to do it.

Her heart was beating like a drum as she proceeded through the process. She took a deep breath and dove to the bottom of the pool. Then she struggled to bring her 'victim' to the surface. When they reached the surface, he was so big it was hard for her to get her arm across his chest to tow him. She was submerged several times as she struggled to get him to the shallow end of the pool. When she reached the end of the pool, she knew it would be difficult getting him out of the water. She placed him parallel to the side of the pool and holding his head with her left hand she rolled his body with her right using the bottom of the pool as a solid base. Her 'drowning victim' gave a grunting noise as she did so. 'Oops,' she said quietly to the 'unconscious' man, 'I hope I didn't hurt you.' she whispered.

'I'm fine,' he whispered back.

Jenny did run into problems though when she attempted to give him simulated artificial resuscitation. She was supposed to rock from his head to his chest to check his breathing but was terribly worried that one of her heels would dig into her throbbing tailbone. When the examiner asked her why she was doing that step so awkwardly, she finally admitted to him that she had a fractured tailbone.

'You what!' he exclaimed. 'And you towed that huge man all that way with a fractured tailbone? My God woman, why didn't you tell me – I would have had you explain verbally what you would do.' Her 'victim' also shook his head in amazement. Jenny then went to her swimming bag and gave the examiner the copy of the letter from her doctor.

She was pleased to know that she would not be required to be a 'victim' in case the person 'saving' her bumped her tailbone.

When it came time to let the students know the results of their tests, Jenny was very pleased that he gave her an extra commendation because of her injury. The one that clapped the most was the man she had towed the length of the pool. Jenny clutched the document in her hands and just beamed. She felt such a sense of accomplishment.

Marjorie had also passed, so they knew they could both progress to the next stage of training towards becoming swimming instructors. They gave each other a big hug.

Suddenly two of the students threw the examiner into the pool then pushed each other in until the pool was full of students, instructors and the examiner. The only one who was not shoved into the pool was Jenny, so she made a shallow dive and got in herself – smiling as she surfaced beside the examiner. What a great and momentous night that had been!

Twenty-three

When Jenny arrived home from the pool she was bubbling over with excitement; she'd done it! She'd passed her exam with a fractured tailbone. As she tucked in her sons, Mark asked, 'Did you pass Mom?'

'I did!' she said proudly.

The children could see how excited she was and gave her a big hug. She kissed them goodnight and went into the living room where Russ was watching television. He continued watching television and never once either that night or later, asked her whether she had passed her test.

Two weeks later she and Marjorie began their swimming instructor lessons. These were held on Wednesday nights, so again it was also convenient with Russ's schedule. Jenny made the same arrangements with Denise in case Russ refused to stay at home with the children.

She and Marjorie both earned their teaching licences and began working at the local pool as swimming instructors. Although Russ objected strenuously, Jenny worked at the Civic Centre two afternoons a week while the boys were at school. Agnes babysat Debbie while she was working. Occasionally she accepted evening classes while Denise watched the children.

Marjorie worked the full five-day week teaching school children how to swim. Her children were all in full-time school, so she was able to be home after school. She was often working at the same time as Jenny, and they enjoyed each other's company.

When the head instructor at the pool saw how competent Jenny was at teaching, she gave her three special groups to teach. The first was a group of adults who were quietly referred to as 'panic victims.' These were people who had suffered a traumatic experience associated with water and were terrified of it. Most hated getting their faces wet and some had taken two or three sets of ten lessons and were still terrified of water. Most were still determined to learn how to swim in case any of their children ran into trouble in the water.

Jenny solved some of their panic problems by being in the pool with them whenever they went into deep water. At the beginning of their first lesson, she had them stand along the side of the pool at the shallow end with their arms holding the side of the pool. Then she demonstrated how she wanted them to put their faces in the water and blow bubbles. At all times they would keep their feet on the bottom of the pool and their arms held securely onto the side of the pool. They were to practice this at home using their kitchen sink for the coming week until their next lesson.

'What I want you to do is fill your kitchen sink with water and practice this in the safety of your own kitchen. Do it at least twice a day, making sure of course that you have a towel to dry off after you have done it. For those of you who work during the day, do it before you have your shower in the morning and possibly again in the evening some time.'

At their second lesson they were asked to pick a black hockey puck off the shallow end of the pool. Most tried but couldn't reach it by just bending down.

'Why do you think you can't pick it up?' Jenny asked.

'I guess we have to get our feet off the ground to get it.' one portly student replied.

'I think I might have to push myself with my feet to get down there.' replied a petite mother of two.

'I guess I will have to get my face wet.' answered another.

'What do you think is keeping you from getting the puck?' Jenny asked.

The answer was shoulder shrugging.

'The reason you can't pick it up is because you have two balloons keeping you at the top of the water. Those balloons are called lungs. Whenever they're full of air they usually float you to the top of the water. If you panic however, you may blow out all your air and can sink in the water.'

She watched them nod their heads. 'Men have more difficulty with buoyancy than women because they have more muscle mass than women. Women on the other hand have more subcutaneous tissue; fat. Sorry ladies, that's the truth, but it does help you float easier than men.'

They all laughed, and she went on. 'There are enough pucks at the bottom of the pool for all of you. I'll show you how you'll have to

120

push yourself down to the bottom of the pool, so you can reach the puck.'

Jenny demonstrated how to do this then added, 'Now one at a time, I'd like each of you to pick up a puck. Who wants to go first?'

They all had a try, and some were surprised that even though they thought they'd pushed themselves down enough to grab a puck; they floated to the top before they could reach it. If anyone seemed to be floundering Jenny righted the person until the student had his or her feet securely on the bottom again. They practiced this for the next fifteen minutes until they felt comfortable diving down and getting their bodies fully submerged.

The next week, while they stood at the side of the pool, she had them practice holding their breath. Using a timer, she was able to let them know that holding their breath for a minute was not difficult. Then she had them jump one at a time into deep water.

'Most of you will be able to hold your breath for well over a minute. So, don't panic when you jump in. You will pop back up to the surface in well under a minute, so won't need another breath for some time. By the time you need a breath, your lungs will have brought you up to the surface.'

They were instructed to take a deep breath and jump, then relax and let themselves float to the surface. They knew Jenny was nearby in the water if they had any problems.

When they had all done this a few times, they all cheered at each other. Most of them never thought they would be able to master their fear of water. By the end of ten lessons, Jenny had them jumping off the low diving board and swimming across the deep end of the pool.

Her second special group was toddlers; most of them being three- and four-year-old's with three to five in each class. She called them her 'tadpoles.' Most Canadian children did not obtain swimming lessons until they were in school, but the swimming pool where she taught believed that children should learn to get used to water when they were toddlers.

Whenever they were in the water, they wore special floatation jackets that had been hand made by the instructors. These harnesses were circular bands of cotton fabric that had pockets all around the device that held pieces of Styrofoam. The circular bands were clipped together at the back of the child with big plastic clips. Straps were sewn to the circular band to fit over the child's shoulders that would keep the floatation device securely held around the child. As the child became more and more confident in the water, lighter Styrofoam pieces were inserted, or some pieces were removed, until the child was able to swim without any floatation assistance.

The pool officials seriously advised the parents not to use the little blow-up arm flotation devices because they could easily slide off the child's arms. The paramount rule was never to leave children unattended in a pool.

Jenny had fun working with the toddlers and before long had them jumping off the low diving board into the water. She was always there to see that they were fine once they bobbed to the surface and would watch them until they reached the side of the pool before the next toddler jumped.

The third group she taught were high school boys. Their regular instructor was away for several weeks, so Jenny took over their classes. At the first lesson, she asked them to swim four lengths of the pool using four different strokes. The boys did nothing but fool around; did not swim properly at all. After a few minutes she blew the whistle, beckoned them out of the pool and had them congregate at the side of the pool. She decided she was going to teach them a different kind of lesson.

'What would you do if you came home from school, heard a scream and found your mother lying on the basement floor? She's had an electrical shock and isn't breathing.'

They all shrugged their shoulders.

'How many of you have young brothers and sisters?'

Several raised their hands.

'What would you do if you found him or her floating face down in a wading pool or lying with a plastic bag over his or her head? He or she's not breathing.'

'What would you do if you found your father lying on the living room floor? He's had a heart attack and is not breathing.'

Again, they shrugged their shoulders, but their faces showed that they were now listening carefully to Jenny.

'Well, for all of these situations you would have to know how to do artificial resuscitation and the steps to take for CPR, coronary pulmonary resuscitation. How many of you know how to do that?'

'I saw it demonstrated on television one day but can't say I really remember how it should be done.' replied one tall teenager.

'I'm going to teach you how to do it.' she said as she looked around the group.

She showed them how to do it then had them simulate the action without really breathing into the other's mouth or pushing hard on the chest. She commended them on paying such close attention to the lesson. Then Jenny noticed the head instructor watching her with the boys and when she was finished teaching them CPR, she quietly pointed out to the boys that the head instructor was watching. She said, 'I want you to show her how well you can swim. Now get back in the pool and do lengths of the four strokes you were supposed to do earlier, but this time do them properly!'

They all took off and really burned up the pool doing the four strokes. When they had finished, Jenny praised them on how well they had done during the entire lesson.

'Will you be our instructor next week?' one boy asked.

'I think your regular teacher will be away for a couple of weeks. But I hope you will all behave for her like you behaved for me, because there's a lot to learn about swimming that can save not only your own life but help you be strong enough to save someone else's.'

Later, the head instructor took Jenny aside and asked, 'What the devil did you say to those kids? They were very serious and not clowning around while you taught them CPR. How did you get them to do that? And they really burned up the pool at the end of the lesson.'

'I just gave them all a scare showing them they weren't prepared, should they run into anyone, especially a family member who isn't breathing and will likely die without their help.'

After that, Jenny was given regular teen classes to instruct. Word got around at the school and both male and female students asked whether she could be their instructor. Jenny's self-esteem rocketed. She had made the right decision by getting her swimming instructor's license.

I can do it! The sky's the limit!

Twenty-four

Jenny knew that she was now physically and emotionally strong enough to ask Russ for a divorce. She knew that he would not take this well but was not prepared for what happened next. 'We'll see how far you get without me!' he screamed as he stormed out of the house, slamming the door behind him.

Three days after she told Russ she wanted a divorce Jenny went to the bank to withdraw some money for groceries and clothing for the children. The account was closed. Russ had closed their joint account and had opened another in just his name the day after she'd asked him for a divorce. He knew she was penniless – and had trusted him to do the right thing.

'How was he allowed to do that?' she asked the teller, 'It was a joint account! Shouldn't he have had to get my permission to remove the money?'

'No, you both had signing authority on the account.' replied the teller.

As she left the bank empty handed, she pondered, 'What am I going to do? I have no money. Russ likely thinks that it will be impossible for me to move out if I don't have money to live on. But what am I going to do? I don't want to go to my parents for help again.'

Then she realised that she still had her credit card and hoped that Russ hadn't closed that as well, so at the grocery store, she filled her basket with essential items and went to the checkout counter. When she presented her credit card, the clerk asked whether she wanted some extra cash. Jenny shrugged her shoulders and decided, 'What the hell – all they can do is refuse it.'

'Can you make that an extra hundred dollars?' she asked.

Jenny held her breath while the clerk processed her credit card and breathed a sigh of relief when it was accepted. At least she had that way of paying for things she and the children might need. Then she went to the department store and bought the children new runners and clothes that she had planned to buy for them with the credit card. She wanted to keep the cash for transactions that were too small to use the credit card such as the children's lunch money and allowances.

Later, when the credit card bills came in, she hid the invoices from Russ and paid the minimum amount with the extra cash she withdrew on the card. Russ didn't seem to be worried about where Jenny had obtained the money. Jenny thought that Russ likely thought she'd received the money from her parents.

He refused to leave, would come stomping home from his four to twelve shift – turn the stereo on full blast and even tried to rape Jenny.

Russ then proceeded to do everything in his power to make her leave the home that they had purchased with the proceeds from her car accident.

One night, after she'd asked him for a divorce, Russ came home from work well after midnight. It was obvious from the noise he was making that he'd been drinking. He turned the stereo on full blast, which woke the entire family. When the boys came upstairs, he shouted at them to get back to bed, and finally went into the master bedroom and collapsed on the bed. Jenny got up and turned the stereo off and went downstairs to comfort the boys.

Russ refused to leave the home. So, Jenny moved into her sons' room and put the boy's beds in the rumpus room downstairs.

Another night reeking of alcohol, he came into Jenny's bedroom and tried to force her to have sex. Jenny had been asleep but fought him off when she realised what he was trying to do. However, she had little success at repelling him because he now weighed two hundred and thirty pounds. She twisted and turned trying to fight him off, knowing she had to be quiet otherwise the children might wake up.

Mark, who was then eleven, was sleeping in the basement with Bruce. Somehow, he heard her struggles and came upstairs with a golf club in his hand, ready to hit his father. Jenny saw him over Russ's shoulder and yelled, 'No Mark, don't!' Russ turned around and glared at Mark.

Jenny said, 'Look at what you're doing to your children. You should be ashamed of yourself!' Russ got up, staggered past Mark and slammed the bedroom door so hard the entire neighbourhood must have heard it. Mark started to sob, and Jenny held him and hugged him. 'Thanks for being there Mark.'

They heard another door bang and realised that Russ had left their home. Jenny took Mark downstairs and put him to bed. When she returned to her room, she propped a chair against the door in case

Russ tried again. She heard him come in again an hour later, but he went directly to the master bedroom where he slept.

One day when she was getting an outfit out of their master bedroom closet, she noticed a rifle leaning against the wall. She identified it as the rifle the police had confiscated for three months when Russ had been hunting illegally at night.

Russ knew she was deathly afraid of rifles or guns of any kind and Russ normally stored the rifle at Antonio's home. She checked and saw that it was fully loaded. 'How dare he leave a loaded gun in the house within reach of the children!' she thought angrily.

She carefully removed the clip then looked around wondering what she should do with the bullets. She knew she couldn't just put them into the garbage, so looked around the yard. Grabbing a shovel, she buried the clip deeply in a corner of the back garden. The next week she checked the rifle and was angered to see that it was again loaded. She repeated her earlier action and buried the clip in the garden knowing that Russ was doing this to scare her into leaving their home.

When she found the rifle fully loaded a third time, her mind snapped. Instantly, she was in a blind rage and decided that when Russ came home in two hours, she was going to finish him off with his own rifle. How dare he treat them this way? The children would still be at school, so they were safely out of the way. She sat on the bed holding the rifle and started rehearsing in her head how she would do it. Would she just wait till he came in the door and let him have it, or would she allow him to explain why he had endangered his children so severely. Then she realized that he would just try to talk her out of it and would likely be able to overpower her before she had the courage to follow through with her threat.

So, she decided she would blast him as soon as he got home. He would come in the back door with the groceries, so she would hide in the living room. She even visualized him falling to the floor with his blood spattered all over the wall behind him. This vision so appalled and shocked her that she dropped the rifle then immediately gasped when she recognised that it could have gone off when she'd dropped it.

She was trembling all over so went to the kitchen and made herself a cup of tea to calm herself down. Then she re-thought what she was planning to do and knew that she could not kill her children's father.

But what was she to do? She started by unloading the rifle and buried the bullets in the back yard as before.

When she returned to the house, she was still blindingly furious with Russ for doing this to her and his children – so mad that she did something that she would never have contemplating doing if she hadn't been pushed beyond the breaking point. After returning to the bedroom, she grabbed the rifle, stomped down the stairs to Russ's basement workroom and went on a rampage. She picked up a sledgehammer and smashed the rifle into a hundred pieces, then looked over at Russ's workbench. There, where it had been for four months, was the vacuum cleaner that Russ had promised to fix. When it was smashed to pieces, she did the same to all the other items he'd promised to fix for her. When her rage was over, she lowered the hammer and surveyed the mess. Her rage had gone, and she knew that Russ would not be able to leave the loaded rifle in their home again. Then she left the room and all its mess for him to find. He never commented about the mess – just left it where it was.

Twenty-five

During the next three months, Jenny carefully examined Russ's past behaviour. She knew she'd felt terribly depressed and unhappy during most of her marriage but always believed that it was something in herself that caused her unhappiness. However, after Reverend Thompson explained that what Russ was doing to her was a form of wife abuse, she spent considerable time at the library researching the topic.

The books about spousal abuse opened her eyes. Not only did they identify the signs that pointed to abuse and how to deal with it, but most advised that it was best for the person to leave the abusive relationship. She recognised that Russ was guilty of doing many abusive things both before and after she'd asked him for a divorce.

Jenny learned that abusive men were often oblivious to the sexual needs of their partners and meeting their own sexual needs was all that was important. Abusive men also fail to recognise the signs when other men abused their wives or others. For instance, he refused to step in when his friend Grant had hurt Betty, his pregnant wife. He also ignored the fact that Barry, their older neighbour was abusing his own wife, Jenny. In fact, he thought Barry's actions were funny and did not think it was necessary to defend Jenny against his actions.

Abusive men keep their wives financially dependent. Jenny had to account for every penny she spent and was not allowed to have an income or separate bank account of her own. Russ wanted Jenny to stay home with their children, so she was not allowed to work even though she wanted to. When Jenny defied him and took a part-time job to earn money one Christmas, he made it clear that she was still responsible for the complete care of the home and their children and their babysitting costs would come out of her salary.

Abusive men isolate their wives from others. Slowly, but surely Jenny's friends drifted away, because Russ would not socialise with them. He had few friends of his own, so she was very lonely. Russ made it clear that his job was to work and hers was to stay home and look after their home and children. She had the full responsibility for the care and upbringing of their children.

Not only had Russ abused her, but Jenny realised that Russ abused his children as well. He almost ignored them when he was home. He rationalised this by saying he would spend more time with them when they were older.

The only time Russ interacted with Debbie was to spoil her and give her anything she wanted even though Jenny had forbidden it. This left Debbie confused about what she was or wasn't allowed to do.

Russ took delight in encouraging the boys to fight and wrestle with each other. Although Bruce was younger by sixteen months, he and Mark were often asked whether they were twins. Bruce was as big and as heavy as Mark. While Mark's personality was more intellectual; Bruce's was more of a rough-and-tumble style than intellectual. Mark liked learning and reading. Bruce enjoyed roughhousing and being active. It was obvious to Jenny that Mark hated it when his father insisted that they fight. When Mark was older, he refused to fight saying, 'Why would I want to fight with Bruce. He's my brother. I don't want to hurt him, and I don't want him to hurt me just for nothing!' and he walked away.

Russ then called him a 'sissy' because he wouldn't fight.

Instead of being with his children, Russ spent his time puttering with his tools in his basement workshop. Although he could have worked a day sift at the railway with weekends off, he decided that Wednesday and Thursday were the nights he wanted off. So, the children were in school during the week and he was not home except for Wednesday and Thursday evenings. On Saturday and Sunday when the children were home, he ignored them as usual, then headed off to work later in the day.

Russ's shift work left Jenny at home on the weekends when most couples were socialising with each other. Russ and Jenny's social life was almost non-existent, but when they did go out, it was to his choice of tavern that had a live band. Most of the people got up to dance. Russ knew that Jenny loved to dance, but she was forced to sit and watch everybody else dancing because he refused to do so. If she danced with other men, he would be calm at the tavern, but took out his rage on her later by forcing her to have very rough sex.

Once Jenny recalled telling him, 'I would never think of taking you to a restaurant and not allowing you to eat. That's the same as you, taking me some place where people are dancing, and you won't dance. That's a form of torture to me. You can dance but refuse to do so.'

Twenty-six

The day after Russ tried to rape her, Jenny decided that drastic action was needed. She could no longer wait for Russ to move out. Russ's behaviour was deteriorating to a dangerous level, and she had to get away from him to protect not only herself but her children as well.

Because Russ kept obtaining continuances for the separation to be finalised, Jenny was afraid that he would learn about her use of the credit card. Her car was so old that she knew it wouldn't last long, so she knew she had some big expenses coming up. So, she decided to speak to the welfare people to see if they could help her out financially until Russ was forced to support them. She made an appointment and when they called her name, she left the children in the waiting room. Her caseworker was Sally McCormack and Jenny liked her right away. Sally could see how stressed Jenny looked and had seen her lovely well-behaved children sitting in the waiting room. 'What do you want us to do to help you?'

'I've asked my husband for a divorce and want to stay in my home, but my husband refuses to leave. I'm really worried about my son Bruce. He's obtaining counselling and is in bad emotional shape because of the tension in our home. His doctor has advised me not to work until Bruce is better. I've lost ten pounds in three months and I can't afford to lose any in the first place.'

'Well then, I guess you'll need an alternative place to live in. Would you like me to see if I can arrange that?' she asked.

Jenny knew that she couldn't withstand much more tension and knew that Bruce and the other children couldn't either, so she agreed to have her arrange for alternative accommodations. Jenny knew she would likely have to live in a place far below the standards of the children's present home but felt it would be worth it. Then another thought occurred to her, 'But how will I move there?'

'We'll provide a moving van to move you there.' Sally explained.

'And we won't have any money to buy groceries and things the children need for school. How will I pay for those kinds of expenses?' she said wringing her hands.

'We'll give you a monthly allowance for necessary expenses.' Sally added.

Jenny couldn't believe that this was finally happening; that she was finally able to leave Russ. She breathed a big sigh of relief. 'Could you arrange all that for me please?'

'We'll do everything we can to expedite this. I know of a place that was available a few days ago. Let me check to see if it's still available.'

'Oh yes. Please do. The sooner we move the better.' Jenny added excitedly.

Within less than a week all the arrangements had been made. Russ had been in the habit of driving directly to their cottage at the lake after his Tuesday four-to-twelve shift and normally didn't come back until the morning of Friday to be ready for his next shift. Before leaving for work on the Tuesday nights he began loading a trailer with furniture from their rumpus room to take to the lake. The first Tuesday, he took the sofa set Jenny had recovered then took the end tables that matched it the week after. The next of his weekends, he took an old beer fridge. Jenny began to wonder if he was planning to move down to the cottage but knew she couldn't take the chance that this was not his plan.

So, because he would likely be gone from Tuesday at 3:20 pm till Friday afternoon as usual, Jennie decided that the best time for her to have the moving truck come was the next Wednesday morning. Sally confirmed the arrangements and for the rest of the week Jenny began secretly packing boxes and hiding them in the children's closets. She stored a bunch of empty boxes at her brother Jeff's home. Her father had agreed to come and help her move, so flew in on Tuesday morning. Jeff picked him up at the airport and drove him over to Jenny's at four o'clock after Russ had gone to work. He brought the extra boxes with him then took Debbie back with him so Jenny, the boys and her father could get on with the packing.

Jenny hadn't told the boys what was going on until their grandfather arrived. She explained the situation to Mark and Bruce, and they began packing boxes of toys and clothes from their bedroom. They seemed relieved that they would be getting away from Russ and soon.

By ten o'clock, the boys were so tired they were weaving on their feet. Jenny sent them to bed and she and her father continued packing until all the boxes were filled. They knew they would need more boxes, so her dad took Jenny's old car and drove behind the local grocery store and scavenged the boxes that were in a bin at the back.

By the time the moving truck arrived at eleven the next morning, they had finished breakfast and had packed all the rest of the bedding and belongings.

Jenny didn't feel guilty about taking the furniture because most of it was hers anyway. She had bought the bedroom suite in the master bedroom, the kitchen table, the living room suite and the carpet in the living room with her own money. Over the years, on special occasions such as birthdays and Christmas, Russ did not give Jenny personal gifts. Instead he gave her appliances, so she felt these were hers as well. He'd given the refrigerator to her one birthday, the washer and dryer he'd given to her for Christmas. The same went for her toaster, her kettle and television.

When Jenny arrived at the townhouse, she was amazed at how nice it was. She'd expected a run-down place, but this one was brand new. She looked around and marvelled at their new spacious kitchen, dining and living room that were on the main floor. There was a small bathroom off the kitchen that she knew would be handy for them all.

Upstairs, there were three bedrooms. The boys as usual would be sharing a bedroom, but Jenny gave them the master bedroom, so they would have more room. The boys were finally able to put their single beds side by side instead of having them set up as bunk beds. They loved their new bedroom. Jenny didn't need much room herself so settled herself in one of the smaller bedrooms.

The only concern she had was that there was mud everywhere. The sod still hadn't been laid, nor had any of the greenery been planted.

Just after dinner, Jeff delivered Debbie and she loved her little room and promptly got busy unpacking her toys. It wasn't long before her head was drooping, and her grandpa helped her put on her pyjamas and she dozed off in her new bedroom, her favourite teddy clutched in her arms.

A few days later, Martha arrived driving her little Austin 1100. She'd driven all the way from Victoria, so was very tired. She was pleased to see that Jenny and the children had such a nice home.

Ian and Martha stayed for a week, and when they were leaving, her mother asked Jenny to hold out her hand. In it she placed the keys for her Austin and the registration slip showing that Jenny was now the owner of the car.

'We can't bear the thought of you driving that old relic any more. We want you to have a car that's reliable.' explained Martha.

Jenny's looked incredulously at Martha then burst into tears. 'How am I ever going to pay you back for all the kind things you've done for us?'

'You'll find a way in the future somehow. But don't worry about it. Your Dad and I have another car at home and because we're retired, we really don't need two cars. I didn't want to see you doing without a car. I'm sure you and the children will make good use of it.'

That evening, her parents flew back to Victoria. After she and the children had driven them to the airport and the children were in bed, Jenny looked around her new home and felt such a sense of peace she burst out crying with the joy of it. She felt as if she had escaped from jail and had a sense of freedom she hadn't felt in years.

Her parents had been so good to her. One thing that always puzzled Jenny was why they had not spoken to her about their concerns about the cultural differences between her and Russ. They had never talked to her about it and she wondered if things would have been different if she had been warned before her marriage. If they had discussed their concerns with her, would she have picked up and confirmed those differences simply by watching the interaction between Russ's father, mother and brother? Would she have noticed how Russ gave in to his father's wishes? In hindsight, she wished that her parents had spoken up. On the other hand, she would not have her children, so some good came from their union.

Twenty-seven

So, they settled into and loved their new home. It wasn't long before the sod was laid, and the greenery planted. In fact, the landscape men let Mark and Bruce help plant some of the flowers. Life was good!

Jenny hadn't realised how much pressure she and the children had been under when they lived with Russ – how the children had to watch that they didn't anger Russ. The change in their behaviour was remarkable. They squabbled less, slept better and seemed to enjoy life far more. And they smiled more. Even though they were dirt poor, they managed to be happy and enjoyed their new sense of freedom.

One thing Jenny did not know was that every cent the welfare people gave her would eventually come out of *her* portion of the value of the home she had bought.

After Jenny was settled in her new home, she decided it was time to phone her friends and former neighbours to let them know how to get in touch with her. She needed a support group to help her through this difficult time. What she needed were others to believe in her and understand her, but she was sadly disappointed to learn who were and were not true friends.

The person that stuck by her was Marjorie Stewart. If it hadn't been for her support, Jenny would have felt totally deserted by those she thought were her friends. Marjorie couldn't do enough for her and helped her through the tough transition. Jenny blessed the day that she'd met her at her swimming class. Marjorie encouraged her to continue teaching swimming and they often met for coffee and chats. One day when Jenny was a bit low about the desertion of her friends, Marjorie said, 'You've learned an important lesson. You've learned who your real friends are. They've shown their true colours by their desertion of you. Remember, life is tough, but you're even tougher. You'll do fine.'

To obtain some support, Jenny joined an organization called Parents without Partners. At one of the meetings, she met Gordon Berry who was also separated from his wife. He really missed his children. He met and hit it off with Jenny's three children. One summer day, Gordon asked whether she and the children would like to take a ride to Lockport, a small community located just north of the city of Winnipeg.

The boys were very excited to see Lockport and were ready to have fun that day. They were enthralled watching the locks work. Jenny packed a lunch and they enjoyed the afternoon walking around the area and having a picnic lunch. Having been there before, she knew there would be grassy hills the children could slide down, so she brought three flattened cardboard boxes.

Jenny smiled as she watched her children as they laughed and raced each other down the hill on their pieces of cardboard. It was good seeing them having so much fun. Just after five thirty Jenny called the children and told them it was time to go home. They begged for two more slides and she nodded. It was close to six o'clock by the time they left. Soon they were back at her home and she made dinner for them all. Gordon left when the children went to bed completely tired out from their busy afternoon.

That night as Jenny was watching the ten o'clock news, she was horrified to hear the news report saying that just about the time they were leaving Lockport, a family of four in a canoe had attempted to go over the weir, but their boat had capsized. All four were subsequently rescued, but because nobody on shore knew CPR, two of them died.

'I was right there!' she almost screamed at the television. 'I could have saved them! Why couldn't we have left fifteen minutes later!'

She phoned Gordon and told him the sad tale. He too knew CPR and they commiserated about why things happened the way they did in life. Both spent restless nights thereafter wondering what would have happened if they had still been there at the time the family had gone over the weir.

Twenty-eight

It took two years for Jenny to obtain a divorce. Shortly after she left the home with her children, Russ moved in with another woman, leaving their home empty most of the time. Jenny was advised by her lawyer not to move back, because Russ would likely return and keep up his abusive behaviour.

Jenny knew that in the 1970s, the only way she and Russ could get a divorce would be for her to charge him with adultery. She also knew that she would need concrete evidence to prove it.

It would cost a lot to hire a private detective to follow him. Her biggest problem was how to pay for a detective. Then her eyes spotted her diamond engagement and wedding rings. 'I wonder how much they would be worth?' she pondered.

That day she went to a pawnshop and learned that she would get five hundred dollars for the set and took the deal. Then she spoke with a detective who was recommended by one of her friends. She had been assured that the detective was good and didn't charge an arm and a leg. When she met him, Jenny liked him immediately He had a kind face and listened carefully as she told him her story. He probed for more details and Jenny could see that he was saddened by the problems her husband had caused her. 'Yes, I'll take the case.' he said. 'You can pay me on instalments if you need to, but I'm going to get this guy!'

He followed Russ for ten days and was able to establish that he was living with another woman in her home and just went home to their matrimonial home on Friday nights when he had his weekly visit with his children.

At the beginning of June, Jenny and Russ went to court to settle their divorce. Jenny was very nervous being in the same room as Russ and when she had to testify she told the judge about the mental cruelty he'd submitted her to, his swearing of a vendetta against her, of having her followed when she went out socially and about how he had been living with another woman for over a year.

When Russ took the stand, he took out a notebook and started itemising the times Jenny had been out on evenings attending parents without partners meetings. When asked, he admitted that he had hired someone to follow her. He itemised the furniture she had taken from the home and how she had left very little for him. Jenny just sat shaking her head. 'How pathetic he is.' she thought.

Jenny learned that Russ had put the cottage into his own name even though she had hammered nails the same as he did when building it. Russ had borrowed fifteen hundred dollars from her father to build it, but never paid it back.

It was Jenny's detective's testimony proving that Russ spent his time living with another woman except when he saw his children that the judge approved of the divorce on grounds of adultery. He awarded $225 a month maintenance to Jenny for the children and stipulated that Russ would have the children every second weekend.

Jenny realized that to do this Russ would finally have to change his shifts, so he had weekends off when he had the children.

It tore Jenny's heart to realize that despite her patience and years of perseverance, her marriage to Russ had not worked out and for a long time, she felt as if she was a failure. Then she reminded herself that if she had not married Russ, she would not have her three beautiful children. She also reminded herself that her dream as a teenager was to get married and have children. Her marriage to Russ might have failed, but she loved her children with a passion, so she had fulfilled half of her dreams. They were her reason for living.

She also realized that she had never felt passionate or intimate with Russ because of his insistence on rushing through the sex act. Emotionally, he always kept Jenny at arms-length and seemed unable to show intimacy towards her or their children. Russ was too introverted to risk the chance that someone could touch his inner core and protected himself from any close relationship – including that of his wife and three children. With Jenny, he never *'let her in,'* but held himself emotionally aloof from such feelings.

Twenty-nine

One morning when Jenny woke up, she decided some changes were required now that she was heading towards single life. Russ had always insisted that she wear her hair long. She had hard-to-manage hair and this involved a lot of extra effort - effort she felt could be better spent enjoying life. His insistence on her keeping it long had always gnawed at her and she felt annoyed every time she had to fuss with her hair. One of the first things she did when she and the children were on their own was to go to a hairdresser and get her hair cut short into a pixie cut. Because she had small delicate features, the style suited her to perfection. She felt even more free from Russ, because now she could just 'wash and wear' her hair without the constant fussing. This proved a boon to her when she went back to teaching swimming.

Jenny had little money to spend on entertainment for herself and her children, but soon she found many places where she could take the children that didn't cost much money.

They found a small man-made lake not far from their home and spent many a day enjoying the water and the sunshine. They drove to Lower Fort Garry, to the Lockport Dam and attended several free concerts. Because they lived near the Assiniboine Downs racetrack, she made a point of taking the children there on 'Ladies' Day.' Jenny didn't believe in gambling but did love horses. Because children got in free, it was a lovely inexpensive evening for them all. Their treat of a hot dog and soft drink capped the evening. They didn't bet of course, but they did pick their favourite horse before each race and had fun when their pick turned out to win. It was a lovely summer and that fall the boys enrolled in a nearby school. Mark was in grade six and Bruce was in grade four.

Both boys were paperboys and made their pin money that way. One day Bruce came home with his face scratched and bleeding. 'What happened?' Jenny asked in concern.

'Kevin and Billy Watson pushed me off my bike while I was delivering papers. Because I had just picked up my newspapers, it was awkward to ride my bike and I got tangled up in it when I fell. But I gave one of the boys a good bash, but the other one grabbed my face and scratched it.' he said as he pointed to his bleeding face.

'Where do these boys live?' she asked.

'They live in our complex – in number 34.'

'Well, I'll speak to their parents. They're nothing but bullies.' she said emphatically.

After she cleaned up his face, she took Bruce with her and left Mark with Debbie. She knocked on the door of unit 34 and a rather shabbily dressed woman answered the door, wiping her hands as she came. 'Yes?'

Jenny explained what had happened. 'Oh, so he's the bully that bashed my boy!' she yelled.

'No. Your two boys pushed Bruce off his bike when he was delivering his newspapers.' As she spoke, she could see two boys standing behind the woman. They were obviously one or two years older than her boys.

She continued, 'Then they started hitting him and Bruce fought back. But look at the dirty fighting your son's use – two against one and they're both older than Bruce. Look at how they scratched his face.' she said as she pointed to Bruce's cheek.

'Well, I still think it's your boy that started the fight.' she said as she stood with her hands on her hips.

'It was still two against one – surely you can't condone that kind of behaviour.' Jenny enquired.

The woman backed up and slammed the door. Jenny realised that the woman was not going to back down and she was wasting her time trying to reason with her. 'Those apples didn't fall far from that tree.' she thought.

As they walked back to her home Jenny asked Bruce, 'Are you sure that's the way it happened?'

Bruce looked her in the eye and said, 'Yes, Mom. I'm not lying. That's how it happened.'

When Jenny got home, she took her boys aside and spoke to them. 'It looks like the neighbour boys are street fighters and fight dirty. From now on, I want you both to deliver your newspapers, but together. Once you've delivered one set then deliver the other one. That way you'll be together, and they can't gang up on you. Okay?'

Both boys nodded.

'And another thing – with these boys only, you have my permission to bash them back. Someone has got to teach them a lesson and if you two are together, they won't be able to gang up on you.'

That evening Mark and Bruce practiced how they would fight back should the boys start trouble. 'The most important thing we have to do is to get off our bikes, so they can't tip us over.' said Mark.

Two days later, the inevitable happened. The Watson boys started trouble again. 'Sissy, sissy, sissy.' they chanted to Bruce. 'Had to get your mother to fight for you – what a sissy!' they taunted.

'Well it won't happen again.' said Bruce as he placed his bike on the ground.

'Oh yeah!' shouted Kevin and threw a fist at Bruce. This time Bruce was ready and dodged the punch but grabbed him around the neck and threw him to the ground.

Billy tried the same tactic with Mark and ended up on the ground. Both Bruce and Mark landed two-fisted punches and the Watson boys suddenly realised that they couldn't intimidate these two younger boys. They ran off holding their faces and tummies.

'And don't come back!' shouted Bruce, the more pugnacious of the two.

They had no more problems from the two bullies except for dirty looks any time they saw each other. In time, Mark and Bruce were able to deliver their newspapers alone again.

Jenny learned that a neighbour in the complex had a small crank-up tent trailer for sale for only seven hundred dollars. The family needed to buy a larger one for their expanding family and were only offered five hundred for it in trade. It slept four, so would be perfect for Jenny's family to use for camping. Jenny enquired and learned that her little Austin would not have trouble pulling it because of its low pulling weight. But how was she going to pay for it?

'I don't have that kind of money. Could I pay for it a bit every month?' she asked the owner.

'Maybe we can make a deal.' the woman replied, 'I have two girls that need care before and after school. Would you be interested in looking after them in exchange for buying the trailer? We'd be willing to pay you ten dollars an hour to do so.'

'You've got yourself a deal.' replied Jenny as she accepted the keys for the trailer. Because they would require a stronger hitch for their new trailer the husband installed their old one on Jenny's Austin. So, they were all set for summer fun!

That summer they drove to many lakes where they could swim and enjoy their holidays. The boys were especially fond of the breakfasts of bacon and eggs that Jenny made on their little barbeque. They all had sleeping bags, but Jenny's and Debbie's could be zipped together to form a double sleeping bag.

Thirty

One afternoon Jenny received a request from the principal of the boy's school. He asked her to come to his office that afternoon. He said, 'We've been having problems with your son Bruce. His attention span is very short, he gets angry and blows up quite often and is falling behind in his school work.'

'What do you suggest?' Jenny asked.

'We have student counsellors here and I would like to have him assessed. Would you agree to that?'

'Yes, I would. I've noticed the same tendencies in him at home and he gets very agitated if I correct his behaviour.'

The counsellor recommended that Bruce be checked neurologically to see if something neurological was causing the behaviour. The Neurologist examined him and asked Jenny, 'Has he had any bad knocks to his head?'

'He's had a few falls, but nothing serious,' she replied, 'but he had a difficult time when he was born.' She explained about the electrical shock he had received before he was born.

'That could explain it. I'll do an electroencephalogram and see if there is any damage.'

After the test was completed, he explained that Bruce had a brain disorder that probably stemmed from the shock he'd received. He prescribed medication that would alleviate the problems.

The medication worked wonders for the troubled boy. He did better at school and got along with his friends and siblings. When he was taking his medication, he was a model child. However, Russ would do anything in his power to harass Jenny – even harm his children while doing so. When Jenny told him about Bruce's medication, his comment was, 'There's nothing wrong with that kid! He just needs a clip on the ear, so he'll behave better.'

After the divorce, Russ was allowed visitation with his children every second weekend. Shortly after the visits began, Jenny realized that the Bruce's erratic behaviour was getting worse.

Jenny was concerned – seriously concerned. She'd obtained her divorce from Russ just two months ago, but he was still tormenting her life. The courts said that Russ could have his three children every second weekend. Even though he had almost ignored the children during his marriage, he had asked for increased visitation rights with them. Jenny knew he hadn't done this because he wanted to spend time with them, but simply because it was another way to torment her.

When Bruce's behaviour deteriorated after his visits with Russ, Jenny learned that Russ had refused to let him take his medication during his allotted weekends. This resulted in a resumption of Bruce's off-the-rails behaviour that lasted for days until his medication kicked in again.

One day, after Bruce had returned from his weekend with Russ, he was especially agitated and began fighting with Mark. Jenny had been upstairs when she heard them fighting. She rushed downstairs and saw Bruce straddling his brother on the sofa. He repeatedly pounded his fist into Mark's face as hard as he could. Mark's face was a bloody mess. Jenny rushed over to Bruce and grabbed him around the waist to pull him off and thrust him into a living room chair. One look at Bruce's face made her blood run cold. He looked belligerently at her and Jenny was shocked by the almost insane look he gave her. She pulled away from him wondering for a moment whether he was going to hit her as well.

'Go to your room,' she shouted at him as she bent over Mark's bleeding form. Bruce stomped loudly up the stairs to his bedroom.

Jenny examined Mark and saw that blood was streaming out of his nose and mouth and knew that he needed medical attention. She got him a towel to put on his face, then said, 'I'll be right back. I'm going to get Mrs. Henderson from next door to have a look at you.' Then she went outside and knocked on the door of the duplex next door. Lorraine was a nurse, and Jenny was glad to see that she was home.

Lorraine Henderson gently examined Mark and as she looked up at Jenny, she stated, 'I think he will need stitches in his lip and his nose could be broken. So, I'll look after Debbie and Bruce while you take Mark to the hospital. Just give me a minute to tell my family what we are going to do.'

Jenny phoned Dr. Sims to tell him she was taking Mark to the Hospital. He said he would meet her there. Mark had facial X-rays taken and was told that his nose was not broken. However, he required four stitches on the right of his top lip. The doctor asked him to check to see if any of his teeth were loose and Mark gingerly wiggled them then shook his head. He had bitten his tongue and that was very sore and made it difficult for him to talk.

Dr. Sims took Jenny aside and asked how it had happened. He had recommended that Bruce see the psychiatrist and knew that he should be on his medication daily. 'I'm really concerned that Bruce has gone off the rails so badly. Do you have any idea why that has happened after he's done so well on his medication?'

'His father refuses to let him take the medication when he's with him every second weekend. Bruce comes home so wound up that it takes me two days to get him back to normal.'

'Give me his phone number and I will talk to him and stress how important it is for Bruce to take his medication.'

That evening Jenny reluctantly phoned Russ to tell him about Mark's injuries, and to encourage him to ensure that Bruce continued to take his medication. While she was talking to him, she heard a click on the phone. Jenny learned later that Mark had picked up the extension phone to hear what his father was going to say. Unfortunately, he overheard Russ's shocking comment, 'It's about time Bruce cleaned his clock! That beating has been a long time coming if you ask me.'

'You're disgusting!' shouted Jenny as she hung up the phone. She looked up the stairway and saw Mark standing there with tears running down his face. 'I'm never going to speak to him again.' he sobbed through his bandaged mouth.

Because of this, Mark refused to have anything further to do with his father even though the family courts insisted that Jenny send him to his father's every second weekend.

Mark stayed home the next weekend Russ was to have the children. That weekend, Russ spoke privately with Bruce.

'Would you like to live with me?'

Bruce looked up at his dad not knowing what to say.

'You'll have a room of your own and I'll get you a new bike,' Russ said using bribery as encouragement

Poor, gullible, eleven-year-old Bruce nodded his head. When he returned home after the weekend, he told Jenny what was going to happen.

Jenny knew that this offer had not been made for Bruce's benefit, but was done solely to hurt her. However, she decided to let him do it because she expected him to be back with his family in a short time.

So, he and Mark divided up their toys and Bruce waited for his father to arrive. Russ arrived, gave dirty looks to Jenny as he and Bruce carried the boxes of his belongings to his van. He left Bruce in the car and approached Jenny. In a menacing voice, he renewed his ongoing vendetta to Jenny by saying, 'I have the house, the cottage, the car, the bank account and now I have Bruce. You're going to end up with nothing!' Then he swung around and got in his van.

After Russ had left with Bruce, Jenny just sat on the sofa with Mark and Debbie at her side. She knew she couldn't take much more of this kind of pressure. That night she phoned her parents, Ian and Martha to discuss the situation with them. Jenny decided that she had to move to another city; that she couldn't take any more of the tension of living in the same city as Russ. She knew he meant his vendetta and didn't want to give him the opportunity of taking Mark and Debbie away from her.

As expected, her mother said, 'Come here. You know you're welcome here anytime.'

'No Mom, this is something I need to do on my own. It seems that there is lots of work in Alberta. I think I will go there and see if I can get a job.'

'Whatever you want dear but know you can always count on us for help.' added Martha sadly.

It was summer holidays, so Jenny packed Mark and Debbie in the car and started driving westward. Mark was now almost thirteen and Debbie was six. When Jenny and her family got to Calgary, Alberta she rented a motel and purchased several local newspapers. Then she scoured the want ads and found an advertisement for a legal secretary. She phoned the office and was offered an appointment for that afternoon. Mark agreed to look after Debbie while she was gone.

At the interview, Jenny met the lawyer, Mr. Ruby and was pleased to learn that he was also from Winnipeg. He specialised in finalising home real estate sales. Jenny had kept her typing skills up but was quite rusty in the shorthand area. They hit it off right away and he offered her the job.

'I'll have to return to Winnipeg for two weeks or so, but as soon as I can find a place to stay and to move my belongings, I could start.'

'Have you found a place to rent?' he asked.

'Not yet, but I'll get busy looking as soon as I get back to my motel.'

'As you know, I'm associated quite closely with the real estate market. I know of a place that might suit you and your two children. Why don't I call the lady who owns the place and see if she can let you see it today.' he replied.

'That would be wonderful. How kind of you to save me that trouble.'

Jenny and the children examined the home he recommended and were pleased with it. The rental unit was the upstairs of a two-storey home. It had a living room, dining room, kitchen and three bedrooms. The landlady, who introduced herself as Nancy Kelly, was an elderly widow who lived in the lower unit. When she finished showing Jenny around the unit, she said, 'If you rent the unit, I would be able to keep an eye on the children both before and after school while you worked.'

Jenny glanced at the children and they both nodded. They already liked the kind lady who would live in the same home as they.

'Would we be able to park our tent trailer in the back yard?' asked Jenny.

'That would be fine, there's lots of room to park the trailer and our two cars in the back.'

'That would be wonderful. I'd like to rent the unit to start in two weeks, the 15th of August. We'll be back then in time for me to start work. Where is the nearest school for the children? Mark will be in junior high school and Debbie will start Grade one.'

Nancy got out the phone book and looked up the phone number of both schools. Jenny talked to both school administration staff and enrolled her children for the start of the school year in September. She knew that she would have to obtain Mark's school records from his present school in Winnipeg but didn't think that would be a problem. Because this was Debbie's official first year in school, she didn't have any school records to collect. Although the schools were two blocks apart, she arranged for Debbie to stay at the school until Mark could come and collect her. He would also be able to walk Debbie to school in the morning.

It all happened so quickly and smoothly, that Jenny knew she'd made the right decision to move to Calgary and start a new life for her family. That night she phoned Ian and Martha with the good news and the next day drove back to Winnipeg.

At home, Jenny ordered a moving truck to come the next Monday and they all began packing boxes. She went to the school and obtained Mark's school records then informed the family court workers that she would be moving with Mark and Debbie to Calgary. She was tempted to phone Bruce to give him her new address, but the last thing she wanted Russ to know was exactly when she would be leaving. Instead, she decided that it would be better to give Bruce that information later when they were settled in Calgary. Jenny planned to invite him to join them, so the children could be together again.

Thirty-one

On the Thursday night before their intended move, Mark rushed into their home. His eyes were as big as saucers as he approached Jenny in their kitchen. 'Mom. Mom. I just saw Dad driving down our street! He's spying on us.' he said excitedly.

'Did he see you watching him?' Jenny asked with a concerned look on her face.

'No, I don't think so. I just saw the back of his van, but it was him.' he said earnestly.

Mark was interested in cars, so Jenny believed him when he said that he'd seen his Dad's car.

'Why don't you keep watching to see if he comes back.' she suggested.

'Okay Mom. But I'll hide, so he can't see me.' he said as he went out the back door. He crept around the side of their rented home and stood in the shadows where his father, Russ, would not be able to see him.

Debbie was already asleep in bed, so she was glad she hadn't been awakened by her brother's loud voice. They'd had enough turmoil in their lives lately and she didn't want six-year-old Debbie to face any more of it. And now with only a few days till they left for Calgary to start their new life, Mark had spotted Russ cruising her street. Jenny knew Russ would do anything to stop her from leaving.

'What am I going to do?' she thought. 'The moving truck isn't coming until Monday. By then he might be able to stop us from leaving and all our plans would be for nothing.'

Thankfully, most of their belongings had been packed in cardboard boxes and she had enough boxes to pack the rest of them. Then, Jenny did what she'd been forced to do for many years – she contacted her parents for help. They agreed to come right away and spent most of the next two days taking turns driving their car from Victoria, British Columbia to Winnipeg.

As soon as they arrived that Sunday afternoon, Ian advised Jenny, 'Pack the kids in the car and just go. We'll make sure all the packing is finished and return the key to the resident manager.'

'Then we'll join you in Calgary.' added Martha.

Ian handed Jenny some money to pay for motels because the furniture would not arrive until Wednesday. By midnight that night, Jenny, Mark and Debbie were across the Saskatchewan border and heading for Calgary.

Early Monday morning in Winnipeg, the moving truck arrived to pick up their belongings. Shortly after the van had left with the furniture, Ian and Martha were standing outside the unit. They were just about to head for the office to give the keys to the resident manager when a woman approached the unit.

'I'm looking for Jenny Carponi,' said the woman.

'I'm sorry, she's not here.' Martha replied.

'I have a court order banning Mrs. Carponi and the children from leaving the province.' the woman said as she tried to hand Martha the document.

Martha stepped back and refused to accept the document and said, 'You'll have to come back another time if you want to serve this document. Mrs. Carponi is not here.'

The woman returned to her car and Ian and Martha began their long road trip to Calgary. Her parents chuckled as they drove towards Calgary knowing that they had thwarted Russ from causing any more damage to his family. They stopped at a motel along the way and had a well-deserved rest.

On Wednesday, they'd just reached Jenny and the children's new home in Calgary when the moving truck arrived. They all pitched in and soon had everything unpacked and settled. Ian repaired a few things in the apartment, then he and Martha drove back to Victoria a couple of days later. Jenny started her job the next Monday and hired their downstairs landlady, Nancy Kelly, to care for the children for the next week until they were to start school.

So, they all started a new life, and were finally free from Russ's tyranny. For the first time in fifteen long years, Jenny felt free from Russ's tyranny – at least so she thought...

Thirty-two

When the divorce was finalized, Jenny was dismayed to learn that she would only receive $4,000 for her portion of the home which Russ still lived in. This was the same amount she had received after her car accident and had used for the down payment so they could buy their first home. She was dismayed that she and her children had ended up with no additional money after fifteen years of marriage. But she had most of the furniture which she felt was hers anyway. When the $4,000 arrived, Jenny started looking for a home they could live in and was pleased to find one in the Duggan area of Calgary. It was a tiny three-bedroom home, but it had lots of interesting aspects to it. The rumpus room floor was formerly a bowling alley floor so was very thick and provided lots of insulation on the basement floor. It had obviously been installed when the home was built, because it weighed a ton. The room also had black iron sconces on the wall and had a swinging split door also made of black iron leading into a tiny laundry area. Although the home was to the east of Calgary, they had a view of farmland with horses on it. Because Calgary was built in a bowl, they had a view of foothills that were on the other side of Calgary and couldn't see downtown Calgary at all except at night when the city lights could be seen reflected in the sky,

The price of the home was $26,000 and had a $14,500 mortgage on it. Jenny realized that she didn't have enough money with her $4,000 down-payment to buy it and did not qualify for a full mortgage on the home which would be for $22,000. As she usually did, she asked her parents for advice. They were pleased to send her the additional $7,500 she would need to buy the home and take over the mortgage. They agreed that she could pay off their loan by putting $200 monthly instalments in a bank account they opened for that purpose. This would be hard for her until it was paid off, but she and the children would again have a home of their own.

In the meantime, for two years, Russ did not comply with the maintenance order, did not contact his two children in Calgary, and did not send any money to Jenny. During that time, she and the children wrote faithfully to Bruce, sent him birthday and Christmas gifts. In several letters Jenny asked him to join them but received no word back from Bruce. They didn't receive acknowledgement for his gifts or letters, so they stopped sending them. Several times Jenny phoned Russ's home, but he refused to let her talk to Bruce, saying he was in bed, at school or simply not home.

She didn't learn until years later that Russ had not given Bruce their letters and gifts and had not informed him about the phone calls. In fact, Bruce didn't even know where they were and felt completely deserted by his mother, brother and sister. What a terrible thing to do to a young boy and his siblings and how hard it must have been for Bruce to think that his family had deserted him.

Two months after she and the children moved to Calgary, Martha and Ian came to visit just before the October Thanksgiving weekend. Jenny prepared the traditional turkey dinner but noticed that Mark wasn't very hungry. He'd been feeling under the weather for a day or so but didn't look at all well that day.

'Mom I really feel sick,' he said just seconds before he bolted for the bathroom to be sick.

Jenny felt his head and realized he was sweating profusely - yet felt cold and clammy. She quickly went downstairs to ask Nancy if she could recommend a doctor she could call. Nancy suggested that because it was a long weekend, it would be better to take them to the emergency ward at the nearby hospital.

The doctors examined Mark and said they were going to admit him because his blood tests showed that his white cells were elevated showing he was fighting a serious infection. For days, Mark couldn't seem to keep anything down and the doctors advised Jenny that they needed to take a bone marrow sample to test him for leukaemia.

'Oh no. You don't think he has leukaemia, do you?' she said in horror.

'Not really, but we need to rule it out.'

Jenny asked them to let her know when they would do the test. Her boss, Mr. Ruby knew that Mark was in the hospital and was kind enough to let her to take some time off if she needed to care for him.

When she went up to the hospital after work to visit Mark, she learned that they had done the test without letting her know. Mark sobbed as he told her how painful it was. They had obtained the bone marrow sample from his sternum and he said he held the nurses hand so tight she winced.

In two days, the results came back that Mark did not have leukaemia, but he did have hepatitis. Everyone in the family, including Ian and Martha had to have very painful hepatitis shots. Mark was home in two days and recovered within a week.

Later in life, he had such rich blood that it was a shame that he couldn't donate blood, but because he had been diagnosed with hepatitis he could not donate. When he was an adult and married, a routine blood test showed that he had not had hepatitis after all, so remained confused as to why he had been so sick that Thanksgiving holiday.

Their first Christmas in Calgary, Jenny was surprised when she received a phone call from her brother Jeff who lived in Winnipeg with his wife Marion.

'Hi Sis. I've just arrived in Calgary. Marion and I have split up and I'm at loose ends this Christmas.'

'Well come on over,' Jenny almost shouted and immediately invited him to stay with them for the holidays.

When Jeff arrived, he had lovely, gifts for Jenny, Mark and Debbie. After the children were in bed, Jeff said, 'I told Russ I was coming here to see you for Christmas and offered to bring his presents for the children. He told me he wasn't sending them anything and wouldn't consider having anything to do with them until they moved back to Winnipeg.'

'He's a very angry man and is terribly upset with me that I dared to defy him and leave him. He's so used to being in charge, that he can't accept that I have a mind of my own and don't want any part of him.' Jenny replied.

'I couldn't believe that a father could act so callously towards his children. How could he not send them gifts for Christmas?' he exclaimed.

'Even though Russ knows where we are, he has had no contact with us since we moved here, and we haven't had any contact with Bruce. Every time I phone, Russ refuses to let met talk to him. Do you know what's going on there?'

'It's impossible for me to know what's going on with Russ and Bruce. As soon as you left for Calgary, he refused to have any contact with your side of the family. So, before I came here, I just went to their home and forced Russ to talk to me. Bruce was at school, so I didn't see him.'

'Well, I guess now you really know what a vile, evil man he really is. Maybe now you will understand why I left him. He has a mean streak in him that's a mile wide and he'll do anything to hurt me. It looks like he's trying to do that through his own children. What a childish and mean way to act.'

'Do you want me to take Bruce's presents back with me?' he asked.

'That won't be necessary. We mailed them to him in November, so he should have them long before Christmas.'

But of course, Bruce was never destined to receive those gifts.

The children enjoyed having their uncle with them for Christmas and he helped make it a nice Christmas holiday.

Thirty-three

Two years after her divorce was granted, Jenny realised that she would have to do something to make Russ take responsibility for his children and make his payments for the children's upkeep. She took a week off work, hired a babysitter and drove back to Winnipeg. Mark and Debbie didn't come back with her, in case the courts forced them to stay in Winnipeg. To take Russ to court for back maintenance, she knew she'd need to hire a lawyer. Because she didn't qualify this time for a Legal Aid lawyer, she contacted another law firm close to where she used to live in Winnipeg and was given an appointment.

When she arrived at their office, she was surprised to notice that most of the staff in the office were staring at her. After she was escorted into the lawyer's office and shook hands with him, she was surprised by his first comment, 'I'm sorry Mrs. Carponi, I can't represent you. You see our firm now represents the new Mrs. Carponi. There would be a conflict of interest if we took your case. We thought you were Cloe Carponi when we made the appointment to see you.'

Jenny sat in the chair stunned by what she'd heard and the full implications of what his statement meant. 'So, they finally made it legal, did they?' she said almost to herself rather than to the lawyer, 'Decided to stop living in sin in front of my son.' she added.

'I guess I'll just have to get another lawyer then.' she added as she stood up and left the lawyer's office. Her face was a bright red as she passed through the outer office, where the staff again watched her every move.

So, Russ had finally married Cloe and had moved her and her daughter into Jenny's former home. *'At least Bruce will be able to have some continuity in his life and will be back living on the crescent with his old friends.'* she thought.

Later that day she found another lawyer, Walter Scott who agreed to take the case. Walter informed her that she would not likely have to appear in court unless Russ denied that he had reneged on sending her the court-allotted maintenance payments. This was a relief, because it was difficult for her to leave her job in Calgary so she could attend a court appearance in Winnipeg.

The case went to court several months later, and Russ admitted that he had made no maintenance payments to Jenny because he didn't have access to his children. Walter sent her a letter explaining the court's resolutions. Russ asked that the court change his maintenance payments from two hundred and twenty-five dollars per month to one hundred and seventy-five dollars per month, now that he had custody of Bruce. They agreed. The document also stated that Russ was forced to make his payments directly into the court. The court would then forward those payments to Jenny. The good thing was that if Russ was in arrears for two successive months, he could go to jail. That way she did not need to have any future contact with Russ.

But Jenny sighed in frustration as she read the next resolution. The money Russ owed for the two years' back maintenance was not being sent to Jenny as it should have been. Instead those funds were being placed in a trust fund for Mark and Debbie. The children would not be able to access those funds until they were eighteen. It appeared that Russ had won this battle to keep Jenny from receiving the money and it was obvious that he had wangled the courts so Jenny would not see a cent of those funds.

But thankfully, he was out of her life forever! When Mark and Debbie reached majority – the funds were given to them, but Jenny requested that they not thank their father for the money, because that money should have been given to them years ago to help them buy necessities.

Thirty-four

One Saturday, Jenny asked Ruth, a new friend, over for coffee. Ruth was a highly skilled career counsellor, who found careers for people who had been injured and couldn't do the kind of job they'd been in before their injury or accident. Jenny decided that she would be the perfect person to give her advice. Once they finished drinking their coffee, Jenny asked, 'Ruth would you be willing to be my career counsellor? I would have to pay you in instalments though, because I'm barely getting along financially.'

Ruth replied, 'I've watched you struggling with your secretarial job and know you're capable of much more. It would be a pleasure to help you out, but I won't help out if you won't let me do it for free.'

Jenny was overwhelmed and had difficulty holding back her tears of gratitude. 'I'll pay you back somehow – just wait and see!'

'You'll pay me back by following through on what I suggest,' Ruth replied as she smiled at Jenny.

The next day, Ruth brought over the forms Jenny needed to complete so she could identify the right career for her. After she had completed all the necessary psychological, IQ and aptitude tests, Ruth identified five occupations, that with a bit of training, Jenny would likely enjoy and be good at.

Jenny looked at the list of alternatives and exclaimed, 'I wouldn't want to become any of these!'

'I didn't think so,' said Ruth. 'You 'fudged' the tests. You answered the questions the way you thought you should answer them instead of asking yourself honestly. 'What do I really think?''

'I guess that's exactly what I did. I'm so programmed to ask myself what other people want from me that I've forgotten to ask myself what I want to do. Let me do the tests again and see if I come up with some proper choices.'

After she had analysed the second results, Ruth said, 'It looks as if there are five suitable occupations you can go into. The first on the list is to sell goods or services. Your persuasive powers are off the scale. What do you think of that kind of work?'

'Right now, I don't think I could sell myself out of a paper bag. I don't have enough confidence to sell things. What's my second choice?'

'The second one is marketing. That's an occupation where people analyse the market and determine target markets for products, then determine the best way to approach potential buyers to actually buy the item.' Ruth explained.

'That sounds interesting. What do you suggest I do to find out more about that occupation?' Jenny queried.

'I always advise people to interview at least two people in an occupation and ask them what they like and dislike about the occupation, what kind of education they require, what kind of companies they've worked for etc. The reason you would interview two people is because one of them might be in the wrong job.'

'I'll do that before I make a decision. What are the other choices?' she prompted.

'The next one is public relations. I think you would be well suited for that field, but unfortunately there aren't many positions available in that occupation – in fact there are too many well-qualified people in that field who are still looking for jobs. So, I don't think you should even consider that choice.'

'I guess you're right.'

'Fourth on the list is human resources. That job has lots of variety in it; recruiting, training, classifying jobs, wage and salary surveys, writing job descriptions, managing performance appraisal systems, employee relations and even disciplining and firing employees. How does that one sound?'

'I like the fact that it has a good mix of detailed work and contact with people. I think I'll interview a few people in that field. What's the fifth choice?'

Ruth laughed as she said, 'The fifth choice is small appliance repair. You scored high on electrical and mechanical knowledge.'

'Yes, I guess all those years as my father's assistant has helped. I seem to have no problems keeping my clothes dryer, my car, my lawn mower and my appliances working fine. However, I don't think society is ready for a woman to work in that field. I think I'll pass on that one.'

Later, after Jenny had investigated the occupations, she realised that her favourite was as she had initially thought - human resources.

'Why did you choose that one?' Ruth asked.

'I like it because of the variety in the job. Mainly I like the people contact but also think I can handle the amount of detail required from my experience as a legal secretary.' she admitted.

'That's good that you've been able to find something that will suit you. Next you need to write down specific goals you must make to ensure that you keep focused and on your target.'

'I've never set goals before. Where do I start?'

Ruth asked, 'Well, do you want to recruit staff? Classify jobs? Look after company benefit plans? Work in employee relations? Be involved with training and development?'

After much soul-searching, Jenny decided to aim for the top; for a position as Head of a Human Resources Department, knowing that at this time, there were very few female heads of *any* departments. But she felt she had the stamina and drive to reach her goal.

Ruth didn't laugh at this lofty goal. Instead, she encouraged Jenny to chart a path so she could reach her objective. She asked, 'For instance, what education would you require and how and where would you obtain it? What kind of training and experience would you need to run a human resources department and where would you be able to find such a job? Who would look after your children? How would you find the time to do all the things you had to do?'

It took Jenny several weeks to list all the goals she would have to make and how she was going to achieve them.

At their next get-together, Ruth asked, 'How long do you think it will take to reach that goal?'

'Probably about fifteen years,' Jenny replied.

Later when she had finished her planning, she had another meeting with Ruth who surprised her by saying, 'Before you set out on this venture, you need to set a backup goal as well.'

'What? I've already planned about fifteen years of my life and you want me to plan another goal? Why do I need to do that?' Jenny asked in astonishment.

Ruth explained, 'Let's say you've planned a trip to Hawaii; you take the trip and wonder why you feel so depressed when you get back. It's because you had no backup goal waiting on the back burner for you to start working on when you were close to achieving your first goal.' She also advised Jenny to specialise in more than one area of work and not put all her eggs in one basket.

When asked what her backup goal would be, Jenny decided it was to have her own company that would offer human resource services to companies too small to have their own human resources departments.

As she came closer to achieving her first goal, Ruth encouraged her to develop a specific plan for achieving the second one. 'Make sure as you go along, that everything you do in your private and business life is aimed towards achieving those two major goals.'

Ruth then urged Jenny to set a time frame for achieving her second goal. Jenny estimated that would take twenty years to have her own company.

Jenny began concentrating on achieving her first goal of becoming a Human Resources Manager. It took her a long time to determine how she could reach the sub-goals she wanted to reach. Her first sub-goal was to determine what education she'd need to get her where she wanted to go. Because she'd married so young, she had only a high-school diploma, so knew she'd have to obtain specific training. She read all the university and college brochures, and interviewed others in the field, and decided that instead of going to university full-time, she would obtain college training by taking courses in the evenings after work.

'How can I afford this training?' she wondered. She looked around her home and saw lots of items that she really didn't need, so the next weekend she held a garage sale to pay for her first semester fees.

Once she had registered for her courses, Jenny approached several firms to see if they would be willing to take her on as a trainee. She knew that a small company probably wouldn't be able to take the time to train her, so she targeted medium-to-large sized companies, where she could learn the most up-to-date human resources systems.

In the meantime, Jenny kept her secretarial job and was thrilled when a recruiting firm offered her the job of finding employment for part-time workers. She was so excited that she called Ruth with her good news. They celebrated that evening with a bottle of wine.

'I knew you could do it!' Ruth said, 'and it's just the first step on your ladder to your dream job.'

Jenny was a bit apprehensive when she started her job with the recruitment firm. They found full-time jobs for candidates, but her responsibility was to fill part-time clerical positions that occurred because staff were ill or on holidays. Jenny would interview potential candidates, who were more than likely married women wanting to work only part-time to earn extra money. When Jenny started working with the firm, they had an average of forty-five part-time workers hired out to companies at a time, but she soon increased that to eighty-five.

One of her responsibilities was to speak with Human Resources Managers of larger companies to explain their service and encourage them to use her company's holiday and illness replacement employees. Many subsequently used the company's services.

During one of these interviews, Jenny spoke with Marcie Jacobson, head of Human Resources for a large international oil company. After their interview, it was lunch time, so Jenny asked if they could have lunch together. She decided to pick Marcie's brain to find out what she had done to get to her position and explain her own ambitions. Marcie was hesitant, but helpful and after their lunch, Jenny returned to her own office.

It was just about closing time that afternoon, when the owner of the employment firm, Lydia, asked if Jenny would like to join her for a drink at a local restaurant. Jenny was pleased and went willingly. However, her pleasure turned to horror when her boss said that she was being fired. Jenny knew she had done an excellent job, so couldn't understand why she would do such a thing.

'Why? Aren't you happy with the way I'm doing the job?' Jenny asked as she fought off tears. This was the last thing she would have expected to happen that day. She was also mortified that her boss had chosen such a public place to fire her.

'I refuse to have an employee on my staff who recruits herself to one of the companies we deal with.' her boss replied with fire in her eyes.

'What do you mean? I've never done that.' she replied emphatically.

'I beg to differ.' her boss said then added, 'Marcie Jacobson called me this afternoon and said that you had applied to work there.'

'Well, she lied. At lunch, I only asked her what steps she had taken to get her own position. I didn't ask her for a job!' she said indignantly.

'We obtain a lot of business from her oil firm, so I have to believe her. I want you to come back to the office with me and clear out your desk while I prepare your last pay cheque.'

Jenny was openly crying now. 'How am I going to manage?' she wondered. 'How will I feed my kids?'

When she and her boss returned to the office, she was relieved to see that everyone in their office had gone for the day. Jenny cleaned out her desk, accepted the cheque and left the office.

Later, when Jenny had more knowledge of Human Resource laws, she realized that this had been a wrongful dismissal.

Jenny just sat in her car crying. She was in no shape to drive home. She drove to a nearby park and sat in her car until she could regain control of her emotions.

The next day, Jenny set out to find another job. She read the newspapers and phoned competitive recruitment offices to the one she worked in, and left her name as being available for full-time work. Because Calgary was booming, the unemployment rate was very low, and she was sure she could find something suitable within a short period of time. Her final paycheque gave her two extra weeks' severance pay, so she hoped that by then she would find something suitable.

Thirty-five

When she scoured the paper, she noted that a large international firm that offered part-time replacement employees was looking for someone to start a branch of that company in Calgary. Jenny didn't think she was qualified enough but applied anyway. She was astounded when she received a phone call from Houston, Texas asking her if she could attend an interview the next week in Calgary. She would pick Morris Bailey up at the airport and drive him to his hotel, where they would have the interview.

When she picked Morris up at the airport, he marvelled at how advanced Calgary was. He had expected that he would see igloos and people would be riding horses. When Jenny drove him into downtown Calgary, he couldn't get over how big and modern it was. He obviously had no knowledge of Canada and its people. Jenny had to work hard not to laugh at his ignorance.

After their interview, Morris offered Jenny the job. She would have to do many things. The first was to find a suitable location for their office. Then Morris would send her all the brochures she would need to advertise the new branch. She would order office furniture, supplies and equipment.

Morris added, 'Jenny we will need you to go to Detroit, Michigan for training. That will take two weeks. Will you have any problems going out of town for that long? We will pay for any of your expenses such as babysitting.'

When she got home from the meeting, she told Mark and Debbie about her new job. Then she asked Mrs. Kelly, her downstairs neighbour to come up.

'Would you be able to look after the children for two weeks while I'm away? Mark really doesn't need much help, but Debbie does, and I need someone to be here to keep things on track.'

'I'd love to do that,' she beamed. She was a very lonely widow and had been so helpful to Jenny and her children.

So, it was arranged, and Jenny was off to Detroit, Michigan for training.

Jenny was extremely busy setting up the company and hiring two full-time staff members. One employee would hire office staff – the other trades positions. Morris asked her if she could do short training sessions with her staff. She agreed to do so and began putting together some training programs. One was *'Time management,'* and another was *'Stress management.'* They were so well received by her staff that she contemplated whether she could do sessions elsewhere. Jenny approached several extension and continuing education departments of local colleges and universities who agreed to have her present them in the evenings after work. They were again well received, so Jenny began writing more. She loved training others – watching their eyes light up as they absorbed the new information.

One college asked her if she could put together more programs for business staff. She complied and kept writing and presenting seminars for years. And so, began what would end up being a big passion in her life.

Another local college asked her if she could write sessions relating to supervision. She called her session *'Survival Skills for Supervisors and Managers.'* It took a whopping nine hundred hours for her to research and prepare that three-week seminar. Unfortunately, the college was not interested in such a long session, so she cut it down to one week.

'It's still too long,' they said.

So, she finally condensed the training to take only three days.

The research she spent preparing the three-week course wasn't a loss, because she was able to break the session into separate segments that would take anywhere from three hours to a day to present. She continued marketing these to local colleges and universities through their adult education sections. Both the supervisory skills session and the mini seminars were overnight successes.

Jenny enjoyed her job with the employment firm but realized that there was no possibility of progressing further within the company. It was then that she saw an advertisement and was hired as a Personnel Officer to hire the full-time staff for a large industrial trailer firm in Calgary. It was a rapidly expanding firm, and she felt that she would have the opportunity of obtaining more senior positions with the international company. Two years later, when a position for International Recruitment for Europe became available, her boss promised her the position. However, shortly after that, she noticed that there was an advertisement in the newspaper for that position. She asked to speak to the owner of the company and explained the promises she had been given by her boss. She then explained what her boss had said to her when she questioned the advertisement. 'He said that he didn't think a woman would be suitable to fill this position. Could you please investigate this for me?'

He promised to do so.

She ended the conversation by stating, 'If I don't hear from you within two weeks, I will be handing in my notice.'

She did not hear from him again, so gave them her notice.

Jenny searched for two weeks and applied for a recruitment job in Edmonton with the Attorney General's Department of the Alberta Government. She was reluctant to move her family there, because Mark had just enrolled at the University of Calgary, but it was a high-paying job and she needed a job to support her family.

It was a busy two weeks, selling the home in Calgary she'd bought three years before for double the amount she had paid for it. The value of homes had skyrocketed because of the oil boom in Alberta so she had a quick sale.

Then she tackled the job of transferring Mark to the university in Edmonton. They both went up to Edmonton to complete the enrolment and find a suitable home. Mark wasn't happy about having to change universities but adjusted soon after he began at the University of Alberta.

Mark and Jenny went house-hunting, and both looked at each other when they viewed a vacant three-bedroom home with an unfinished basement. They both loved the home and they would be able to move right away. Jenny put a bid on the home and obtained a mortgage for the remaining amount.

Mark was well advanced with his knowledge of carpentry and wanted the opportunity of building a rumpus room in the basement. Within a year it was finished including a bedroom, a laundry room, a bathroom and a rumpus room. Everyone was pleased on how it turned out.

On her first day at work, she met a woman who also was starting that day. Linda Pender and she became a close friend of Jenny's for life.

Debbie was enrolled in a nearby school; Mark started university and Jenny began her job with the Attorney General's Department. Her job involved travelling all over Alberta, mainly on day trips, so she seldom had to be away overnight. During those trips she accumulated many frequent flyer points. Mark ensured her that he could stay with Debbie overnight and would get her off to school in the morning during the times she had to stay overnight. *'What would she do without him?'* she thought.

Jenny had many adventures performing her job. She flew all over the province interviewing people for positions in the court system. Most of the time, she travelled on larger jet liners.

Jenny had two unusual situations occur while she was working for them. The first happened when she and two others were to interview candidates for court clerk positions. Her boss advised her that because the roads were in such terrible condition, she was to go to the Municipal Airport in Edmonton to board a four-seater Cessna that would take her, a court reporter and a judge to St. Paul to interview candidates for positions at their courthouse. It was a rather bumpy ride there and back, and it wasn't until they were travelling back to Edmonton that the judge stated, 'Thank God we made it!'

Jenny nodded in agreement, 'Yes, it was rather a bumpy ride wasn't it?'

'No. I said that because we made it back in one piece. Didn't you know that an identical plane was taking a court crew to St. Paul last week when it crashed, injuring all of those on board?'

'No, I didn't! If I had known, I might not have accepted this assignment.'

On another unusual situation, she interviewed several people for a position as Bailiff for a courthouse in Edmonton. When she screened the applicants, she saw that one of them was a former MI5 officer from the UK. When she interviewed him, she asked him why he was applying for the position. He replied, 'I hate being retired and am still interested in solving crime, so this will allow me to keep in touch with the court systems in Edmonton.' When she made the short-list of candidates for the job, she included this man. When he and the Judge met each other – it was wonderful for her to see how *'in sync'* they were, and he was hired on the spot. They became close friends, more than simply being employed as judge and bailiff.

Jenny enjoyed this position very much, but it was at this time that she realized that she had only learned the recruitment part of human resources. So, she began looking elsewhere to gain the knowledge and training she needed.

Her next position was in a large Human Resources Department of an Oil company where she learned what they could teach her about human resources. She started out in recruitment and watched how her co-worker did her job as Classification Officer 1. Her job was to classify positions and allot a salary range to that position. Above her was a Classification Officer 2 position who did virtually the same routine for classifying higher-level positions.

Jenny noticed that a Classification Officer 2 position was available and put her name in as a candidate. When the Human Resources Manager called her into her office for an interview, she asked why she had applied for that position when she had not completed the Classification Officer 1 level.

'Ask me any question you would normally ask a Classification Officer 1, and if I can't answer them, I will drop out as a candidate.' Jenny replied

The HR Manager soon learned that Jenny could indeed answer the questions as well as any of the other candidates and decided to offer her the job.

Next Jenny went to another large company and learned how they did everything, but this time she was hired into a more senior position. Jenny found that there were many different approaches to Human Resources - such as different methods of writing job descriptions, evaluating positions and conducting performance appraisals. 'Now I'm getting somewhere!' Jenny crowed to herself.

I can do it! The sky's the limit!

Thirty-six

Jenny had several Human Resources positions after that – each one allowing her to gain knowledge of different aspects of Human Resources. Because Jenny knew exactly where she wanted to go, and how she intended to get there, she reached her first goal long before she expected to. She had underestimated her abilities, as most women do.

Within six years of setting her first goal, (nine years ahead of schedule) she was appointed Human Resources Manager of not one, but a group of twelve construction companies in Edmonton, Alberta.

Jenny reported directly to the president of the company, John Hawke who she estimated was approximately her age. John was a true entrepreneur and had taken his company Hawke Production from being a small company that manufactured construction site dwellings, to one with twelve subsidiary companies. They had never had a Human Resources Department before. Jenny was to set up and run the department.

John explained that she was the only female executive in the company and might run into resistance from some of the executives about the need to write job descriptions for every position.

On her first day, John called a meeting with his executives. When Jenny entered the room the group all stood up to shake her hand. John started the meeting by explaining what Jenny had been hired to do.

'She will be implementing the most up-to-date human resources policies and procedures that all our companies must follow. I know you guys might balk at doing some of the work, but Jenny has assured me that she will do everything she can to make the transition easy for us.'

Ted Boothe, the head of the Leasing division of the company looked at Jenny and asked, 'What kind of things will you be implementing? Most of us have very little time for extra work.'

Jenny looked at him, realizing that he seemed a bit belligerent, 'The first thing I will do is see which policies and procedures are in place in each of the divisions. You can all help me with that.'

They all nodded as she continued, 'Next, I'll review all the job descriptions you now have in place and help you to update them, so they fit with legal requirements of our province.'

'Why is the government getting involved?' Ted, the Marketing Manager asked.

'The government will expect companies to comply with new legislation that compares the value of one position against another. All positions will show a salary range, and all those working in that position will have to be paid within that salary range. For instance, male chefs and female cooks who do basically the same kind of work, must be slotted into the same salary range.'

'Wow!' George Simmons, the executive in charge of the transportation department said. 'I can see that we might have been breaking some of the new employment laws in our companies. Some of our companies have different salaries for people doing the same type of job.'

'It will also ensure that people working in the different divisions who are doing essentially the same kind of work, will be paid appropriately. The job descriptions will also make it easier for you to discipline employees if they don't do what their job description says they are supposed to do. That will stop you from feeling guilty if you must discipline or fire an employee because of bad performance.

I will need a list of rules and regulations employees are expected to follow. These rules and regulations will be put into a handbook that each new employee will receive when they start with the company. After they have had an opportunity of reading the manual – say in a week's time – they will sign a document stating that they understand the rules and regulations.'

John asked, 'What kind of rules are we speaking about here?'

'Rules such as the mandatory wearing of hard hats, safety boots and glasses.' Jenny replied.

They all nodded their heads. They all asked many questions and Jenny left the meeting feeling the men all understood why the processes she would be implementing would be necessary. She ended the meeting by saying, 'As we go along, I will do everything possible to help you write descriptions and do performance appraisals.'

After the meeting, John had his wife Bonnie take her on a tour of their facilities. Jenny had to put on safety equipment. It felt funny to wear construction boots instead of high heels. John's wife was beautiful and graceful and very friendly, but she was disturbed when they entered the facility that made the construction site trailers. Two of the employees whistled at them. Bonnie walked over to the two men, introduced herself and explained who she and Jenny were. The men gulped and apologized for their unacceptable behaviour.

'Just see that it doesn't happen again. Women are to be shown respect,' were Bonnie's parting words.

When they finished exploring the facility, Bonnie said, 'You must let me know if that happens again. John won't tolerate that kind of behaviour towards female staff.'

Jenny was very busy the next few months as she assisted the executives in writing job descriptions. She had been approached twice to deal with employee relations situations and slowly but surely gained the respect of the executives.

Jenny oversaw recruitment for full-time employees. Reporting to her was Sandy Clarke, who oversaw hiring hourly employees. He came to her one day explaining a problem he had hiring cabinet makers who would complete trailers that were going to Saudi Arabia. They wanted high-quality furnishings for their construction-site offices.

'I can't get enough employees who have the quality we need to fulfil this order,' he complained.

'Sandy, I think I have a solution to your problem. Why don't we hire a full-time well qualified cabinet maker and have him or her train our staff to do the work. There's also a special government program that can assist us by paying a portion of the salaries for women who wish to work in construction.'

Sandy nodded, then asked, 'Do you think John will go for that idea?'

'I think he will because the salary of a full-time cabinet maker will be offset by the money the government will give us for training the women to do the job. Also, it's been found that some of the best cabinet makers are women. They're much more precise in completing elaborate furnishings.'

'Great,' Sandy replied. 'Do you want me to speak to John or do you want to do it?'

'I think I had better do it, because I have all the information relating to the government offer.'

John was in favour of the idea and encouraged Jenny to put in an application for six female apprentices.

'We've had no luck in the past two years in hiring a cabinet-maker from Canada. I think we will have to go international in our recruitment to fill this position.'

Jenny agreed and began sending information to recruitment firms in the US, England, Germany and the Scandinavian countries. It wasn't long before one applicant was chosen from Sweden. He spoke fluent English but would not be available for two months.

By this time, the government had sent eight women to be interviewed for the training and Sandy had hired six of them. The only hitch was that they needed to start right away.

John agreed that they should work in the general carpentry area until the cabinet maker would be available from Sweden. The women agreed. All of them wanted to learn general carpentry as well as the specialized art of cabinet making.

Three weeks later, Jenny received an urgent message that one of the women had been injured on the job and to call for an ambulance to take her to hospital. The woman had been securing a chain around some lumber that was being lifted by a crane to be put on a pallet. Her glove caught on the chain and when the crane driver raised the load of lumber, she was jerked off her feet, dislocating her shoulder. She had screamed loud and long until she was lowered gently to the ground by the crane operator.

Jenny rushed over to the woman and assured her that an ambulance was on its way and guided the ambulance officers to where the injured woman was sitting. She was soon on her way to the hospital.

She looked around her and saw by the shocked look on both the men and the women working in the area. After speaking to their supervisor, it was decided to let the crew go home. Most were so shaken up by what had happened that they would not have been able to concentrate on their work.

The foreman explained, 'I've seen this happen before – especially to the men. They can't stand it when a woman is injured. They fall apart. They don't seem to have the same reaction when a man is injured. Not to say they don't care, but their protective instincts don't kick in the same was as when a woman is hurt.'

Finally, the cabinet maker arrived, and the women began learning the trade. Jenny learned that the research about women as cabinet makers was true – they were much more precise at completing elaborate furnishings.

Jenny had begun doing exit interviews with employees who were leaving the company. She was sad to learn that Karen Lewis decided to hand in her notice. She was a dedicated and hard worker who worked in the Credit department reporting directly to the manager, Don Matthews. She placed Karen in a side office where she would have the privacy to complete the document, then discussed the information with her. Karen stated that she loved her job and felt she had done a good job but gave personal reasons to explain why she was leaving the company. Jenny was excellent at reading body language and she could see that Karen was very embarrassed when she asked, 'Could you elaborate a bit more about why you are leaving?' Jenny simply did not want to lose such a good employee.

Karen's face turned bright pink and she looked down as she quietly said, 'I can't work any longer with Don Matthews.'

'Can you elaborate a bit about why you feel this way?'

'He won't keep his hands off me,' she said as she started to sob. Jenny was glad they had privacy as she patted Karen's arm.

'How long as this been going on, and exactly what has he done?'

Karen showed her a list she had written itemizing the times he had touched her. This had started a month ago, and Jenny had not been aware of it.

Jenny couldn't help but remember how she at almost the same age as Karen had been sexually harassed by a Squadron Leader and how relieved she had been when they believed her when she said he had harassed her.

Jenny knelt beside Karen and said, 'If I could guarantee that this would never happen again, and have you work with another manager – would you consider staying? We don't want to lose you,' she added emphatically.

Karen nodded.

'I'd like you to go to the cafeteria and get a cup of coffee while I deal with this matter. Take about a half hour - then come back to my office. By that time, I should have some solutions to this problem.'

Jenny returned to her office, phoned Don and said it was important that she speak with him. 'Could you come right away?' she asked.

'I'll be right there,' he promised. He thought she was going to discuss replacing Karen.

She started their conversation by stating, 'I understand that Karen has given her notice? Do you know why she is leaving?'

'I haven't a clue,' he admitted.

'How have you treated her? Any conflict?'

'None that I know of. In fact, I really like Karen,' he admitted.

'Have you ever touched in any way?'

'I'm a touchy-feely guy, I like touching women,' he said with a grin.

'Do you realize that you have put our company in jeopardy by touching her inappropriately?'

'What do you mean?' he asked incredulously.

'Your actions are deemed to be sexual harassment. There are government laws that protect employees against such actions. Karen could legally charge you with sexual harassment that was serious enough for her to quit her job.' Jenny said angrily.

'Oh my God!' he exclaimed. 'What will happen now?'

'I am going to have her come into my office, and you are going to promise in my presence that you will never act inappropriately again towards any employee and especially not towards her.'

'I'll do that. Please arrange for that to happen.'

'I'm also going to have her transfer over to help George Simmons in the transportation department because his assistant had to leave because of health reasons. You can understand why she doesn't want to work with you in the future.'

'My next job will be to hire someone to be your assistant and I'm tempted to hire a man, so you won't be tempted to continue your harassment. I will be placing a written warning on your file and you need to know, that if this EVER happens again, you will be terminated.'

Thirty-seven

In 1978, the summer Bruce turned sixteen, Jenny was surprised to hear his voice on the phone. 'Can I come for a visit?' He asked.

'Of course!' she almost shouted. It had been five long years since she had any contact with Bruce.

When she met Bruce at the bus station, she was surprised to see that he was as tall as his father – well over six feet. She hugged him and Mark thumped him on the shoulder. Debbie shyly gave him a hug.

When they got to their home, Bruce asked, 'Mom, why didn't you let me know where you were? I asked Dad, but he wouldn't tell me.'

Jenny went over to him and gave him a big hug. Then she and Mark explained that they had sent letters, gifts and had tried to speak to him on the phone, but his father wouldn't let them. 'We didn't know you weren't getting our letters and gifts and finally had to give up trying. We wanted you to come here as soon as we moved to Calgary.'

Bruce nodded his head and said, 'I guess Dad has some explaining to do. Before I phoned you, I told Dad I was going to find you whether he cooperated or not. He finally gave me your address and phone number.'

So, that summer Bruce visited Jenny, Mark and Debbie then went back to Winnipeg to finish his schooling. In 1981, when he was nineteen, Jenny was able to find him an apprenticeship position as a heavy-duty mechanic with her company. Bruce accepted the position, but within six months missed his friends so much in Winnipeg that he moved back to be with his boyhood friends.

Jenny had been employed by the company for over a year and all the Human Resources procedures were in place. She was proud of how everyone cooperated and got the job done in record time.

Unfortunately, in April 1982, many of the oil wells in Alberta had to be capped because it would cost more to obtain the oil than they could sell it for. John asked Jenny to come into his office one day. She knew it might be bad news.

'You've done a wonderful job – and so well, that we can now train someone less qualified to take over. I don't want you to go, so would like to offer you a position in sales and marketing. It won't pay as much as you were getting and would be on a commission basis, but you are too good an employee for us to let go.'

'Let me think about it for a few days and I'll get back to you,' said Jenny as she left his office.

Jenny was especially close to her son Mark who was now twenty-two and had just graduated from college. He had been so helpful when the three of them had started a new life. She discussed the situation with him that night.

'Mom, I know you've been wanting to start your own company. Could this be the time to do it?'

'I suppose it could be,' she agreed. 'I'll have to seriously think about it as an alternative. I do have some slush money in my bank account so could survive for about six months until things start to click.'

'Now that I've graduated, I've been applying for positions. Just today, I received a job offer from a pipeline company, but the job would be in Whitecourt, Alberta which is sixty-three kilometres away from Edmonton. I would have to move there.'

He continued, 'If I took the job, you wouldn't have to worry about feeding and looking after me which would give you more space to pursue your dream of having your own company. And I think it would be a good job for me to take. The company is very progressive and aren't affected much by the oil situation. Pipelines still need to move oil and gas regardless of whether the wells are capped or not.'

She knew that sons needed space when they migrated from child to adult but yearned to continue protecting him. Now that Mark was grown up and an entity of his own, she knew she would have to content herself with occasional visits and phone calls. She had to accept that he was no longer hers – but was a separate entity with a life of his own. But it was hard giving up that responsibility. She transferred her feelings to those of hoping he would succeed in life. She didn't want to be an overbearing mother, so she let him go without a grumble. She still had her fifteen-year-old daughter Debbie at home, so she wouldn't be alone.

The next week, Jenny gave John her notice, but asked to continue doing her job as Human Resources Manager for an additional month. He agreed.

At that meeting, she brought the Don Matthews personnel file and pointed out the written warning. She felt compelled to do so, because she did not want Don to revert to his unacceptable sexual harassment of female employees.

'Why didn't you tell me about this sooner?' he asked.

'I've kept my eye on him for the past six months and he has not stepped out of line once. But I can't take the chance that he will do so again.'

'I will make sure he doesn't' John promised.

In the meantime, she registered her company as Harper Consulting and decided to legally change her name back to her maiden name – Harper. She had reached her second goal in eight years, not twenty years as she had planned. Both she and Mark began their new lives in March 1982.

At approximately the same time as Jenny opened her company, she became aware of a man who had also opened a training firm. He went big – fast – by renting an office, buying a company car and copy machine, hiring a secretary and had a training room attached to his office.

On the other hand, Jenny worked out of her home, did her own typing, took any copying she needed to a copy facility and used the college, university or other company facilities for training. Her overhead was almost nil. After six months, she saw that her company was going to flourish while his folded with a bang.

To put food in their mouths, she knew she needed something to bring home income for the first few months. She spoke with her old employer Daniel Ruby about her plans and learned from him that a real estate firm was looking for someone to work in a high-rise complex that was starting to lease its new apartments.

Jenny spoke with the property owner and learned that she would have quite a bit of free time between showing the apartments to applicants. Her sales site was in one of the empty apartments. She realized that it was a perfect opportunity for her to develop more seminars for the training leg of her company, so brought her typewriter with her to work. She still wanted to go into companies that were too small to have their own Human Resources Manager to set things up for them but wanted to do training as well.

She helped Mark get settled in his rental home in Whitecourt. He was the youngest employee at that branch of the company, and Jenny hoped they would be friendly to him and keep him from getting too lonely.

One evening he called Jenny. 'Mom, I don't want you to panic, but I had an accident with my truck today. I hit some black ice and slid off the road. The truck turned over twice before it landed upright on the tires.'

'Were you injured?' she asked breathlessly.

'My equipment box clipped me on my shoulder, and I'll have a huge bruise – but the hospital checked me out and that's the only injury I had. I have a good seat belt and after my equipment box went flying through the windshield, I was hit by thousands of little pieces of safety glass. I'm still finding more pieces in my hair.'

'How long was it before someone helped you?'

'My truck ended up in a ditch and I couldn't open the doors. I knew I'd be able to climb out through the windshield, but decided it was probably warmer in the truck than outside. I turned on my mobile and reported my accident to the office – and Mom, I couldn't believe it. Within twenty minutes almost every member of our team had arrived to ensure I was safe. And the tow truck arrived shortly after.'

'Was the truck badly damaged?'

'The boss said it would likely be a write-off, even though it is only six months old. Besides a caved-in roof, both sides of the truck had been damaged as it rolled down the embankment.'

'Are you sure you're, all right?' she insisted.

'Yes Mom. And you don't have to worry about me any more – my team at work are obviously looking after me. Most of the staff are old enough to be my parents, so that's a good thing.'

Jenny stopped worrying about her first-born and concentrated on looking after his sister Debbie.

Thirty-eight

In addition to offering companies help with Human Resources issues, Jenny continued offering seminars in the evenings and on the weekends. Later she began preparing full-day seminars.

In 1983, she wrote what turned out to be her most popular seminar called '*Dealing with Conflict.*'

Jenny wasn't aware of the networking that went on between colleges and universities throughout the Canada. Word soon got out about the quality of her sessions and before her company was a year old, she was so busy, she could hardly keep up with the demand.

She was hired to present a seminar for Lakeland College in St. Paul, Alberta. She drove to a hotel the evening before she was to conduct her seminars. Because there were no vacancies in St. Paul itself, she stayed in a brand-new hotel in a nearby town. It was a bitterly cold day and the evening was predicted to be even colder. It was expected to go down to -45° F that night, so she plugged in both her motor and in-car heaters. The next morning when she went out to her car, it wouldn't start. The circuit breakers on all the plugs in the parking lot had tripped because everyone used so much electricity. She spoke with the hotel manager and explained that she absolutely had to get to St Paul because she was conducting a seminar that was to start at 9:00 am.

The manager explained, 'I've called a tow truck to jump-start all the cars – yours will be the first one.'

She thanked him and waited impatiently in the lobby for the tow truck to arrive. It finally arrived at 9:25. The mechanic started Jenny's car and she rushed off to St. Paul. She had phoned the college to explain her problem and promised she would be there as soon as she could. She arrived at 9:45, rushed to the seminar room, apologized to everyone and began conducting her seminar. Her seminar – well - it was her '*Time Management'* seminar. How ironic is that! She was late for her own '*Time Management'* seminar!

She handled it well and explained to her participants that when something like that happened to her participants, she urged them to take a few deep breaths and carry on the best they could. Turn a crisis into something positive rather than grumbling about whatever had happened to cause the difficulty.

Another unusual situation happened when she was conducting her three-day *'Survival Skills for Supervisors'* session at a First Nation settlement in Stony Plain, Alberta. She was well into the morning of the second day of the seminar when there was a horrific bang and the building shook. She knew it was an explosion of some sort so herded her class to the nearest exit. An hour later she learned that the fire was contained quickly. It had started when a First Nation man had removed a gas tank from a vehicle and started welding it in a shop within the building. It exploded. He was taken to the nearest hospital to receive treatment for his burns which thankfully turned out to be minor.

The second thing that happened at the session was that even though the participants knew that the sessions were to run from 9:00 am until 4:00 pm with coffee and lunch breaks, they wandered in and out whenever they pleased. After lunch on the first day she said, 'You are all here to obtain certificates for the three-day Survival Skills for Supervisors session. If you are not here on time or miss some of the classes, you will not be given a certificate.

They looked at her in surprise. They normally had no interest in time at all, but finally understood what was at stake if they weren't there when they were supposed to be there. At the end of the session, two out of the twenty participants were not given certificates. They complained bitterly, but she had warned them.

She had been booked to do seminars for the Medicine Hat College when the head of the extension department asked her if she would do additional days of training in-house for a local company. Jenny agreed to do so. For eleven days straight, she presented seminars in Medicine Hat and was exhausted when she got back to Edmonton.

She had not taken a vacation for years and she felt restless. She had lots of frequent flyer points, so she decided to take Debbie to Hawaii during her school Easter Break. One morning when Jenny was lying on the beach in Honolulu, she realized why she felt so lethargic. She had reached her two goals but had not made others. On the spot - she set another goal which was to expand her company to become international. She looked around at the lovely beaches and lifestyle in Hawaii and thought, 'Would this ever be a lovely place to work.'

Before she lost her nerve, she returned with Debbie to her hotel room and began phoning all the universities and colleges on the island. The next day she had an interview with the University of Hawaii, and that same day she signed her first contract to work internationally.

Her first session was her three-day *'Survival Skills for Supervisors'* session that was held at the Maui Community College (an affiliate of the University of Hawaii).

The room set-up was unusual – much of it was underground. Her participants sat on seats that were like an auditorium, with each row higher than the next. Jenny stood at the bottom as she presented her session. She was only one hour into the seminar when a participant spoke up, 'Jenny, could you take a step back?'

'Why?' she asked, and the woman pointed to Jenny's shoe. On it was one of the biggest cockroaches Jenny had ever seen. She stepped back and the bug dropped to the floor but didn't scuttle off. Jenny took a Styrofoam cup off a nearby table, plopped it over the errant bug and continued with her presentation. Everyone laughed as the cup started walking across the floor. Ten minutes later it was coffee break and she asked one of the male participants to slip a piece of paper under the cup and take the intruder outside. It lightened the day for everyone.

At the end of the second day of her three-day session, she asked the participants (who were mainly of Hawaiian descent) to come the next morning wearing native dress. They did so and one of the men placed a lei around Jenny's neck. Pictures were taken of the group. Later, Jenny jokingly told her friends that she had been lei-eed in Hawaii.

Later she presented seminars for the University of Hawaii in Hilo and Kona. By 1986, she had so much business in Hawaii, that she opened a second branch of her company. She was now presenting seminars to hotels and through private training companies on several of the Hawaiian Islands.

Thirty-nine

Jenny had certainly accomplished a lot, but somehow there was something missing. She had been so busy striving to achieve her goals, that she had paid little attention to her personal life. She had no one to share in her success or wrap their arms around her on a cold night. Because of her experience with Russ, she was a little apprehensive, but when her friend Brenda convinced her to register with an on-line dating service. What a scary thing that turned out to be, because she kept being warned by other friends that it was a dangerous thing to do. She played it safe – got a Hotmail address using her middle and maiden name as being her name. She chose a name for herself – RightGal and corresponded with the men several times to learn more about them. If she felt the fellow was a good candidate, she agreed to meet him for coffee. She always told Brenda where she would be meeting him and would phone with her so Brenda could appear on the scene if things weren't going well. This worked out well, and Jenny did the same for Brenda when she wanted to meet a new man.

Jenny's learned to watch men to see whether they truly liked women or had a disdainful attitude towards them. She also watched how they treated people in the service industry. For instance, when she met a potential male for lunch, she watched how he treated the waitresses. If he used a paternalistic or a power play attitude towards them or put them down by his actions or words – he was immediately taken off her list as a possible friend.

Jenny had several short dates with men, but still hadn't found one that really made her feel comfortable in their company. They were all nice men – but no bells were ringing for her. There was also the problem that she was travelling so much it was hard to start and continue a serious relationship.

In August 1993 Denise, a co-worker of Jenny's asked her whether she would be interested in meeting one of the single men her lawyer husband worked with. The man's name was Bill Masterton and he was fifteen years older than Jenny. He was a widower, had lived alone for several years and was eager to get back into dating again. Bill was highly thought of in the legal field and was a part-time judge in criminal court, so Jenny felt she would feel safe with him. Arrangements were made for them to meet at the Westin Hotel for dinner. Jenny approved of the restaurant because it was up-market and she'd not likely have problems with him should things not work out.

Bill was waiting for her when she arrived. She noted that he had silver hair and had a distinguished look about him. Although he was several years older than she would have chosen, she was impressed with his manners and bearing. They talked for a while and enjoyed a lovely dinner of steak and prawns. At the end of the evening, Bill asked whether he could see her again. When she said, 'Yes,' he asked whether he could see her the next night.

'Tomorrow's my birthday.' said Jenny.

'Have you made any plans?' he asked.

'Not really. Some friends have invited my daughter and I over for lunch on Sunday, but I don't have any plans for tomorrow night.'

'Could I take you out for dinner then?

'Yes, that would be nice. What time?'

'I'll pick you up. I'd like the opportunity of seeing your place, because I understand there are some nice units in the building. I'm looking for a place to buy as an investment, and that might be a good location to buy.'

Jenny lived in a high-rise apartment that was very secure. Her living room / dining room had floor to ceiling windows that overlooked a river valley and being on the sixteenth floor with no obstructions in front of the unit – found it a lovely apartment. She agreed to have him pick her up at seven o'clock the next night.

When Bill arrived, he kissed Jenny on the cheek and presented her with a dozen long-stemmed red roses. Jenny was impressed. She gave him a tour of her apartment and he said he would seriously consider buying one as an investment. They chatted for a few minutes, then left for the Sky room Restaurant in the Chateau Martinique. This restaurant served lovely food, had a small band and dance floor. They had a lovely evening, discussing their businesses, their families and other topics. Jenny felt very comfortable with Bill.

He took her home and after they arrived at her floor, he took her keys and opened the door for her. They had a quiet cup of coffee because her sixteen-year-old daughter Debbie was sleeping. When Bill left, he promised he would call her the next week to set up another date for the following weekend.

The next morning at ten o'clock Debbie answered the phone. 'It's for you Mom.' she said.

It was Bill. He said, 'Good morning. Tell me, do you always give virtual strangers the keys to your apartment?'

'What do you mean?' Jenny replied.

'Well I had them in my pocket. I almost came back up to your apartment to give them to you but kept them instead. I seriously contemplated teaching you how dangerous a thing it is to do. I contemplated coming to your apartment in the middle of the night and letting myself in.'

Jenny was mortified that he would even consider such a thing and wondered why he had pocketed her keys. She was furious but she calmly said, 'I don't understand why you kept my keys. I need those keys because I can't drive without them. Debbie and I need to leave for my friend's place before noon. Can you bring my keys to me before then?'

'Sure I can – I'll be there in an hour.'

She hung up the phone and turned to Debbie who had been listening to the conversation. 'That was Bill. I'm very upset right now. Last night when we got home from the restaurant – I thought he was being a gentleman when he took my keys to open the door to my apartment. What I didn't notice was that he didn't drop them on the table or give them back to me. You were sleeping, so we had a quiet cup of coffee – then he left. He just told me that he still has my keys. But it was what he said next that really has me spooked. He said that he seriously considered teaching me a lesson by letting himself back into my apartment later last night.'

When Bill arrived at her building, he buzzed her apartment from the lobby of her building. Instead of buzzing him up – she met him in the lobby. She put her hand out for the keys and once she had them, she said, 'I'm glad you didn't come to my apartment last night because you likely wouldn't have walked out.'

He looked at her in surprise.

She added, 'I have Karate, Tae Kwan Do, and Judo and I know how to use them. If you ever come near me again – I'll use them! Goodbye.'

She turned around and left him in the lobby of her apartment.

As soon as she arrived back in her apartment, she started shaking when it dawned on her that he could have copied her keys. She quickly called a locksmith to come and change the locks on her door. It cost her a fortune because it was a Sunday, but it was worth it to feel safe again. While she was waiting for the locksmith to come, she called her friends to tell them they would be a bit late for their luncheon. What a way to celebrate her birthday! And he was a judge!

At work on Monday, she took Denise aside and explained what had happened and advised her to never recommend him as a date with another woman. Denise was mortified and promised she would speak with her husband about it.

Over the years Jenny had several relationships, some became intimate, but there was always something about the relationships that made her realize that the man she was with was not the 'one.' Many of them were intimidated by her forceful, energetic and driven personality, others wanted her to be more passive or change her in other ways to fit the mould they saw as a future wife. One even seemed to think she could look after him financially. Jenny continued to search for that special individual who would accept her the way she was.

Forty

On Monday, April 7 1987 Jenny had just returned to her hotel after presenting the first day of a three-day *'Survival Skills for Supervisors'* session for the Medicine Hat College when the phone in her room rang. It was her mother, calling from Victoria. Jenny soon realized how upset she was when she blurted, 'He's gone. He's gone. Your father just died!'

Jenny had been talking to Ian on Wednesday, five days before, and knew he'd had the flu. On Thursday, Jenny made plans to fly to Victoria the weekend after she did the seminars. Her mother explained that by Saturday, her dad was much worse, so she took him to the hospital where they admitted him. Martha explained that on Monday she was there at 3:00 o'clock, when a doctor entered Ian's room and with a solemn face said, 'I have tragic news for you. You have acute leukemia. It's time to contact your family because it is very aggressive.'

'How can that be?' Ian exclaimed. 'On February 27th, I had a full medical because I will be 80 at the end of this month and needed it so I can continue driving my car. Everything was fine – the blood test came back okay. How could it have progressed so rapidly in five weeks?'

The doctor replied, 'This is a very aggressive form of leukemia and possibly took hold right after your tests were done. I'm sorry I have such bad news for you. We will do everything to keep you comfortable.' He patted Ian's arm then left the room.

Ian and Martha were in shock. Ian said, 'I guess you need to go and phone the kids.' Martha nodded, gave him a big hug and a kiss and promised she would be back after she had phoned their children.

She phoned her daughter Susan who lived in Vancouver and she promised she would come over on the ferry that night. Her son Jeff who lived in Winnipeg said he too would fly there as soon as possible.

'When I phoned you. Debbie said you were doing a seminar in Medicine Hat, so I decided to call you later at your hotel to let you know. Then, at 4:30 the hospital called me to say that he had died! I can't get over how fast he went. Can you come?'

'I'll be there as soon as I can,' promised Jenny.

Thankfully, she was able to find the home phone number for Peter, the man who had contracted her to do the seminars for the college. When he answered, Jenny cried as she said, 'Peter, I've just learned that my father died today, so I need to go to Victoria as soon as I can, so will have to postpone doing day two and three of the seminar.'

'I'll arrange that. Don't worry about it. My secretary is still at the college. I'll have her phone all the participants and we will arrange for the extra two days to be done as soon as you are back in Edmonton.'

'I'll pay for the extra plane fare to come to do them,' she promised.

'In the meantime, what can I do to help?' he asked.

'I haven't phoned the airline yet to see when I can get flights to Victoria. I'll call you later when that's arranged.'

Jenny called the airline and learned that there was a flight that would take her to Calgary at 7:30 the next morning with a connecting flight to Victoria that would have her arrive in Victoria early that afternoon. She called Peter, and he promised to pick her up in time to get her to the airport.

Jenny phoned Mark in Whitecourt and told him the sad news and asked him if he could book flights for himself and Debbie to get to Victoria in a couple of days. He promised he would talk to Debbie and get back to her that night.

Jenny phoned the hotel reception and told them what had happened and that she would be leaving two days earlier than expected. She was packing her suitcase when Mark phoned to say that he and Debbie were booked on a flight on Wednesday. She then phoned Debbie who was crying hard throughout the call. She confirmed that Mark would pick her up on Wednesday to take them to the airport.

Ian was laid to rest that Friday. It was a very sad time for everyone, but it was good to have so many relatives, friends and neighbours at the funeral. When Jenny thought about his death, she realized that this was the way he would want to go – fast – not with a lingering disease. He was a heavy smoker and worried about lung cancer.

Jenny returned to Medicine Hat two weeks later to complete the two days of seminars. Peter had been busy and was able to book two more days of seminars for her to do, so the college paid for the plane tickets to and from Edmonton.

Forty-one

In 1986, Jenny had been watching women in the workplace, and noticed how few of them were given the opportunity to advance to supervisory, management or executive positions She decided to do some research on the possibly of putting together another seminar. To do so, she interviewed over 700 managers to see why they weren't promoting more women. Only five of these managers were women, which showed how few women were in top positions. Her research identified that women were responsible for almost eighty percent of the reasons why they were not promoted. Jenny learned that they were making crucial mistakes. When she presented her seminars, she was often asked by women who were miffed at her because of her comment that they were holding themselves back from promotion.

She replied: 'What do you reply when your boss wants you to go to another city for three-days?'

Most of the women replied, 'I would have to say that I can't do that. Who would look after my children?'

'What would you reply if you were asked to work overtime unexpectedly?'

'What would you reply if your company wanted to transfer you to another city?'

Twice more, she got the same reply.

'Well, ladies – what you have just said will keep you from getting promoted – ever! You must follow the same rules as men, who will likely not refuse to do any of those things. So, your first task is to make sure there is someone able to look after your children should you have to work overtime or go away for two or three days and you might have to discuss the issue of being transferred to another city by your company. Be prepared for these eventualities.

Then, you must look at the positions men are in and the education and experience they needed to move into those positions. Most clerical or support positions are dead ended, with no set progression up the ladder in a company. You will notice if you look at a company organizational chart, that support positions are shown as an adjunct to a 'real position' that can lead to promotions.

How many of you have had career counselling? If you haven't, you should do so. A good career counsellor will help you identify your transferrable skills and give you twenty to forty careers you could investigate that use those transferrable skills.'

Her sessions were so popular, she decided to put her findings into a book and in1985 she submitted her book to publishers. The book's title was *'How women can succeed in business.'* It took two years for the book to be accepted by a Canadian publisher. She received the book offer one week after Ian died in April 1987, so she dedicated the book to him. It saddened her that he had not known she was on her way to become a successful author.

The book was released in English and French, in both Canada and France. After its release, the publishers arranged for her to do a book tour throughout Canada and it became a best-seller. This resulted in her being interviewed by television, radio and newspapers to discuss her book.

Her publisher asked Jenny if she had another book she could write. Her seminar *'Dealing with Conflict'* was such a success by this time, that she decided to write that book. As she composed the book, she pretended she was conducting a seminar and used the same wording she used with the participants. It took her only four months to write the book.

Her publisher accepted the book and was able to have it translated for international publishers to sell Jenny's book. It became an international best-seller and was available in twenty languages. Over the years it also enabled Jenny to present that seminar to over sixty thousand participants internationally. Copies of her book were often included when she conducted her sessions.

Jenny began writing newspaper and magazine columns and had quite a following. Most of her topics revolved around helping people manage difficult situations. As she wrote more and more books, she was asked to discuss them on radio and television. She was often consulted regarding Human Rights, Equal Opportunities and Discrimination in the workplace.

Forty-two

In 1989, at the age of twenty-two, Debbie accepted a position and moved to Vancouver. This left just Jenny at home, but it allowed her to travel further and longer than she had when Debbie was still at home.

As Jenny got closer to the age of fifty, she became more and more anxious as she watched women presenters on television being given the boot simply because of their age. She wondered if this would happen to her as a female professional speaker. To offset this, she marketed her seminars even harder.

In the early 1990s, Jenny bought her first computer – a Commodore 64 and within a year upgraded and began communicating with additional international colleges, universities and training firms. She developed a website and began marketing her sessions on-line. She soon added additional clients. When a college or university booked her to do sessions, she sent the information to several large corporations in that city. For years, the Insurance Institute of Ontario booked her to do sessions and soon their satellite offices in London and Mississauga, Ontario did as well. She also conducted many for the Manitoba Health Organization.

She presented her first seminar in Sydney, Australia in May of 1990. Her second book, *'Dealing with Conflict'* was released in Canada, then, in 1991 that book was released in Australia and New Zealand. The Australian publisher, arranged for her to be on television, radio and articles were written by journalists for newspapers in Sydney and Melbourne. Many of these interviews were seen across Australia.

While she was there, she did a seminar at a new training facility in Sydney and was honoured when she shook hands with the man who was there for the official opening of the training facility. He was in the process of taking over the position as Prime Minister of Australia, Paul Keating.

She then went to the Australian Police Staff College in Manley to present her *'What am I going to do after retirement?'* session for senior police officers who were retiring. Jenny urged them to become counsellors for officers who had been exposed to very traumatic events and possibly do the same for members of all the emergency services.

Melbourne was next on the book tour and she was able to take three days off to visit a new friend in Melbourne. She had never tasted lamb before, and her friend cooked lamb chops for her the night. They were delicious.

The next day she would fly to Auckland to continue her book tour. However, when Jenny woke up the next morning, her stomach was rumbling, and she had to make several trips to the bathroom with a severe case of diarrhoea. Thankfully, her plane did not leave until after lunch, so the worst was over by then. Thereafter, she had the same reaction whenever she ate lamb, a staple food in Australia.

In Auckland, she was met at the airport by a lady who would be driving her to the places where she was to be on television and radio. One television interview was arranged for that evening and Jenny was told that the program would go live across New Zealand. Jenny had to warn her publicist about her stomach problem, and that she needed to know where ladies rooms were, in case she had more diarrhoea. Thankfully she felt much better, because there were five more interviews the next day. Next, she flew to Wellington where she did the same. By this time her publishers were able to tell her that her book was a hit and was selling well across Australia.

In1992, Brian was the first of her children to march down the aisle and later his only child, a daughter, was born in 1999. In 1992, Mark's company transferred him to Edmonton where he had a two-storey home built. In 1993 he was married. He and his wife adopted a new-born daughter in 2000. Debbie was the last to marry in 1997. She and her husband had two daughters. So, all told, Jenny ended up with four beautiful granddaughters.

In November of 1992, Jenny's next conquest was to combine a book tour with presenting seminars in Great Britain. She presented her 'Dealing with Conflict' sessions in Manchester, Leeds, London North, Birmingham, London South, Dublin and Glasgow. Her UK publisher arranged for her to do a book tour and again she was on television, radio and was interviewed for newspaper articles.

When Jenny got to Glasgow, she had an additional day before she was to fly back to Canada. She decided to take a taxi to the Paisley Abbey where they had a genealogical section to see if they had any record of where her father had lived, before he emigrated to Canada when he was only seventeen. One lovely lady was so helpful that knowing that Jenny was from Canada, drove her to the site where the home he had lived in was situated. It had been torn down and there was now a long row of multiple dwellings. She took a picture of the street sign and the woman kindly drove her back to her hotel. Jenny gave her a big hug to thank her for her kindness.

When Jenny got home, she was able to show the pictures of the Glasgow homes and the street sign to her father's sister who was then ninety-four. Her aunt thanked her for doing that for her. She had never been back to Scotland after she emigrated to Canada a few years after Ian Harper had done so. She died shortly after.

After Ian died, Martha deteriorated rapidly and was soon diagnosed as having Alzheimer's Disease. It became necessary to put her into aged care for her own protection when she put an electric kettle on the stove and turned on the burner. She died in 1994 at the age of eighty. Two years later, her son Jeff (Jenny's brother) died within a month after being diagnosed with bone cancer. It was a sad few years for Jenny.

After Jeff died, Jenny realized that almost her complete support system had disappeared. She lived alone, was often lonely, and realized that she needed another form of support system besides her children, so spent much more time with her female friends than before. Emails were sent back and forth with her friends Marjory and Brenda in Winnipeg, and she re-connected more with her cousins. One cousin, Ann was just six weeks younger than she and lived in the suburbs of Vancouver. Jenny often passed through Vancouver to go to and from her Hawaiian office, so stopped off to visit her and they often exchanged emails.

She contacted other cousins; Bill lived in Gimli, Manitoba, Gina lived in Winnipeg, and Carol lived in Ottawa, Ontario. They had some wonderful visits and Jenny's loneliness lessened.

Forty-three

In 1993, Jenny offered her first seminars in South Africa. While on this trip, she kept a journal describing her adventure that included sessions in Singapore, Malaysia and Australia. She described that seminar tour as follows:

'I was mentally exhausted even before I left Canada! The plane finally landed in Kuala Lumpur after a gruelling thirty-one hours and I still had another twelve-hour leg to get to Johannesburg. To help with the jet lag, I spent two days in Kuala Lumpur then flew the twelve-hour flight to South Africa. My plans were to go first to South Africa via Kuala Lumpur – then back-track to Kuala Lumpur and Singapore to present more seminars. Then on to Sydney Australia where I was to present my second set of seminars in Australia.

In January 1993 (a year before Apartheid ended in South Africa) I was surprised to open a letter from a training firm in Johannesburg. They were interested in having me offer several seminars for them in early May. I agreed to do so, if they arranged for me to do some free seminars for Black groups. They agreed to do so.

One day later, I received another letter – this time from a training firm in Singapore that wanted me to do a speaking tour that would include Singapore and Kuala Lumpur, Malaysia. I told them my availability and they agreed on the dates. My complete tour would start with two weeks in South Africa, one week in Singapore, one in Malaysia and the final week in Australia.

When my plane landed in Johannesburg, the training firm representative, Deanne Martinson and her husband Nathan met me at the Johannesburg airport. They were Afrikaans (of Dutch descent). Over breakfast, Deanne gave me the itinerary for my training sessions. Besides the planned five days of seminars in Johannesburg, she had arranged for me to offer two free keynote speeches for Black women's groups in and around the Johannesburg area.

Deanne gave me time to look over the itinerary then looked apprehensive when she stated, 'I've been contacted by another client who's interested in having you offer your three-day Survival Skills for Supervisors and Managers session. It will be for the KwaZulu Government. You'd have to fly to Durban. Are you interested?'

I agreed and she made plans for us to go to Durban the next week.

That evening Deanne and four other members from her seminar firm took me out to dinner. I was astounded by the way they treated the Black waiters and waitresses. They talked to them as if they were dogs – belittled them for the least little thing and generally treated them like dirt. I was overwhelmed with shame at their behaviour – but they were my bosses, so had to remain silent. Later in the evening, I excused myself to go to the ladies' room, and pulled aside one of our waitresses that had been treated so shabbily. She looked at me fearfully and I could tell that she expected much more of the same kind of behaviour. I had five rand (the South African currency) in my hand and gave it to her saying, 'I'm from Canada and the other people at the table have hired me to do seminars for them. I'm disgusted at the way they have treated you and the other staff and wanted you to know that I do not approve of it.'

The young woman was overwhelmed and said she couldn't accept the money. I insisted she keep it. For the rest of the evening, whenever a waiter or waitress came by our table, they gave me a big smile and a thumbs-up sign. It made my day.

The five days of seminars went well. On Saturday, when Deanne picked me up to drive me to my first session for Black women, I was surprised to find Nathan at the wheel. As he drove, Nathan explained that we had to take a circuitous route to the hotel. He'd learned that the authorities expected an uprising against the Whites to occur along the normal route they would take to get to the hotel venue. They expected bloodshed because Black slums surrounded the area. He planned to be present at the session then would drive me back to my hotel immediately after I presented my keynote address.

I was fully aware of the turmoil and the killings that were happening in South Africa and had considered this before I had agreed to go. My opinion was that I had to die sometime, but I wasn't going to half-die all my life by not living life to the fullest.

The next day, I understood why Nathanial had been so apprehensive. The newspaper article read, 'Black gunmen kill three South African Whites.' The killings had occurred within three blocks of the conference hotel! To say I was shocked would be an understatement.

After my seminar on Tuesday, Deanne drove me to the airport for my flight to Durban. For some reason, I was going alone – not with her as she had planned. She explained that she had too much work to do in Johannesburg – but I learned differently as my visit to the Durban area progressed.

196

I had been instructed that Jerome Ndluvu, a representative of the KwaZulu group was to meet me at the airport. After I cleared customs, I searched for him, but after probing the airport for over an hour, I hired a taxi to get to my hotel. Thankfully, I had some South African Rand to pay for it because the taxi did not accept credit cards.

I arrived at my hotel at 10:30 p.m. I was tired and rather miffed at the lack of assistance I was receiving from the client. I also wondered whether Jerome would be picking me up in the morning as expected, so I made sure I had the Deanne's phone number handy in case I was left stranded again. I had no idea where the seminar was to be held – just that I was to be driven to the seminar site. I had unpacked the things I needed for the next few days and was getting ready for bed when I received a phone call. It was Jerome telling me that he would pick me up at 7:00 a.m. the next morning.

I asked him why he was not at the airport to pick me up. He said he was there right now. I said that my plane had arrived more than three hours earlier. He didn't respond. Instead he stated that it was a forty-five-minute drive from my hotel to the Black township of Hammarsdale. The seminar was set to start at 8:00 a.m. and he would pick me up at 7:00 a.m.

The next morning, I was ready and waiting at the front of the hotel be 6:50 a.m. but Jerome didn't appear until 7:35. When he drove up, I was introduced to two other Black men in the back seat who were also attending the seminar. They were all dressed in suits and looked very presentable. It wasn't until later that I realized that they were my bodyguards – each had a gun in a holster under his left arm.

We were soon out of Durban and onto a rural highway. The countryside was full of rolling hills that were lush with trees and green crops. Jerome identified points of interest along the way. About twenty minutes into the drive, Jerome motioned to some buildings that were high on a hill, about a thousand meters away from the highway. He explained that they housed Black workers who worked for different businesses in Durban. Part of their wages paid for their housing. They were driven in vans to and from their dormitories and their jobs in the city.

Most of these men lived many miles away from their families and did not own cars. Because most were working for minimum wage, they couldn't afford to travel to their rural homes and families more than once or twice a year, so their women and children were left to fend for themselves.

We eventually arriving at a large barbed wire surrounded compound. Four men, wearing full battle fatigues and carrying AK47s greeted us. One of them approached the car, while the other three aimed their rifles at the car. The guard stood by Jerome's door surveying the interior of the car and stated with a heavy South African accent, 'Your papers.' His eyes widened when he spotted me – a White woman.

Jerome handed him some papers that the guard read carefully. 'I see you're here to attend a seminar. What's she here for?' he asked – pointing to me.

'She's the one who's giving us the seminar.'

The guard menacingly walked around to my side of the car and said, 'You – out of the car!' Apprehensively, I complied then watched him close the car door and stand back from me making sure that he was not between me and the three other guards who swung their rifles to point directly at me. 'Oh God! What have I got myself into?' I thought and was afraid that I was going to be shot.

'What's the name of your seminar?' asked the guard as he glanced down at the papers Jerome had given to him.

'Survival Skills for Supervisors and Managers. We'll be here for the next three days.' I replied, trying not to let him see how nervous I was. I glanced at the three other guards and saw they were still pointing their rifles at me.

'You have an accent. You're an American, aren't you?' he snarled at me.

I looked him in the eye and angrily stated, 'No, I'm not – I'm a Canadian!' I thought, if I'm going to be shot – I'll be shot as a Canadian.

The guard stood there for what seemed like minutes, then his face broke into a smile, and as he gestured me towards the car door he stated, 'Welcome to South Africa!' I wonder to this day whether I would have been shot if I had been an American.

As our car drove through the compound gate, I asked Jerome, 'What was that all about?'

'Two weeks ago, they received a bomb threat, but don't know when the attack might take place.'

'Oh great!' I thought, 'Out of the frying pan, into the fire. What am I doing here?' Then I felt very disgusted, because Deanne had not said anything about the problems in the area and suddenly realized that this was probably the reason, she decided not to come to Durban with me. I felt like a sucker for having trusted her and her company and was very angry at her for not giving me a chance to pull out of the arrangement.

When we entered the main building, I noticed that the seminar room was unusual. It slanted downward from the door and had hard wooden benches set up like bleachers. The only difference was that each bench had a narrow table attached to it.

It was 8:45 a.m. before everything was ready for the seminar, but the participants continued to arrive, so I couldn't start the seminar till 9:00 a.m. I introduced myself to the group and apologized to them if they had problems understanding my accent. One participant replied, 'We don't have any trouble with your accent – we're used to American accents because many of our television programs are filmed in the United States.'

The participants were very attentive, and the day went well. They insisted on calling me 'Ma'am.' They were very respectful to me in every way and hung on every word I spoke. I felt that they had little respect for themselves. I was glad that Apartheid would end next year.

Workers in the area were accustomed to having tea breaks in the morning and afternoon, but instead of just providing tea, they provided sandwiches as well. Jerome explained that most of them had not had breakfast. Black women, who reminded me of 'Aunt Jemimah,' served the food. They all wore a standard uniform of kerchief, long-sleeved blouse, long full skirt with a bibbed apron over top. None of them made eye contact with anyone in the room – instead looked down at the floor as they prepared and set out the food.

At the afternoon tea break I noticed that there was no sugar on the table for the tea so asked one of the serving women if she could get me some. The woman gave a quick, frightened look at me and scurried out of the room. When she returned with the sugar, her face was beat red, and as she looked down, she said in a quiet voice, 'I'm sorry Ma'am. It won't happen again.'

'You didn't have to rush off like that to get it. Thank you for bringing it to me so quickly.' The woman looked up in surprise. Apparently, she expected to be reprimanded for what she thought was a serious mistake.

From then on, whenever the women entered to room to serve tea or lunch, I caught them taking shy looks at me. I caught one doing so and smiled back. The woman's face reddened, and she turned her face towards the ground as she scurried away. 'What a horrible way to have to live.' I thought. 'Nobody should be made to feel subservient to anyone. Thank goodness things are going to change, and maybe I can be part of that change to help them pull themselves up both emotionally and educationally.'

The session finished at 4:30 and I pitied the men who'd had to sit on the hard, wooden benches for so long. I asked Jerome about it when they were driving back to my hotel.

'They need to have the hard benches, otherwise they would fall asleep.'

I was always mindful of when I 'lost' my audiences and I honestly felt that I had not done so even for a minute during the day. It wasn't until the end of day three of my seminar that I was mortified to learn that not only were the wooden seats hard, but that they slanted forward so the participants had to fight to keep from sliding off the seats. Another disgusting practice.

The next morning, Jerome arrived at 7:30 and we arrived in plenty of time to start the second day of the session at 8:30. The day went uneventfully. I noticed that one of the participants was more comfortable asking questions in class. Because of the difficulty in pronouncing their names, participants put initials on their name tags on their desks. The one who dominated the class – known as BW, was in his early thirties, was of shorter stature than most of the others, but had a rather cocky attitude. He was still very respectful, but he dominated the class. At my seminars, I normally would say something to a person if s/he dominated the class, but hesitated to do so, because of the cultural differences of this group.

On the drive back to the hotel, I questioned Jerome. 'Who is BW?'

Jerome looked up from the road and gave me a questioning look. 'He's a supervisor in the Electrical Department. Why do you ask?'

'Well, he dominates the class, and I've been debating whether I should speak to him about it or not.'

'I wouldn't do that if I were you. You see, BW is the son of our chief.'

'Whoops. I almost stepped into that one.' I thought.

'And the big fellow sitting beside him is his bodyguard.' I had noticed the larger man sitting beside BW but hadn't thought anything about it.

When I arrived back to the hotel after class, I tried calling Deanne but by then her office was closed. I had prepared myself to give her a chance to explain what was going on, why she had backed out of coming to Durban and why she hadn't warned me about the situation. I realized that with her office hours being 9:00 a.m. to 5:00 p.m. there was little likelihood that I would have a chance to speak to her before I returned to Johannesburg on the Friday night.

That evening when I went to the dining room of the hotel for dinner, I noticed that BW's bodyguard was sitting alone at a table. I asked him if I could join him and he shyly agreed. It wasn't until later that I realized that Whites and Blacks did not sit at the same table and it was probably quite uncomfortable for him. However, we had a wonderful conversation. He was articulate and knowledgeable. He told me all about life in South Africa and encouraged me to go on a safari on my next trip, so I could enjoy seeing all the animals. I thanked him for keeping me company adding, 'See you tomorrow.' We parted and I went to my room to prepare for the next day's seminar.

The next morning, we had been driving for about twenty minutes when I noticed that a car had been travelling even with their car for some time. When I glanced over, I noticed that the driver was a white man. He was miming something to me 'Are you all right?'

I quickly assed the situation and realized that he probably thought I was being kidnapped by the three Black men. I smiled, and mouthed the words, 'I'm fine – I'm fine.' And punctuated my reply by making the thumbs up sign. He waved and drove on. I looked around to see if anyone in our car had noticed the exchange, and Jerome said, 'He was obviously looking out for your safety.'

At the end of this, the final seminar day, I was rather overwhelmed when BW's bodyguard stood up and thanked me for coming so far to help them learn. He then touched on how brave I was to travel alone in a country so far from and different in culture from my homeland.

The participants all stood and clapped while I blushed furiously. One by one – they came up to the front of the room to shake my hand and express their own personal thanks for the seminar.

When they left the room, Jerome escorted me to an office and introduced me to a distinguished-looking black man. Because of Jerome's heavy accent, I didn't catch the man's name. It was only when I returned to Canada that I realized that I had been introduced to Chief Mangosuthu Buthelezi, the Chief Minister of the KwaZulu and president of the Inkatha Freedom Party. The next year he contested Nelson Mandela for the leadership of South Africa. I also learned that the participant BW was Chief Buthelezi's son. I was saddened several years later to learn that both BW died from AIDs.

When Jerome had picked me up at the hotel that morning – I had checked out of my hotel room, so Jerome and the two other men drove me directly to the airport to catch my plane. I told them that we had time for me to treat them to a cup of coffee. It was then that Jerome explained that it was not customary for Whites and Blacks to sit at the same tables – that they were expected to stay in their 'place.' Then I understood how uncomfortable it must have been for BWs bodyguard at the hotel restaurant. I thanked them for their help and boarded my plane.

On the flight from Durban to Johannesburg, I read an article in the Durban newspaper that again confirmed that life was not as peaceful as it appeared in South Africa. The different tribes were still battling with each other. In the article, the KwaZulu police reported an incident at KwaMashu, a black township close to Hammarsdale. Four black people had been shot and killed the day before, shortly after they had been tried in a 'people's court.'

Deanne and Nathan met me at the Johannesburg airport. When we got to my hotel I asked, 'Can we stop for coffee? I have something I need to discuss with you.' A guilty look passed between Deanne and Nathan and I knew that they had an idea what I wanted to talk about. I confronted Deanne with my findings. She made all kinds of excuses about not coming to Durban with me, but it was obvious to me that she was lying. I told her how disappointed I was that she hadn't warned me about the problems I might run into.

'We were afraid that you would back out and we'd have to refund their fee.' She explained.

'You have a duty of care as a seminar group to ensure that your international speakers are kept safe and aware of possible problems. I hope in our future negotiations that you will be up-front with me.' Deanne promised to do so.

The next day I was to do my second free session for Black women. This was at a regular monthly meeting of over 300 female clerical workers in the black township of Soweto, a suburb of Johannesburg. I had been warned by the Canadian government not to go to Soweto but was on my way there before I even knew where the venue was. Deanne and Nathan had not specified that it was in Soweto – just a township near Johannesburg. Again, they let me down.

My topic for this group was Goal Setting: Step by Step. I asked my audience to write down their dreams, their career aspirations and the goals they hoped to set and how they would make them happen. I elaborated on the tremendous opportunity that would be coming for black women in South Africa. After Apartheid ended in April 1994, not only would black citizens be able to vote but they could buy their own homes, property and businesses. No longer would they need a white intermediary to sell their produce, carvings, figurines, artwork and crafts. They could sell their wares directly to the public or retail businesses. They could even sell directly to overseas clients without a white intermediary taking most of their profits.

Women would be offered a degree of freedom that they had not been able to acquire in their lifetimes. They would be out from under the control of both the white and black men in their lives. Presently, many of them were left with the full responsibility of caring for and raising their children without the help of the fathers. Illegitimate children were everywhere, and the absent fathers seldom helped with the financial or emotional upbringing of their children.

While the mothers worked, they had little choice but to let the children fend for themselves. They would now be able to earn enough wages through their own efforts, to afford adequate care for their children. What an opportunity!

I had made sure there were adequate microphones in the aisles and invited the participants to tell me their dreams and aspirations. One by one, they proved that they were ready. I said, 'I'm so proud of you – you're ready – very ready to take advantage of the opportunities that will come your way.'

The M.C. of the event suggested that as an honour to me, a white woman, that the group show me the African symbol for the future. I was brought to tears when they sang the African freedom song and put their fists in the air. This South African Freedom Song was about the anti-apartheid movement. I thanked them for honouring me that way, then was whisked away by Nathan and Deanne back to my hotel.

The next morning when I was reading the local Sunday newspaper, I read that twelve people had been arrested for public violence in Soweto the afternoon before. I realized that I had been in Soweto at the time of the violence and had just missed being in the middle of a serious clash between blacks and whites. I doubted if angry blacks would have waited for me to speak to realize that I was not from South Africa and was very much against Apartheid.

Monday, after a quick brunch, Deanne drove me to the airport for my twelve-hour flight back to Kuala Lumpur to continue my seminar tour of Singapore, Malaysia and Australia.'

Jenny returned to South Africa in 1996. By this time Apartheid was over. While she was in Johannesburg, she contacted several of the women who had been at her goal setting seminar in 1993. They had spoken about their dreams of starting their own companies and Jenny was happy to learn that three of them had done so. One of them said she had kicked her husband out, because he was always working in another city, and did not financially support his children – just seemed to get her pregnant again when he came home once or twice a year.

After Jenny finished presenting her seminars, she was driven to the Mabula Game Lodge that was two hours north of Johannesburg. They were setting up a training centre and asked if she could come to see the lodge and go on a three-day Safari. She witnessed lion feeding and on the last day, she rode on horseback and was surprised that the wild animals didn't recognize that people were on the horses. She saw all the Big Five animals the lodge had bragged about.

Singapore and Malaysia

Jenny continued in her journal after her May 1993 visit to South Africa:

'I arrived in Kuala Lumpur and the next day, presented my seminar, 'Dealing with Conflict' then flew to Singapore and conducted another 'Dealing with Conflict' session. Then I was a keynote

speaker at a secretaries' conference. My topic was, 'Career Development for women' and I was able to sell several of my 'How Women can Succeed in Business' books.

Then I flew to Australia to present more seminars in Sydney and back home to Edmonton.

I can do it! The sky's the limit!

Forty-four

In 1996, Jenny's body took a beating. She had been going from Edmonton to Singapore – back to Edmonton – on to Australia – back to Edmonton – on to Singapore – back to Edmonton. The only thing wrong with this was that Edmonton was in the middle of winter and the temperature was -30ºC while Singapore and Australia were +34ºC. Jenny found she could not get warm when she came back to Edmonton. Her hands and feet never seemed to warm up, and the long winters were distasteful to her once she saw how lovely it felt to be in warmer climates. She was also very afraid that she would fall on the ice in Canada. Her doctor had warned her that if she fell the wrong way, she could be back in a wheelchair.

By this time, she was 57 and knew she did not want to spend her retirement years in a cold climate. So, she began the lengthy process of emigrating to a warmer climate. She didn't want to emigrate to the United States even though she had an office in Maui, Hawaii. Then she thought of South Africa and decided she was the wrong colour. How about the Middle East? That was a definite no no because she was a woman. She decided that Australia was the place she would prefer and began the paperwork to emigrate there. Unfortunately, she ran into what she called *'the bureaucrat from Hell'* who worked in the Australian Emigration office in Vancouver British Columbia. Jenny wasn't sure which category she would fit the best so asked for the paperwork for five categories.

When the parcel of paperwork arrived, there was one set missing – that for *'Distinguished Talent.'* By this time her books were being sold internationally and she had written many more. She phoned the emigration office and spoke with the woman who had sent the paperwork.

Jenny said, 'Thank you for sending four of the sets of paperwork. Unfortunately, there was not one for *'Distinguished Talent.'* Could you please send that one to me?'

The woman replied, 'You wouldn't qualify.'

'How do you know I wouldn't qualify?'

'You just wouldn't qualify.' She insisted.

Jenny hung up in disgust and wondered what she should do, then picked up the phone again – this time phoning the Australian

Consulate in Ottawa. She couldn't get through but was given a FAX number to send her information. This was done immediately.

Two days later the woman in Vancouver phoned her and took a strip off her for going over her head to the consulate.

So, Jenny had to try another way to enter Australia. She made a trip to Brisbane, talked with a firm there and they were interested in sponsoring her to teach their employees how to conduct training programs. The paperwork was filled out, but Jenny was disappointed in late November 1997 when she learned that she had been denied entry because the age a worker could be brought into the country had to be 45 or younger – she was now 58.

Jenny was very disappointed and realized that she might have to try to emigrate to another warmer climate. Because it was so close to Christmas, she decided to wait until the new year to try again.

In Mid-December 1997, she was flabbergasted when she received a FAX from the Emigration Office in Sydney telling her that she had been accepted for emigration under the *'Distinguished Talent'* category! Jenny was over the moon and started making plans to move. She knew she had to wait for the paperwork to arrive via the Vancouver office. She phoned there and spoke with the same nasty woman who said she would be doing the paperwork. Jenny understood that the paperwork should only take about ten days, so waited every day for the paperwork to arrive. It didn't arrive until the first week in March. The *bureaucrat from Hell* had done it again!

Jenny emigrated and arrived in Australia on March 22, 1998 but ran into another huge glitch. The stevedore's on the Sydney wharfs went on strike in early April 1998, just as Jenny's office and personal effects were to be delivered from there to the Gold Coast of Queensland. In the meantime, she made a quick trip to Sydney to see if she couldn't speed up the delivery of her goods. While she was there, she went to the Emigration Office and spoke with one of the supervisors. She had made a detailed list of all the problems *the bureaucrat from Hell* had caused her and others, keeping well-qualified Canadians from emigrating for eighteen months or more. He promised to investigate the issue. Before she left, she asked him if he would let her know what was done about the problem employee. He promised to do so. Two weeks later she received a short email from him that stated very simply, 'There is one less Aussie in our Vancouver office.'

It took until mid-June for her possessions to arrive on the Gold Coast. While waiting, she concentrated on opening another branch of her company, buying office furniture, kitchen and living room suites and everything else she needed that she had not shipped to Australia.

She had brought her computer with her on the plane and didn't waste any of those months while she waited for her goods to arrive from the Sydney dockyards. Instead, she kept herself busy writing more books and marketing her seminars both locally and around Australia. Her home in Edmonton had been sold and she started looking for a place to buy.

Although she marketed heavily in Australia and had already presented many seminars there, somehow, now that she was a *'local'* they didn't seem interested. Several companies called but expected her to present the seminar for nothing. As they said, 'But you can sell your books at the seminar.'

Jenny finally got fed up with that attitude and lashed out, 'Would you expect your accountant or lawyer to do work for free? That's how I make my living – presenting seminars. Why would I do them free for you?'

She decided that she would continue to pursue more international clients and soon succeeded. South East Asia was only a short plane ride now – far different from when she had to spend up to thirty-one or two hours travelling from Canada. Besides regularly doing seminars in Singapore and Malaysia, she was approached by several training firms in Dubai, Abu Dhabi, Oman and Bahrain.

At the second set of seminars she presented sessions in Dubai, she followed the training group representative into the training room. He opened the session by explaining where the men's and women's washrooms were, when and where the lunch and coffee breaks would be held. While he was doing this Jenny sat at a side chair and perused the audience of thirty or so people. She noticed that six of the men were in Arab caftans and headpiece. The representative gave an introduction of Jenny's accomplishments and the men looked pleased at her long life of presenting seminars. However, when he mentioned her name and she stood up to greet her participants she noticed a distinct change in their facial expressions and body language. She learned later that the flyer advertising her two-day session had listed the seminar leader as being Jason Carponi and these men had come from Saudi Arabia where women must be veiled. This was not the case in Dubai and Abu Dhabi. Jenny always made sure she was covered to the wrist, ankle and neck when she presented sessions there.

As usual, when she worked in the Middle East, she started her sessions by saying, 'I'm not entirely clear on all your customs and your culture. So, if I do or say something that you find offensive, please let me know so I don't repeat the error.

It took until after the first coffee break for the men to lower their crossed arms and start to listen to what she was saying.

At lunch, a long table was set up for all the male and female participants. One of the men from Saudi Arabia sat across the table from her. He smiled as he announced to her that this was the first time in his life that he had shared a meal with any female other than is mother, sisters, wife and daughters.

'Does it bother you?' Jenny asked.,

'No, not really. It's just different.' He admitted.

That afternoon, because of these six men, she got up her courage and adlibbed by asking the following questions of the participants:

'Do any of you attend meetings with men from Europe or North America?'

Several hands went up including a couple from Saudi.

'Do you shake hands with them?'

'Of course.' Was the answer.

'What if the business person is a woman?' she added.

All six men shook their heads indicating 'No.'

Then Jenny went on to explain about handshaking. 'Originally shaking hands was used to show a stranger that they were extending their empty weapon hand and came in peace. Later the handshake became a promise that the dealings between the two would be honest and up-front, no gameplaying and they could trust each other.

'If you don't shake the hand of women from Europe or North America, they will wonder if you are going to have honest and truthful dealings with them. So, without knowing it, you may lose a large contract with a client.'

She demonstrated with one of the female participants how *not* to shake hands with women. By giving a wimpy handshake or just holding the tips of her fingers. She also explained what some aggressive men did to show dominance when they shook hands. These men would turn their wrist while shaking hands placing the other person's hand facing upward in a subservient position while theirs was facing down in a dominant position.

The men all nodded their heads when they heard this information.

On the second day during the afternoon coffee break, the man who had sat across from her at lunch the first day asked if he could talk to her. She took him aside and he placed a plastic bag in her hands. 'This is for you so you can learn more about our customs and culture.'

In the bag was a leather-bound Koran along with several booklets about the Muslim religion. Jenny was overwhelmed, thanked him and promised him she would read the material.

She would not forget this group especially when all six men from Saudi Arabia came up to her, thanked her for the seminar, and each one shook her hand. What a prize that was for Jenny.

When she got back to Australia, her travel agent (who was a Muslim woman) jokingly asked her if he had proposed yet? She went on to explain that Muslim men could have up to four wives.

'Nope' was Jenny's quick reply.

Jenny continued to increase the numbers of countries where she offered seminars in New Zealand, Thailand, The Philippines, Germany and Hong Kong.

In three years, she presented a whopping forty-nine seminars in Indonesia.

In January 1999, the European Central Bank was established with their head office in Frankfurt, Germany. They contacted Jenny to see whether she could present her *Dealing with Conflict* session for them in April 2000. The bank found that because their staff came from so many different countries, with different customs and languages, they were running into problems.

Jenny arrived in Frankfurt and was to go directly to their office rather than to a hotel. She took a taxi which let her off at the address. However, as she lugged her heavy suitcase behind her, she couldn't find the building she was looking for. She stopped a female bystander and asked, 'Do you speak English.'

'Yes, I do,' she answered in perfect English. Jenny was to learn that many people in Germany spoke fluent English. The woman pointed to a building across the street and Jenny thanked her.

The bank representative put her luggage in a corner of his office. 'First let's get some lunch then we'll return to the office. The group that you will be training will join us to be taken to the venue by bus,' he explained.

A few hours later they arrived at castle hotel that overlooked the Rhine River. It was a wonderful setting and it was a shame that Jenny had so little time to explore the castle. She was shown the meeting room where the session would begin the next day, and was given a lovely room. Everyone was to eat together in the dining room, and the next two days would be spent at her session.

Jenny's seminar is very interactive with lots of class participation. But as hard as she tried – she couldn't get them to participate. By the end of the second day, she was exhausted because their lack of participation made it necessary for her to adlib and add extra material to her two-day session. Otherwise it would have been over a half-day early.

The participants were asked to fill out an evaluation form. Jenny was anticipating that most of them would be negative, but she was amazed that they loved it. It was then that she learned that all the participants were Economists who had master's degrees. They were used to attending lectures where they had no opportunity of joining in with the discussions.

In November 2000 Jenny was asked by a hotel in Bangkok to present five days of seminars for their staff from hotels they owned in South East Asia. The venue was different from the hotel where she stayed, so they sent a taxi each morning to take her to and from the venue. The hotel had warned her not to hail a taxi off the street, but to order one through them or the seminar group. She understood why they were so concerned when she read an article in their newspaper about tourists being 'gassed' through tubes coming from driver's seat. When they were unconscious, they were robbed and/or raped and dumped at deserted locations.

On the last day of the seminars, Jenny entered the taxi they had ordered and suddenly realized that the driver was holding a small towel over his face. She knew instinctively what was going to happen. *'What should I do,'* she wondered. *'I can't jump out of the car because we're going at least sixty. Should I put the driver in a headlock and insist that he pull over?'* Then she realized what she had to do. Even though the air quality in Bangkok is terrible, it would be better to be breathing that stale air than what could be the dangerous air that was being pumped into the back seat of the taxi. So, she rolled down both back windows and hoped she would survive. Soon, the taxi drew up to the front door of the hotel. She immediately got out as a hotel staff member opened the door.

She looked at him and pointing at the taxi exclaimed, 'He tried to gas me. Please call the police.'

The taxi sped off, but Jenny was able to write down the licence number. She'd also noted the name of the driver while she was in the car. She asked the attendant if he could tell her where she could find the manager of the hotel. After explaining the situation to the manager, he phoned the police. They said they would investigate but seeing she would be flying home the next morning, they likely could not charge him.

'How can that be the case' she asked the Manager. 'All they have to do is pull him over and find the gas cylinder he must have in his taxi.'

'By now, he will have thrown it into a garbage bin knowing that you had caught him trying to gas you,' he replied.

'So, that's how things are done in Bangkok,' she thought.

I can do it! The sky's the limit!

Forty-five

Jenny made yearly trips back to Canada to see her family, but it was an arduous thirty-one-hour plus trip and as she got older, she told her family that it was their turn to fly to Australia. Only Mark, his wife and daughter came once.

In early January of 2009, Jenny learned that Russ had been in an accident. His truck had hit black ice and had rolled several times down an embankment. His neck was injured, and he ended up in a wheelchair. Jenny wanted to say, 'Now you know what it feels like to be in a wheelchair' by but it was not Jenny's nature to be mean spirited and she, more than anyone, knew what might lay ahead for him.

In early 2009, Bruce was having problems with his right shoulder and in June after having extensive tests, he sent Jenny the following email:

'Hello. I went for further tests today at the neurologist. Sit down before reading further. It is not good news. They are about 97% sure that I have Lou Gehrig's disease as they call it in the USA (ALS as they call it in Canada and Motor Neuron Disease in Australia). They are waiting for a couple more tests; a third MRI on my brain this time. We have not told Carolyn anything yet! I am still off work until further notice; if I go back at all. I will update you as we know further information.'

Soon the diagnosis was confirmed. Bruce had one of the most devastating diseases one could get. Jenny went on the internet and cried many tears when she learned that most patients lived only three to ten years. She couldn't help but wonder if the shock Bruce had received before he was born, had resulted in him having this horrible disease. Again, she felt great animosity towards Russ, who she felt could be responsible for their son's illness.

Motor Neuron Disease paralyses a person bit by bit, until they can't move a muscle. However, their brain stays fully functional. In most cases this can take three to ten years to progress to the final stages. In this case, Bruce degenerated very quickly and within seven months of his diagnosis, he was in a palliative care unit hardly able to move and was fed through a tube in his stomach. Jenny made a trip to Winnipeg in July 2009 shortly after he was diagnosed and then again that Christmas. At that time, he begged her to help him die. She wished that the laws were different, and he could be put out of his misery.

On May 24, 2010 Jenny was sitting at her computer in Australia when she had the sudden realisation that she needed to go to Canada as soon as possible. Her flight arrived on May 29 and she was able to visit with Bruce for the next three days. She winced when she first saw him. Bruce looked like a tall, thin cadaver. His skin was so white he blended in with the sheets covering him. He could not speak or move, but she knew he understood every word she said. On her second visit, she devised a piece of cardboard that had four lines of the alphabet. Because Bruce could still blink, she said he could blink two for 'no' and once for 'yes' when she pointed to letters. With this crude system they were able to communicate.

After a few general comments, Jenny asked, 'Are you afraid to die?'

He blinked once. 'Are you afraid you will choke to death?' she asked watching him closely. Again, he blinked once, and she could tell that he was close to tears.

She reassured him, 'I've talked to your carer about this and he assures me that this will not be allowed to happen. As you know you are monitored 24/7 and if you started to choke, he would be here in a flash.'

One thing Jenny had learned was that often terminal patients needed to obtain permission from their families so they could let go and allow themselves die. She added, 'You have fought long and hard and I know that you wanted to die six months ago. It's time to let go and allow yourself to drift away. If you allow yourself to do this, you can then go peacefully in your sleep.'

She watched as tears ran down his face and she gently wiped them away. When Jenny left him that night, she kissed him, told him how much she loved him. She wished she could hug him, but it was far too awkward to do so. Twelve hours later, on June 2, 2010, Carlie phoned to say that Bruce had died during the night.

The next day, Jenny received the stunning news that Russ was paying for the funeral and was banning her from attending it. She was booked to return to Australia on June 8th, so there would have been plenty of time for her to go to his funeral. However, Russ booked the funeral for June 9th. She realised that after thirty-seven years, he was still fulfilling his vendetta and was still hurting her by not letting her say her final farewell to her son.

She couldn't believe he could be so cruel and tried to find out why Bruce's wife Carlie was allowing Russ to make these decisions about his burial. But Carlie kept her phone on answering service and refused to talk to Jenny. Jenny even tried sending emails to Carlie asking to see her granddaughter on the weekend before she flew home to Australia, but there was no reply, so she was denied such a visit. And, she was completely devastated emotionally because Mark and Debbie did nothing to stop their father from following through with his plan to ban her from the funeral.

Jenny was staying with Marjory, who suggested that she have her own wake for Bruce. They invited close friends and relatives to Marjory's home that Sunday, and they all said their goodbyes to Bruce and comforted Jenny.

As Jenny flew home, she realized that she was in the sky while the funeral was taking place. She smiled as she realized that as she was at 35,000 feet, she was much closer to Bruce than those who attended the funeral. She said a silent 'good bye' to her son and quietly wept.

When Jenny returned to Australia, all the emails she sent to Carlie and Carolyn were returned because they must have obtained new email addresses. This she knew was due to Russ's continued influence and interference. She never heard from them again.

After watching both her mother and son die horrible deaths, she became a staunch believer in euthanasia.

Russ remained in his wheelchair until he died on Christmas day 2013 at the age of seventy-five. For Jenny - the vendetta was finally over.

I can do it! The sky's the limit!

Forty-five

At the age of seventy-five, Jenny realized that she had presented seminars for another twenty-five years after she expected people to stop hiring her. She was glad that she hadn't been given the boot, just because she was a female who was over fifty which seemed to happen far too often to women on television. Even at that age she was still being asked to present seminars and her value as a speaker increased along with her fees.

Jenny kept track each year and determined that she flew an average of 250,000 kilometres a year. There came a point when it became too much of a hassle with the additional security measures. She wasted so much time leaving home in the wee hours of the morning to arrive at the airport three hours early. She finally decided that now that she was seventy-five, she would quit doing international seminar tours. It had been thirty-two years since she had opened her business at the age of forty-tree. She celebrated her seventy-fifth birthday by climbing the Eiffel Tower.

In 2014 Jenny took a cruise on the Aurora. While on board, she had the opportunity of speaking with the man in charge of entertainment on the ship. When he learned about her seminars, he asked if she would do a short *Dealing with Conflict* session for the passengers. She did so, and when she took another cruise on the same ship in 2017, she did another.

After Jenny retired, she continued to write books and by 2019, had thirty-eight books to her credit – thirty-five of them non-fiction (based on the time-consuming research she had done for her seminars). The other five were fiction including a trilogy of books that she thoroughly enjoyed writing.

In 2010, she became a dedicated volunteer with Crime Stoppers Queensland, whose mandate was to educate the public by ensuring that callers to their phone line would remain anonymous when reporting crime. The volunteers also fundraised for promotional material and rewards for calls that resulted in the arrest of criminals.

In February 2015, Jenny was asked to start-up and be chairperson for a new Crime Stoppers area committee on the Gold Coast. Five months after their launch, her area committee was in the black, and she and her committee received many Crime Stopper, the Gold Coast Council and Police awards.

Jenny continued doing talks, but this time they were focused on explaining what Crime Stoppers was all about. Groups such as Rotary, Probus, Lions and View Clubs learned that they could remain anonymous and if the criminal was arrested, they could qualify for a reward.

Jenny's dedication to giving her *'all'* to everything she attempted earned her many achievement awards in both Canada and Australia.

Jenny often had to pinch herself when she thought of how different her life became from what she'd expected it to be. Never, in her wildest dreams, would she have believed she'd have the lifestyle she enjoyed so much, living in such a tropical paradise. Her many books were being sold internationally; her training firm had grown tremendously and eventually there were three international branches. Who would have thought that one day clients would pay enormous fees for her to present her seminars, fly her first class around the world, pick her up at the airport in limousines, have her stay in first class hotels, pay for her meals and all other travelling expenses? What a life she had built for herself! Quite a change from the uneducated and abused young woman she had originally been before she left Russ.

www.ingramcontent.com/pod-product-compliance
Lightning Source LLC
Chambersburg PA
CBHW022140240626
47153CB00007B/2440